KICKDOWN

KICKDOWN

A NOVEL

REBECCA CLARREN

Arcade Publishing • New York

Arcade Publishing books may be purchased in bulk at special discounts for sales promotion, corporate gifts, fund-raising, or educational purposes. Special editions can also be created to specifications. For details, contact the Special Sales Department, Arcade Publishing, 307 West 36th Street, 11th Floor, New York, NY 10018 or arcade@skyhorsepublishing.com.

Arcade Publishing® is a registered trademark of Skyhorse Publishing, Inc.®, a Delaware corporation.

Visit our website at www.arcadepub.com.

10 9 8 7 6 5 4 3 2 1

Library of Congress Cataloging-in-Publication Data is available on file.

Print ISBN: 978-1-62872-967-2
Ebook ISBN: 978-1-62872-968-9

Printed in the United States of America

For Greg

Kickdown, def.: A well will kick or kick down when the pressure of the natural gas overcomes the pressure exerted by the mud column.

1

Jackie Dunbar takes a deep breath, inhaling the wind and mud and snow on the ground and the smell of the newborn calf, and she tries not to think about what might go wrong. To consider failure is always the first misstep. She corrals the calf between her thighs. The tagging gun in her hand keeps slipping from her dad's old gloves so she pulls them off, the snow and wind biting her skin. The animal twists into the ground as if it could escape, as if that were possible.

Large wet flakes fall from the midday sky. A mama cow, the one Dad called Robert Plant, is close enough to smell. Threatening to run at Jackie, she grunts and snorts and flicks her tail. Jackie keeps looking up, keeps making eye contact with the fifteen-hundred-pound animal. She has to be quick. She has to click fast. *Pretend it's a skin staple*, she tells herself. *Pretend Dad is still here. It's going to be fine.*

The baby's ears are soft; the vasculature is subtle, but finally, there it is. Chink-click. The piston threads the cartilage and it's done, a yellow plastic tag secure in the ear. No blood or mess. The calf bawls, but only for a second: surprise is always worse than pain.

Jackie jumps off, and the calf jumps up and totters away. As Jackie starts the motor on the four-wheeler, she whistles through her crooked teeth. Chicken sprints across the field to her side.

He's a good worker, good enough company. She bends over to let him lick her wind-red cheeks.

The relief in being alone with animals. The efficiency of getting a job done without discussion. Her dad would understand. Her older sister Susan might have, once, but not now, not for several weeks. These days, Susan requires watching. So too the vacuum cord, the turkey knife, the baling twine, the pink plastic razor.

"Go on. Load up." Jackie nods at the dog and he hops on back and they drive into the herd, into the land.

Light bleeds through the heavy clouds and settles on the fresh snow. It's going to melt by late afternoon—she's relearned this about spring weather—but for now the white covers the mud and the cow shit, and the ranch is as pretty as she remembered. Beyond the fence line and the poplars, juniper and piñon slope uphill to the mesa and mountains beyond. At the other end of the field, the creek snakes through cottonwood, carving and re-carving its riparian path. She takes another deep breath, inhales it all.

Every stretch of land here holds memory. There's where Uncle Ellis ran over Dad's foot with the tractor. There's where her first 4-H calf was born, on a day so hot the ground hissed when she dropped. Susan showed her how to smoke cigarettes behind that poplar. Jackie wills herself not to look up at the mesa, not to think about what's buried under snow and fresh dirt and pine boards.

Soon enough the snow will be gone and the land will need help and care to remain what it has always been. The ditch road will need clearing. Irrigation pipes will need cleaning and placing. The ranch and the mountains are the only religion she's ever practiced. Its tenets being stewardship, self-reliance, and sacrifice. Here hard work and sweat are equal to prayer.

Chicken leaps off the four-wheeler and races after a heifer; his duty is uncomplicated. He barks and leaps and circles the cow, keeping her away from the ditch. Much of the herd still clusters around the hay Jackie flaked for them a few hours past. She gets off the four-wheeler and walks among them.

Blanca's tits are big and tight; a first-time heifer, she could drop her calf any day now. Una and Dos curl up on the hay and groom each other. Stevie Ray, Jackie's favorite, the most gentle of them all, bends to munch some alfalfa by her foot. Jackie listens to the cows eating around her. *The sound of peace.* She can almost hear him say it again. As long as she is here, as long as she keeps things running, a part of him remains. And if the market stays in her favor, if the calves all drop like they should, they'll make enough to make things right with the bank and the land will stay Dunbar.

Several mountain passes away, her classmates are scrubbing in on surgeries, rounding, taking histories and physicals, being busy parts of the hulking ecosystem of recovery and comfort that is the hospital. If she were there, she'd be making a difference, she'd be different, be the sort of person who isn't from Silt.

It is not something her friends or professors in Denver understand: her being here. She has told them repeatedly that she has no choice. That being here, this life constructed of water and seed and shit, this is what her family needs. What she has not mentioned to anyone is how she hopes this sacrifice might make reparations. She missed too much of his sickness. She missed most of his dying. When Susan had called her on New Year's Eve, telling her the news, telling her she better break fast for home, she had put them off. The drive was only four hours away, but she had put them off. A couple weeks to finish her rotation had not at the time seemed like an unconscionable decision.

No reason to think about it. She spits into the snow.

It's lunchtime when she gets back to the house. Jackie stops in the hallway, outside the kitchen door. The footsteps inside are unsteady, unstopping, too fast. They sound like a bad day.

"You want coffee?" Susan steps across the linoleum, to the sink and back to the fridge, and back again and again. "I made coffee. I think it tastes the way you like it, but it might be too thin. Here. Try it."

The bottom of Susan's faded long-john shirt lifts to expose a shell of a belly. Her red hair hasn't been washed in two weeks and it's got a butter-slick shine. Three unplucked hairs stick out of her chin. Her eyes, the color of dirty water, dart to the window, to the new snow and the fields where new calves take first steps. "I don't know what to do."

"Susie, you're pacing again." Jackie at once regrets the harsh sharpness of her tone. With anyone else she could be kind. She leans against the counter and rearranges her face into something resembling a smile.

"Oh. I didn't realize." Susan exhales several breaths in a row through her pursed mouth, puffing.

"You take your pills today, honey?" The *honey*, she hopes, will soften things, will remind both of them that they are all each other has left.

Susan shrugs. She brushes the table with her arm, knocking a thick book to the floor. A moon-colored watch with a thick leather band, too big for Susan's wrist, clanks against the wood. Jackie can't imagine why her dad would leave it for someone who can't keep track of time.

"You've got to take those pills, Susie."

"They make me feel weird."

Jackie pauses, stops herself from pointing out the obvious. "Why don't you get outside? A walk would help. There's a strong link between serotonin levels and exercise."

"You think I should be doing more around here." She doesn't look up. There are dark circles under her eyes.

"I know it's hard."

"I'm sorry, Jackie. I don't know why I'm acting like this. I don't know what to do." Her voice breaks like she's about to cry, but Susan never cries anymore. Not since those first days when Jackie had finally made it back to the ranch to find her dad stuck in a sickbed that smelled like Windex, his pancreas pocked with cancer and Susan making cup after cup of herbal tea that sat on the TV tray, cold and untouched. Only three weeks from diagnosis to death. He should've had more time; he would've if Jackie had paid more attention, had insisted he see a doctor when she was home at Thanksgiving and noticed how skinny and slow he'd been. But she hadn't. And now, here she is, failing her sister too.

"It's OK." Jackie nods. "You know I can handle things. Go on. It'll be fine."

Susan drifts down the hallway to her room and again, Jackie is alone. It's fine. She can make it fine. She pours the coffee Susan made into the sink and starts a new pot.

At first, it had been impossible to have any time to herself. Someone from some church had organized food, and every day there was another middle-aged lady Jackie hadn't seen in years. They all brought a face saddled with pity and another tuna casserole or macaroni salad. Susan was no help, worse than help. And every time Jackie tried to escape for town, a neighbor would stop her on Dry Hollow Road. Mavis Reed just wanted to say that her sister lost a breast to cancer and isn't it strange how some people pull through and others don't. Pete Johnson talked for a long time about his cousin who died in a combine accident. Jackie'd had to wait twenty minutes for Jim Boyce to push his sheep across the road, and the entire time he talked about his son who died in Afghanistan. As if any of it had to do with Dad.

After the funeral, a small service at the family cemetery up top, the well-meaning had crowded around her with their own need. If she'd opened her mouth, she'd have screamed. But she couldn't let him down. So she did what he would have done. She nodded at their sympathy and listened. She made them feel like they were helping.

She grabs her daily planner off the counter. *Get referral for S. Fix post-holer. Write up research proposal!!*

She picks *Anna Karenina* off the floor where Susan had let it fall and reads the first sentence. She shakes her head. Susan doesn't need to dwell on other people's unhappiness; they, the Dunbars, have enough of their own.

Jackie has never found time for novels. Too often she grows impatient with the protagonist's confusion and stupidity; she usually flips to the end of the book to search for the characters she likes, making sure they survive long enough to make the reading worth her time. What Jackie likes is nonfiction. Journalism is fine, but better are scientific articles. Stories from the real world, how it works and why, elucidating new truths.

She sets to work on the dirty dishes, sweeps the floor, gets everything in order before sitting down at the table with a stack of journal articles on purkinje cells. If she can write a flawless research proposal, if it impresses her attending and she gives her a research rotation, if it helps her land a good residency, all this time away won't matter. Within minutes she is consumed by the miracle of how purkinje neurons adjust muscle tone, how they keep a person from falling down, keep a person steady.

2

Dust covers the attic floor, Susan's palms, the pictures stacked against the beams. Five opened boxes surround her. Somewhere up here is her old copy of *Women in Love*. But no box of books, not yet. It's only a book, anyway. Not a statement of her intelligence. Nothing like that. But she really has to find it. It's here somewhere.

Here is the painting of a butterfly she did in third grade that Mama framed and hung in the kitchen and that Dad replaced five years later with Jackie's science fair poster about eagles. Here is the picture of Granny, wearing a sombrero and smoking a cigarette. Here are Dad's dog tags. And his pipe. And two of his old sweaters. They smell of dust and tobacco. Her heart drops. There it goes, down the well.

She will not fall apart. She is here for the book, not some trip down memory lane. More like a highway than a lane really. She paces. The tired sits on her. Slows her down. Way down. It's like this all the time now. Like she is moving inside a cocoon. Or a spaceship. No one can find her in there. It takes a long time looking until there it is, her own name, *Susan*, written across a box in Dad's small, neat script. She sits down and breathes and sneezes and breathes some more. Her hand shakes as she tears off the tape. Dad's freckled hands carried this, sealed it.

Her clips have gone beige. Their edges curled. He kept them all.

The first article she ever wrote, about clowns visiting the children's hospital in Junction. "Clowning around for a cure," by Susan Dunbar. She'd found a tiny little girl who'd had six open-heart surgeries for the lede. *Jenny Thomas, her chest split by the ridgeline of a purple scar, giggles at the stranger's red nose.* Not the best opener.

An article about a new CAT dealership, another about the smash-up derby, about an ag professor who was trying to engineer the perfect peach, about the first Democrat in twelve years to win a city council seat. *Arnold Mackley is an accidental activist.* She'd thought that was a great line until Ed Hanscom, managing editor, told her it wasn't. She learned to avoid phrases like *win-win* and *fox guarding the hen house*. She learned to write fast and, after a few years, she got better.

In the middle of the box is her proof. "Battling the Blaze"—her story, her byline, top of the fold. A hokey title, not her choice. But the assignment, the idea: it was all hers. Though that's not exactly true either.

She had been standing in Camila's kitchen. The flowers on the curtains were blue, before they faded to the purple they are now, and they were drinking wine from a box. Monica was on the floor drawing something in crayon.

"What's that, baby?" Susan had asked. "What are those flames about?"

"Daddy."

Camila had explained then about the wildfire and how Ray's guard unit was helping out.

"You know Ray, he never says much about anything and the papers never report what really goes on out there. I mean, how do those fires get so big? Don't tell me there isn't something the Forest Service could be doing differently."

And there was the idea. She hadn't known anything about wildfires either, not about the politics of real estate development on the edge of national forests, not about the gazillions in federal dollars spent to fight them, not about how that money creates a culture of machismo, of pressure to work in unsafe conditions. But with Ray's help, she had gotten great access. *Fake it 'til you make it*—that's what they told each other in the newsroom. Day after day, she swallowed her fear and followed Ray into the biggest wildfire of the decade.

Her hands shake as she picks the clip from the box. "Flames spit fire across the dirt road faster than Matt Kampen could run." Pretty good. She is right back there, breathing smoke through a bandana. Suffocating. The wind came from down-valley. And then a baseball bat crack and a pop, and the snag—still smoldering, the needles still on the tree—flew off the hillside. And landed on that kid. What was his name? She should know his name. Alex. She skims the article. Alex Hay. When the tree landed on him she had laughed. It was the opposite of funny, but she had laughed, her anxiety uncontrolled.

"Susan. Stop." Ray had grabbed her arm and squeezed until she swallowed and shut up.

It had been chaos. The helicopter couldn't land anywhere close. And the wind changed again. And with it, the fire turned back on them.

From the safety of the attic, she smiles. It had been so exciting. Exhilarating to not be in charge. Whatever Ray and his buddies said to do, she did. And Alex Hay didn't die. And the fire was contained.

And she got her front-page story.

Welcome to the big time, honey, Dad had said when she brought home the paper. Jackie had driven all the way to Junction to get the guy at the morgue to give her five copies. She'd laid them in a fan on Dad's coffee table.

The night the paper printed, she'd been at the High Spot drinking tequila and playing pool with guys from the newsroom. And there was Kelly, just off a hitch on a drill rig down-valley, watching her put the eight ball in the corner pocket. She won ten dollars off the table. *You lose the next round, you go out with me*. She threw the game. Then she threw everything else.

She'd told Hanscom that she was moving to Wyoming with her fiancé who worked in the gas patch and that she'd be working for the *Pinedale Round Up*. Fake it 'til you make it. Except she never did get that job. The editor, Trip Erickson, wore a goatee and a turquoise bolo tie. *We aren't hiring for full time. Try writing some stories about the state fair. On spec. That means we only pay you if we like it, but I'm sure we will.* She pitched stories about the immigrants who worked ranches when all the white guys had gone to the oil patch. *These aren't the kind of stories people in this town want to read.* She pitched a piece about domestic violence in a bust cycle. She pitched a feature about oil patch wives. *Do yourself a favor, kid. Don't write about anything you care about.*

He had her try out for the copy desk. What she never told Jackie: she flunked her grammar test. Not that she cared back then. Who wants to line-edit punctuation in a corner desk? But it would have been something.

She started trying to get pregnant. And waiting tables at The Pad Rat. She decided her love for Kelly was big enough. Somehow, she did the math wrong. Never got the right parts of life to add up.

The woman reporter on the ten o'clock news is no more than twenty-five. Twenty-seven, tops. She's got a great voice and she's pretty, even with those bangs. Susan sinks deeper into Dad's old floral couch. It smells of dog hair and must. The man did not buy one new thing his entire life.

"I'm going to bed," Jackie says, leaning her head into the room. She looks so much like their mom—same dark eyes, same dark hair and tall, lean frame. Her shoulders round forward: a body made for work, for bending toward the future.

"Aren't you going to bed?"

"No, I want to watch this."

"Looks fascinating." Jackie sets her notebook on the couch, picks up one of the pillows, and beats on it, dust floating into the room.

"No really, it is. Beetles are killing the pine trees in the Rockies. Tens of millions of beetles. They're inside the bark, tunneling in there, having babies that hatch and mature. Mass tree death, it's called. Pesticides don't help. Nothing can stop it."

"Did you call Kelly?" Jackie picks up another pillow and gets to work.

"The trees turn red when the beetles finally kill them. An entire forest of red. That's a good story."

Jackie sits down. Susan should say something else. Keep the train in the station.

"You promised you'd call him," says Jackie.

"He was out on a rig."

If she'd called, he would've been out, so this isn't a lie, not really.

"Why don't you call him now?"

"I'm watching this."

"You should file. He owes you something."

"Kelly doesn't have any money."

He used to say she was the kind of woman he'd want around in wartime. *Darlin', you can make ten dollars last a week.*

"I'm sure he has enough money for drinks."

"Yeah, well."

Her hand taps the edge of the couch as if she were sending Morse code. He kicked the car door when she drove away. Three dots. Three dashes. Three dots.

"I bet you could settle out of court; it would make you feel better to just be done with it once and for all."

"You don't get it."

"What's there to get, honey? That guy sucks."

"Forget it. I'm just tired."

Susan lies down on the couch and closes her eyes. She can feel Jackie standing there staring at her.

When she hears Jackie's footfalls down the hall, away, Susan opens Jackie's notebook and flips to this week. *Find come-along, Susie exercise, Mesa Bank 10 am.* All of those plans in pen, like something that will keep her little sister safe, like proof that she's in charge of her life.

That night, she lies in bed, under the quilt Granny made. Tired. Ready already. The sheep jump over the moon. Or is it over the hay? And really they leap, not jump. The sheep leap over the moon. The cow ran away with the spoon. She scowls in the dark. The cows need her. But Jackie thinks Susan can't do anything. *That guy sucks.*

Kelly's skin tasted like the ocean. The salt made her think she knew him. Dunbars go in for hard work, for sweat. The first month after they met, he fixed her truck and the hinge that never had worked in the bathroom, and he patched her bike tire. His job on the rig had taken him everywhere. She'd never met anyone who'd seen what he'd seen. He would sit back in his chair and grin, and then he'd launch his deep voice and tell her all about it—gators in Florida, caves in Alaska, markets in Saudi Arabia. She got hooked, on his stories and his deep voice. He knew something about everything. The sex was better than she'd figured possible. He was more handsome than Camila's Ray. More worldly than Dad. More wild than a pack of Jackie's boyfriends. He was meaner than all of them too, but she didn't know that then.

She sits up in the dark and finds the Walkman on her bedside table, the tape Jackie brought her from the library already inside.

Imagine yourself in a sun-dappled forest. The woman's voice is slow, stoned-sounding. *It is a cool spring evening. You feel very safe and secure as you stroll through this quiet wooded area.* There are cracks in the ceiling. She waits for the plaster to break. To dust her with asbestos. *Take a deep, cleansing breath.* She wasn't a good daughter. She did a bad job with Dad at the end. *Relax your shoulders and jaw.* She used to do so much: the book club with the other roughneck wives, blueberry pie for sick neighbors, tutoring kids at the elementary school. *A feeling of calm fills you, as though nothing matters.* People liked her for the things she did. The doing is what mattered, what matters. *Let your thoughts go. Let your mind float among the leaves.* She needs a plan. But what can she do?

How do you do? Don't. *You feel yourself relaxing more and more with each gentle and easy breath.* Kelly said: I don't really see you as a magazine-style writer. Kelly said: don't act like a nerd. Kelly said: Your face looks funny with glasses on. You're not exactly Lois Lane. You aren't saving anyone with that article. You need to get a real job. Don't use those ten-dollar words around me. No one's ever going to love you as much as I do. I can't believe I wasted two minutes with you, let alone seven years. *You will not allow any outside sounds to interfere with your relaxation. Only the sound of my voice is important now.* This lady on the tape with the irritating slow voice: this is her career. People—other people, like Susan, but different enough—must find this helpful. Jackie says it should be helpful.

She flips the tape eleven times before dawn. She holds her dad's old watch to her ear, listens to its ceaseless ticking. As the sky turns white, she slips out of bed and into the hall, her feet moving her forward as if they belonged to someone else, someone with something to do.

3

THE DOORBELL SOUNDS ITS two notes as Ray Stark walks into the diner. There's a hot plate of cakes set down on a Formica table. On a wooden peg in the back is his mug, his name written in blue. Today will be different. Today Ray will get coffee, see people, start the day like he used to, start the day right.

He slides into a booth beside Dick Birk. On the wall above them is a stag head, its antlers a six-foot span, and beneath that a framed picture of President Bush, a hierarchy that strikes Ray as fitting. Across from him, Jim Boyce and Jon Amick—guys he's known his whole life—nod at him, grunt hello, and never drop the thread of talk. The three of them hunch over coffee as if it were fire, all of them in wool shirts, their hands red and rough from ranch work.

"You see that storm blowing in from Utah?" Amick says, while Molly fills Ray's mug. "That red dirt'll cut that snowpack quicker than salt. Last thing we need."

"Farm Service agent out of Parachute says he's got a plan if there's another drought year, but you know how that goes." Boyce rolls his blue eyes and slaps the table in the same way his dad always did. "Another big government solution."

"Shit. I ain't ever known you to turn down cash on the dollar."

"With the prices we're getting on steers, my bank book's in a coma."

The conversation around him bends to stock prices and last night's hockey game, and Ray tries to take comfort in it, to care about it. He waits for it to mean something, to touch him somehow. He stares at the badge on his uniform and at his hands, which haven't seen a hard day's work in months.

"You look like crap, Stark. You doing OK, bud?" Amick glances at the other guys, all of them awkward in their concern.

"Sure, sure I'm all right." Ray thinks about the newspaper sitting in the driver's seat of the patrol car, open, like it has been every day of the past five months he's been home, to the page in the back where they list the casualties. "How's your family?"

"Oh, you know. The same." Everyone laughs at that and Ray tries to join in but he can't say he gets it, not really. Outside the wide glass windows, the clouds are thick enough to suffocate the sky. Maria Richardson, pastor's kid, walks by smoking a cigarette, her red winter coat pulling at her belly. The surprise in him dies as quickly as it was born: another one pregnant and stuck here. His wife, Camila, looked like her once. Camila was her once.

Before he went away, before the war, Ray was like Amick and Boyce. He set his clock by contra dancing at the grange in the winter. Farm supply auctions in fall. Calving in spring. Rodeo in summer. Good enough whiskey for sale at the Skyline, every night but Sunday. Good enough coffee every morning at the diner.

Ray stares at the mug in his hands. Maria Richardson's life is now set: a debt run up, and she hasn't even spent a dollar. He tries and fails to not think about certain things. His hands tremble. He clenches a fist in his lap, trying to keep it steady, but it's no good.

"I got to get back to it, guys." He stands up too suddenly, his coffee spilling across the table. "Sorry about that."

"Nothing to worry over." Boyce smiles and mops up the mess with his sleeve. "You're always rushing off these days. Stay awhile. This town ain't got so many problems."

"Not everyone is lucky as you." He throws a wrinkled dollar and a few coins on the table.

As Ray walks outside into the slop snow, Shelly Stewart, her orange face hard, waves him over from across the street. "Hey Ray, come here and give me a hand." Beside her, blocking the driveway into Guns Flowers & Tanning, is a shiny new Dodge Durango and an oil-and-gas guy with all the trimmings: wraparound sunglasses, new down coat, baseball cap with a corporate decal, cell phone glued to his ear. Shelly has her hands on her hips. "This joker is blocking things. Tell him how things work here, Ray."

Ray stays on the opposite side of the street. He tells the guy to go ahead and move. The guy raises his finger as if to say, *You here in this shitty two-block-main-street town aren't worth my time.* Ray nods. Nothing to be done. He shrugs at Shelly, at her confused expression, and gets in his car.

He drives two blocks, through the four-way stop in the middle of town, which is also the edge of town. Silt, named for its soil, wasn't ever good for growing much besides clover. It never tried to be more than that. It took pride in its library and what it went without: stoplights, gangs, big-box stores. But it's different now. A stupid stoplight sits at the end of Grand Avenue; a new restaurant with organic lettuce and something called artisan pizza has gone in. The rental market is too tight for anyone born here, the oil and gas people having snapped up anything decent. Domestic disputes are on the daily. There's more DUIs and meth labs than he's ever seen.

Ray crosses the overpass above the highway and parks at the empty lot behind the new Holiday Inn. Drill rigs rising seven stories into the sky dot the craggy edges of mesas and the wide valley to the west. Miles of new roads crisscross the land around him, connecting hundreds of dirt pads littered with tanks and wells and pipes, scars in the green sloping hillsides.

From here, the Colorado River, the only thing unchanged, shines the color of used nickels and dimes. A hawk circles above the cottonwoods in a long low dip. The willows on the bank are redding up. The ice has started to crack into thin sheets that

couldn't hold a man. When it rains, tomorrow or next week, the creek will swell and turn the color of shit. Up in the ranches, brown water will fill irrigation ditches and flood fields. This is the way of spring. It has always been something to count on.

He finds his cell phone, another thing he never wanted, and calls his wife.

"Hey, honey."

"What's going on? Lilly, don't touch that."

"I just thought I'd check in."

"Lilly, I'm serious. Sorry, she's making me crazy."

"We eating at your mom's tonight?" In the eleven years he's been with Camila, he's never found a foothold in her family. They all speak Spanish over each other, one word he can't catch crashing into the next. They are good people. They help out all the time, especially when he was gone. They call him Raimundo and tell him they love him, but Camila's mom doesn't let down around him, like he's still in trouble for knocking up her brilliant, going-places teenage daughter.

"I told you this morning, I have a PTA thing tonight so we're eating early." A slight Mexican accent laces Camila's speech. "You know family dinner is important to me, Ray. I don't know why it's not important to you too. I know you want the girls to get used to you again."

"Of course it's important to me, Camila."

Ray sighs. When Camila first came to Silt, just her and her little brother living above her uncle's restaurant, she'd learned to speak English by watching *The Cosby Show*, *Family Ties*, and *Andy Griffith* reruns. Her idea of what makes an American family are better suited for a laugh track and a Hollywood screenwriter than for the rise and fall of actual life. No one ever wrote a television show about immigrants or teenage pregnancy.

"Did you know Maria Richardson is pregnant?"

"Of course. Everyone knows that. Lilly, stop it. You're going to end up with gum in your hair."

"Since when is she allowed to have gum?"

"Dinner is five thirty. Don't be late again."

"I better go, babe. It's real busy today."

He takes a long pull on the flask. The hawk arcs above the river, where water pools and stills behind a large boulder. He turns up the volume on *Straight Outta Compton* and tries to feel as brave as the music Wilson had loved. The liquor does what it is made for. He keeps drinking until there's nothing left. He starts up the car and drives the half-mile onto the freeway, the single exit for Silt a blur quickly becoming lost in the rearview.

A doll with one eye missing named Jenny Fox, a teddy bear, a rubber duck, three books, and a water bottle sit on the bed that night between Lilly and Ray. Across the room, under a Cinderella poster, Monica stares at a book while wearing headphones. If a tornado hit, he isn't sure he'd have time to pull them both into the closet. If there was a fire, he could throw the lamp through the window and Monica could pass Lilly down to him. He stares at Monica's arm, wondering if she's strong enough to lift herself onto the windowsill.

"Read this one, Daddy." Lilly, her dark curls falling into his face, puts a book in his lap. He touches her hair to remind himself that everything is fine. For now.

"We just did that one, honey."

"Again." In the time he was away, she grew to be just like her mama.

"OK, sweetheart."

They have been at this going-to-bed business for more than a half an hour. All the nights he missed bedtime don't suddenly come back if he lets her stay up; Camila keeps telling him that. She would say that he's spoiling them. But with his kids, and only with his kids, does he have moments of peace. There is heartbreaking joy or boredom, usually both at once.

"Daddy." She points to the corner of the small room. "There's a spider over there. I think I better sleep in your bed."

On his knees, he checks under the bed, a toy graveyard, and behind her small chair. He gets back into bed and checks behind Lilly's ear.

"That tickles."

"No spider anywhere." He kisses her on both cheeks. "You're safe, Lil."

"When are you going away?"

His own dad had been an outfitter and had been gone a lot: fly fishing in the summer, elk in the fall, big game in Alaska in the spring. Until the season he never came back, sending only the random postcard, until even those stopped. When Monica was born, that first night she'd slept on his chest, he'd promised himself it'd be different. He'd be different.

"I'm not going away, honey. Not ever again."

"Someday I'm going to go to Africa and marry a zebra named Tootsie. You can come too."

"I couldn't miss that."

Cold air seeps through the window near Monica's bed, the window he put in. He piles another blanket on top of her. "Squeeze squash love." He hands her a flashlight from the shelf and winks. "Our secret, OK? But don't read all night. You got school tomorrow."

He stands outside the shut door and listens to their breathing. It gives him the same feeling he used to get watching the cows feed at his gramps's place. Like he can let down for a minute. Like everything's OK in the world.

He goes to the kitchen and pours himself some JD and he stands there, alone in the small dining room he has been buying from the bank every month for seven years. A car passes outside on the county road. Someone's dog barks. Wind in the poplars. The clanking chain from the swing set he hauled home from Shorty's yard sale. Then there is nothing again. He takes a long sip.

He looks out the sliding glass window and sees himself, a man of average build and average height who wears clothes his wife bought for him at Walmart, who looks older than he used to, whose scars are all on the inside.

"Fuck." He's not sure if he says it out loud.

4

IN THE AFTERNOON JACKIE walks down the ditch road from the stack yard through snow and mud. The water runs thick as creamed coffee and the sun cuts a slant of light that burns off the cold. Bits of hay cling to her wool sweater and jeans. She is trying to remember the terminology for efferent and afferent neurons—which ones exit the brain and spinal cord, which approach, and not that it matters today or any day soon, but it bothers her, this forgetting of something she once knew solid. Grief, the great mind slayer.

As she approaches the house, she sees a man at the gate and as the features of his smiling face become familiar, she stops in surprise. When he waves, she raises her hand. She sees that there is no way to get out of this and walks toward him. His dark hair, long in high school, is cut short, clean cut. Gone is any trace of the guy with the penchant for tie-dyes and Mexican ponchos. He's wearing a blue button-down, open at the collar, tucked into jeans, sunglasses on a sports leash around his neck. These are not clothes meant for hard work, which is a sign that perhaps little has changed.

"Tim Layton." She folds her arms across her chest. She doesn't smile. "I heard you lived in Idaho."

"I do, I mean that's what my driver's license says? But I'm on the road a lot. I get through here when I can." He runs his hand through the side of his hair. "Shit. Jackie Dunbar. It's been a long time."

Though he is still handsome, his face has its softness. He is her same age, twenty-four, and it startles her to realize how old he looks for an age that she has wanted to believe is still young. He is smiling too much. It's as if he doesn't remember what happened the last time they spoke.

"We have this modern convenience up here, it's called a phone." She has never had enough manners; to fake anything, even small talk, makes her nervous, as if she were being unreliable to herself.

"I called. No one answered."

"It's not a great day for a visit."

"Come on, Jack. Can't an old friend stop by for a cup of coffee?"

No one has called her Jack in six years. His ring finger is naked. There's no way she's inviting him inside.

"I really have a ton of work to do. Maybe another day?"

"Listen, Jackie, I heard about your dad. I'm really sorry." He touches her arm and she stiffens. "My mom told me I should've brought up some food. I should've gotten up here sooner, I wish I had, I know it's been like what, four weeks already, but I was in New Mexico for work."

She stares at his mouth with a stump-like expression while he strings more words together in a row than she has heard in days.

"I bet your dad was glad to have you back here. People in town keep saying what a nice thing it is that you and your sister are trying to make a go of things. Everyone says how proud your dad would be."

Tim has never had trouble saying the right thing. She shifts her legs uneasily.

"Is it true you lived in Paris for a while?" Shorty had told her that, loudly, one day in line at the post office. And the way she'd said it, Jackie knew what she was thinking: leaving doesn't make you special.

"Well, yeah. That's where I live. Paris, Idaho," he laughs, his left eye twitching.

"Pretty glamorous?"

"Exactly. It's a tiny place but there's sick fishing around there and the mountain biking is killer. I'm building my own place on some land I bought, although it's taking forever because I'm never there. I still don't have a bathroom sink or dry wall in the back room." He trails off, sheepishly as if he could read her mind: follow-through had never been his strength. "Enough about me. How are you doing? How long are you home for?"

To answer either of these questions honestly isn't something Jackie can do. She studies the faint lines beside his eyes.

"Was there something specific that brought you up here?"

He starts talking about mixing business with pleasure, but she stops paying attention. A blur of black and white sprints across the field and down toward the house. As it nears, she makes out a tail and two heads.

"What the fuck is that?" Tim squints as Chicken jumps through two slats in the wooden fence; between his teeth is something gray with long curly brown hair. The eye sockets are empty and the jaw is unhinged.

With his black ears back and his neck covered in slime, the dog drops the head at her feet and sits there panting and proud. Tim has folded into a defensive crouch against the gate. If he were an animal, his ears would be pinned back. He always was made more for town than the ranch.

She smiles, despite herself. "It's just a dog head, our old dog George." She hides her mouth behind her hand and snorts. It's the first time she's laughed in weeks and now started, she can't stop. "You look a little scared."

"You're enjoying this."

"I'm not laughing at you."

"Yes you are."

"Yes I am." Chicken squats in the space between them and takes a shit. "Bad dog. You git." Jackie runs the dog off and shakes her head. "We've been spoiling that damn dog."

Now it is his turn to laugh. "I don't know how I ever left all this."

"I know what you mean."

"What are you going to do with that thing?" He nods toward George's former head tossed in the grass.

"We need some taxidermy in the house. Something for the living room."

"That's a joke? You're being funny?"

"I'll put him back in the ground."

"You want a hand?"

"That's OK. I don't need any help."

"How about company? I have a sixer in the truck." He holds out his hands and something about it, the way he stands, is funny. He always was funny.

She shrugs.

"Why not."

The grave is tossed where Chicken got at it; Dad hadn't dug it deep enough, another sure sign of the decline Jackie had failed to notice. She leans over the bones and hair and dirt and sinks the shovel neatly into earth. Tim sits on the hood of his truck and cracks a beer and watches her work.

"Nice view." He looks past her out to Grass Mesa below. From up here, the wide land swallows a person whole. The peeling paint on the house and the blow-down in the lower field isn't visible. Only the sliver of Dry Hollow Road and the ranches that cling to it, and the red-ribboned mesas beyond. It's a view made for breathing in relief, for making a person feel a sense of their place in the world.

"You all still have that creek?"

She meets his eyes, sees the laughter in them, and quickly returns to the hole in the ground. They'd fished Divide Creek a lot that summer before college. A few times when her dad and uncle were away they'd gone skinny-dipping. She had loved to open her eyes underwater and see the curve of his ass, like something that belonged to her.

"Has your swimming improved?" she asks.

"Has your casting?"

"I don't have time for fishing; I haven't been in years. What are you doing with your life, Tim Layton? How do you have so much free time?"

"I'm a landman. I set ranchers and farmers up with oil and gas contracts."

"I know what a landman does. Good money in that."

"Sure is. Have to admit, I like that part."

"Weren't you going to work at your dad's mill?"

"There was nothing new in it. And I hated all that dust, being inside." He shrugs. "Plenty of paperwork with this job but at least I can get a ride or a climb in most days between house calls."

"Sounds right."

"What?"

"Didn't you always care more about being outdoors than your grades?"

"I wasn't an idiot, I just didn't want to be an astronaut like you did." His look is eager; he's trying too hard.

"Doctor. I always wanted to be a doctor."

"Right. I don't remember you ever letting one thing drop. Except maybe me." He laughs.

Jackie narrows her eyes and shoves the blade into the ground hard enough that it can stand on its own.

"I'm in medical school. I'm just on leave because of my dad dying and my sister. Someone needs to run things."

She stares at him and then she starts to dig with all her effort.

"Are you mad? Is this about me? About that summer?"

"We don't need to talk about it."

"But you broke up with me."

"It wasn't exactly a breakup. I was being practical. We were eighteen. No one needs a long-distance relationship at eighteen."

"You didn't. Not with your full ride to that fancy school."

"You canceled on me the day before we were supposed to leave. We'd been planning that road trip for weeks."

"Did you really care?"

Jackie stops digging. Her chest rises and falls.

The thing is she hadn't cared, not exactly, not after the first few weeks. And if he had ever once called her back or sent any sort of smoke signal, she would likely never have thought of him again. But to be ignored picked at her, it raised the question why and left it unanswered, a thing for her to return to again and again.

She thinks about the version of herself, the one from six years ago, and sees that she can hardly remember what it was like to be her. She looks at Tim. "I guess I did care, but it doesn't matter, not anymore."

"Don't say it like that."

She shrugs. "What's done is done. I think I'm ready for that beer."

Three beers later, she's gotten George's head back in the ground and is sitting in Tim's truck. The cab smells like dirty socks. The floor is strewn with empty sports drink bottles. She has a loose-limbed feeling, like being underwater. They're talking about nothing important, she's not talking much at all. Tim tells story after story about people they used to know or funny things he's seen on the road.

"We're in Wyoming for work, and my buddy can't stop talking about this amazing thing he found at the grocery store called Sirloin-in-a-Can." Tim opens another beer and passes it to Jackie. "I finally open up the fridge to check it out. There's a picture of a golden retriever on the side. He was eating fucking dog food. Fuck, that was funny."

He looks at Jackie like she's the only glass of water he's seen all week. Then he looks at the mountains, and then at the can in his hand. There's a scab on his lower lip, the kind you get from sunburn. He always was too slow. She leans over and kisses him. He tastes like cheap beer and salt and her eighteen-year-old self.

Her head is wedged against the passenger door. With his body pressed against hers, she can feel his heartbeat inside her own belly, can feel it quicken. There is the heat of his mouth and the warmth of the cab. After a while, he touches her cheek.

"You've grown up. You're prettier than you used to be."

Is that a compliment or a slam? Does that mean she's actually pretty or just prettier? Susan was always the pretty one. Jackie closes her eyes and kisses his neck; he needs to shut up. She needs to keep her brain quiet. With one hand she unbuttons and unzips his pants; she is pushing them down with her knee when Tim grabs her leg.

"I feel like I'm in high school," he says, laughing, which isn't the right thing to say at all. "You want to get out of here?"

Jackie pulls down her shirt and moves as far from Tim as she can.

"There's nowhere to go around here. I better get home anyways."

"Sorry. Can't take you home yet. You need a shower. I'm going to wash your hair."

Her head snaps toward him as if he'd yanked her leash. The skin of his fingers against her thigh holds a charge. This isn't the Tim Layton she remembers.

"You go to beauty school up there in Paris?"

He starts with the bottoms of her feet. Then he washes her legs, and between her thighs, and her nipples and her back. The dirt from her body stains the hotel shower. They drink bourbon out of a plastic cup that they rest on the soap dish. When he soaps her hair, he keeps the suds from her eyes, which is a detail she might once have told Susan.

She drops to her knees and pulls him to her in the tub. They don't quite fit together in the narrow short space, and his knee presses into her hip. He tries to lead her out of the bathroom to the bed, but she pulls him onto the thin bath mat. She doesn't need some big romantic hotel bedroom scene.

Afterward, under the bright bathroom lights, they lie on the floor side by side for a long time; they're the same size and her arm fits neatly against his torso. Her mind relishes the pulsing buzz of orgasm. She shuts her eyes and tries to keep the dazed feeling from fading.

"Remember that road trip to Moab?" He traces her ear with his finger; she has to keep herself from swatting it away. Tim goes on and on about the map he forgot and how hot it was and how he wishes Moab was still sleepy like it was then. Jackie remembers it, sort of, but what she remembers more is coming home. Dad had seemed mad. When she offered to make dinner, he'd gone to watch television in his room, which he never did. And when she asked him, what's wrong, why are you upset, he looked small, shrunken. *It's so quiet when you're not here. What am I going to do without you next year?* She'd hugged him and he smelled like he always did, of dust and cigarettes. It had been hard to breathe.

Her eyes get wet. She is not going to fall apart in the bathroom of the Holiday Inn, especially not in front of Tim Layton.

"I've got to go."

"No, stay. We've got HBO. We can order tacos from that new Mexican place. We have so much to talk about."

She explains about calving season and how she needs to check the girls.. Which, it occurs to her as soon as she says it, is actually true. At feeding, Blanca's tail had been flying and she'd been walking fences away from the herd. Dad would never have left a second-year heifer on the verge of labor.

The floor is wet as she jumps up, and she slips, feeling sick from the alcohol, and has to grab the towel rack. Her clothes are in a pile with his and she sorts through them, pulling on what's hers.

"Seriously, Tim, I really shouldn't have come."

"I could make a joke right now." He takes another swig of bourbon from the bottle and stays right there on the floor.

"Get up. I need a ride." She throws him his boxers. "Or let me take your truck."

"Hold your horses, cowgirl; give me a sec."

Tim puts his shirt on inside out. He can't find his keys, making jokes, making a running narration of his movements. He is disorganized and slow. His pink skin looks like it could bruise with mild impact. Jackie watches him as if from a great distance, as if he has nothing to do with her because of course he doesn't.

5

IF SOMEONE ELSE WERE in bed, if Kelly were here, Susan could feel his weight at her back, his warmth, and she could roll over and he would touch her hair and say *Good morning, sweetheart.* She stares out the window at nothing but endless suffocating blue sky. Her skin itches. Her hips need popping. Other people, they're serving a lunch-hour rush, or filing on deadline, or drinking coffee at the diner, or reading stories to a child on their lap. Susan has no reason to get up, to stop looking at the sky. Knit, purl, knit, purl, that's the lining of her stomach. Jackie is outside working hard, doing everything right.

Beside the bed is yesterday's paper. Here is a whole world of ideas. *Listen to this*, she wishes she could say. *The river runs dark and gritty as unfiltered coffee.* Pretty good line for a local paper. Sediment is building up behind Glen Canyon Dam, the 710-foot concrete wall that blocks the Colorado River. So much silt sits in the reservoir behind the dam that the river is backing up on itself, changing its shape and direction, into the floodplains where people like to live. She wants to lean in, over her coffee and pancakes, and say, *You know what I think?* People around here think silt is just dirt. It's not their fault; it's what the Bureau of Reclamation tells them. Nature can be tamed, bent to human will. But control has its limits. Give it time. In a couple hundred decades, all that silt is going to break down the dam.

Susan tosses the paper onto the floor. Tick. Tock. Her watch stares at her. Out the window, the poplars move in the wind. She holds her breath. Listen. No car up the drive. No train in the distance. The apocalypse could've happened, and she the only survivor. She stares at the window and puts her hands on her empty hull of a belly.

The sound of tires against the gravel drive draws her from bed. Into the kitchen, quick quick. And there is Jackie, driving away in a white truck with a man whose face she can't place. Knock knock knock, her fist against the window, but they don't hear, they are gone, and there is only the dust and Chicken barking at the dust.

Susan paces in front of the sink. To leave without saying goodbye isn't polite. Jackie can do this, she can be surprising, though never to herself. But why today, on this terrible sad low day, would she leave without word. Jackie must remember about today, about how six years ago, she'd tucked gardenias into Susan's hair. They had gone to Joann Fabrics to buy a veil, and Jackie had turned to her in the felt aisle to ask if she was really sure. And Susan had laughed with the joy of certainty. Sure she was sure. She had never been more sure.

Her wedding ring didn't have a stone. It had looked so small next to the deodorant in the medicine cabinet, where it stayed the day she left. A note would've been redundant.

She picks up the phone. Sets it back down.

They never said it was over. She didn't pack everything. She just drove to Colorado for Thanksgiving and never went back. And he didn't come after her.

In the bathroom, she washes her face. Puts on lipstick, a coral color that brings out the gold highlights of her hair. He always liked her black tube top; she puts it on. She'll tell him about the silt behind the dam, he'll like that. She'll ask him about the AA meetings. And maybe, if it all goes straight, she'll suggest he visit.

A pony races around in her gut; she dials the number from memory.

"Hel-lo. Kelly Eastman's answering service." A southern accent in Wyoming isn't such a common thing.

"Heidi?"

Heidi Hooten, the welder with the big tits and the cotton candy mouth. Heidi Horndog, the guys called her.

"Oh shit, is this Susan? You been away too long, sweetie."

"Give the phone to Kelly, will you?"

It takes a while.

"What do you want?"

"Well, hi. I don't know. I read something in the paper that made me think of you."

"I ain't heard from you in three months and you want to tell me about the newspaper? Fuck off."

The gruff of his voice used to, at first, be sexy. Billy Goat Gruff. It hadn't taken long to learn to ignore it, to find the cracks in his tone where the sad, vulnerable part of him poured out.

She leans her forehead against the wall; she lets it hold her up. Swallow. Deep breath.

"Sue, I can hear you breathing. What do you want?"

She doesn't know exactly. And the room spins with the question. She should've known the answer before calling. She can see that now.

"I'm sorry. I'm having a hard time," she whispers.

"I know all about your hard time, about your crazy, and honey, the day you left, it stopped being my problem."

The phone weighs a thousand pounds. The ground is made of sediment.

"Why are you being so quiet?" he barks. "Is that it? We done now?"

She hangs up, her chest heaving. The sink. No. The toilet. She sticks her finger down her throat and it burns on the way up. The burn is right; it feels like how she feels.

She should've asked: When can we talk in private? She should've asked: Do you miss me? Even a little? She should've told him about her dad, but then she would have had to explain why she didn't call him when it happened, how she just couldn't. The bathroom is small and dark and there is no place safe for her mind to land.

Quick Quick Quick, think of another thing to think about. The baseboards. The baseboards need cleaning and that is a thing she can do. She gets a rag and the cleaning product and gets down on her knees and makes long swipes through the dust and the dirt. She had wanted her own small child on her lap, a book beside them. To take her or him camping on the lease land. To watch Dad put a fishing pole in a small pair of hands. To feel tiny fingers close around her thumb. To teach someone how to skip, how to ride a bike, how to read. A million other things.

You're crazy, that's what Kelly said when she lost everything for the fourth time. Her plum-sized baby, dead on the bathroom floor. She'd yelled at him to bring a mason jar; she had wanted to keep it, not forever, but for a ritual, to plant it under a blueberry bush or cosmos. Kelly had taken it away, leaving her crying, curled up against the tile. They'd never talked about it again.

She directs herself to the job at hand, to the small satisfaction of a clean surface. She moves on hands and knees down the hall, into the bedrooms, the living room. But her mind will not settle there on the dirty rag. Again, she returns to her conversation with Kelly and what she should've said differently. She climbs onto the kitchen countertop, dusts the tops of every single cupboard. Her thoughts are like dice. Roll again. Find a new way to feel bad.

Inside the medicine cabinet are the two orange bottles from Doc Pitkin. Fuck it. She swallows one white pill and two blue ones, and waits to escape.

6

When Tim and Jackie get back to the house, the sun is sliding down behind Mount Baldy, the clouds are closing in, and the cows have disappeared from view. Tim wants to hug; he wants to give her his number and he is slow, too slow. Jackie's thoughts are in the fields, and the steps she needs to take before getting to the fields, and she rushes from the truck and through the gate. As soon as she gets into the house, it's clear she has, once again, gotten home too late.

Susan sits on the kitchen floor with her back against the wall, her knees tucked up against her chest. She is dressed in summer clothes and she is shaking, her teeth chattering. Jackie drops to a squat before her sister.

"Susie, what happened? What's wrong?"

"Why do you smell like a bar?" Susan looks at Jackie and then looks at the rag in her hand. Her speech is slow, slurred. "I'm so cold. Did you feel that shaking? It felt like an earthquake. It wouldn't stop."

Jackie squints at her sister, at her glassy eyes. The phone is off the hook, making an awful broken hum.

"Why is the phone off the hook? What is going on?"

"I didn't know where you were or when you were coming back. You shouldn't leave without saying good-bye. I called 911. But then John Cox answered the call—do you remember John? He was homecoming king when I won queen? I didn't want to talk to him. I hung up. But the phone started ringing and I didn't know what to do, I didn't know what to say, so I just kept it off."

Jackie pours herself a cup of cold coffee. If she can get the taste of whiskey and sex out of her mouth, she can deal. She swallows an entire cup. Outside the light is thinning, the trees shake in the wind. She needs to get out there.

"Susie, we've got to check the cows."

Susan's eyelids are heavy; they flutter open. "Fuck off." She whispers. The words have hardly any power, except that she's never said them to Jackie before. "Go away. You're good at that."

Jackie flattens her back against the wall and holds up the entire house with her shoulder blades. After their mom died, Susan seemed fine. Everyone said it like an accusation. As in *Jackie, eat something, your sister is fine*. Or *Jackie, you have to start going to school, your sister is fine*. Susan got straight A's and won the science fair for a project about endangered falcons. No one ever saw her cry. But Jackie knew.

The pockets of Susan's jeans, of her sweatshirts, were always stuffed with candy wrappers, bottle caps, envelopes from bills addressed to their mom. She watched her sister at school. Saw her chase a plastic bag across the field and shove it in her coat. None of Susan's teachers or millions of friends ever seemed to notice. *Susie, it's just garbage. You can throw it away. Quit being so weird.* She'd meant to say something a million times. But she hadn't. And Dad never said anything. He never did anything.

For the past few weeks Jackie has clung to the idea that Susan's anxiety will improve, that she will get excited about ranching, so that she, Jackie, can gallop back to medical school, to become a doctor whose only responsibility to the ranch is sending a portion of her monthly paycheck. What fantasy. Tears well in her eyes and she slaps them away. She doesn't have time for this.

"You need to eat something and then you need to lie down. Sleep it off."

She hangs up the phone and lets the door slam behind her. Then Jackie goes out to do what her sister could've done at any point all afternoon.

Jackie rides the four-wheeler across the fields, the sun slipping away, taking with it any warmth from the day. The pair is nowhere to be found. There was the time that she and Dad got to the birth too late. Four coyotes were ripping apart the calf, only halfway out of the cow, hung at the hips. Blue and pink tissue littered the pink snow. Jackie had panicked, raised her gun to shoot, stopped only by her Dad's steady voice calming the heifer, running the coyotes off. He had known to save the cow, to help her birth her dead calf. He had known how to go on from a bad time.

After the light dies behind the mountains and the early evening is all shadow and wind, Jackie finally finds Blanca, off behind a small hill apart from the rest. She is lying in a pool of mucus, shit, and blood. Two hooves stick out of her vagina, the placenta making a web around the calf's legs. The young cow grunts at Jackie to get back, to get away.

"I don't want to be here either," Jackie says.

Blanca grunts again and gets herself up, standing, her tail swinging like she might charge.

"Don't you dare." Jackie stares at the cow's dungeon eyes and makes herself take big even breaths, building herself up big, to be bigger than the cow.

Suddenly, a blue nose slicks out between Blanca's legs. The calf's eyes are glassy. That baby's been in there too long. Jackie needs to hurry. She should've been here an hour ago.

Blanca blinks at Jackie, her eyes wet black stones. *You aren't your dad*, they say. *You don't know what you're doing. You're still a little drunk.*

"You'll be fine, girl."

The cow heaves and twists along her spine. Dad would rope her and snub her down. The come-along rod is awkward in Jackie's hand; it's a thing she's never used alone. She's mid-crouch, trying to decide whether to wait another minute or get in there, when the cow starts like she might charge. Jackie is telling her to stay, in her lowest voice, when a fireball the size of a car explodes beyond the lip of the mesa. It burns a hole into the darkening night. The cow shudders and groans in the glow. Like nothing Jackie has ever seen, as if a cloud burst and flickered across the sky. Then the fire is gone. Jackie edges backward toward the mesa, eyes shifting between the cow and the direction of the flare.

Far below, a black screen of smoke billows in the place of what was flame, casting a net over Dry Hollow Road, Johnson's stock tanks, and Amick's barn. It's the wrong time of day for brush fires. Wrong season. Seconds later, another ball of fire erupts into the air.

Blanca grunts behind her, and Jackie runs back in time to see the calf slip onto the ground. The thin milky coat of the placenta is wrapped around its body like an extra, suffocating skin.

Jackie darts in quick, rips the placenta off the black legs with her hands, and jumps back before the cow knows she's been there. The calf's sleek white fur shines against the hard soil. The torn arm's-length of umbilical cord, ropy and green, flops across her trunk. This is as it should be. Except. The ears don't move. The eyes are unblinking. There's no cough, and no amniotic fluid out of the lungs. Jackie strains into the wind to see a sign of breath.

Come on and pop up. Get on those legs and wobble like a drunk. Jackie puts her hand down the neck of her shirt and grabs onto the side of her breast. She holds herself tight.

A few feet away, Blanca stays down, part of the placenta still hanging out of her like an extra tail. Jackie jogs across the several feet of space between her and the calf and falls to her knees beside the white bundle. It's slightly bigger than Chicken. Jackie tells herself that she has been here before. She's fixed things up, and the gamble has paid. But never alone, never on several drinks. She stuffs this away. This is what it means to be a doctor: to pay attention to everything but yourself.

She inserts her thumb in one black nostril. The nose is cold, soft. Then her index finger slips into the other nostril and jerks twice. The calf wants to move, it wants to breathe, to get up, to nurse. The smell—of blood's salinity, of biological moistness—tells Jackie it's possible.

"You can't die. Get it together."

Another flame bursts into the sky. Blanca bellows three loud notes and looks out her dungeon eye at her baby. Her gray tongue hangs long out of her mouth.

Get out of there, Jackie Blue. It's her dad's voice in her head. She puts her hand on the calf's chest. The heartbeat is there. If she can clear the mucus plug, the baby will breathe and the entire day, the entire winter, will be redeemed. She clamps the calf's mouth shut with her left hand and stops up the right nostril with her right thumb and index finger. Puts her mouth on the other nostril and blows. Breathes quick and blows again, all the air in her body pushed into that dime-sized hole. One more try.

She turns her head to gulp at the air and Blanca's head is down, ears forward, all fifteen hundred pounds running at her. Jackie yanks her hand away from the calf and pushes into the ground. There is snow, sky, mud, clover, snow. She is rolling and then she is not. Blanca whacks at Jackie's ribs with the middle of her forehead, bone to bone. The cow snorts and blows her cud back. The sweet smell of clover, the rotten eggs of methane, all the bile of the cow's gut.

Jackie's breath is broken glass. Her heartbeat a hammer. This can't be happening. This isn't how it goes for her. She moves her tongue behind her front teeth and tastes iron, blood, and the grit of dirt. There is the sky. Another cloud of flame. Yellow and black. It rises. Like a rooster tail, she thinks, before pain consumes her thinking.

7

WHEN THE CALL COMES through his radio, Ray is at the movies. Gary Malin, owner of the Paradise Theater, is a Vietnam vet. Since Ray's been back, Gary's been letting him up to the projection room for the five o'clock show, not noticing his uniform, not asking any questions. It's just their secret, this little arrangement.

"We got a 911 hang up from Dunbars'." John's voice over the radio interrupts the opening credits. "Something sounds off. Hustle up there."

Ray turns up the handheld in his lap, sets his Bud Light on the rug.

"Dunbars? Any intel?" Ray asks.

"Nothing yet. I can't get through."

"Over."

Ray nods at Gary and heads out the door, taking the stairs two at a time. He had wondered after those Dunbar girls but had figured a visit from him would be of little use to them.

Paul McCurdy was flapping his mouth a few weeks back at the Skyline about did Ray remember that hot piece of ass Susan Dunbar and how he'd seen her walking the ditch road with her dog and smoking a pipe. And what a shame that neither sister ever came by the bar. Ray said he'd hardly known them, but of course that wasn't true.

His cell phone rings and he picks up out of habit, wishing right away that he had not.

"What do you need, Mila?"

"I'm just wondering why exactly your patrol car is parked behind the movie theatre again. That's the third time this week."

"Jeez honey, you following me?"

"Please. My mother drove by and noticed. We're all just worried about you."

"Shit, Mila, do me a favor and worry less, will you? Jesus."

"What time are you home tonight?"

"You know what time."

"Will we see you then, or will you be late again, smelling like booze?"

"Mila, I don't have time to talk about this. Really. I got a call."

"Sure you do."

He hesitates. "I hear you, OK? I'll see you tonight."

Fifteen minutes later, his thoughts still scattered from the call with his wife, his life feeling penned in tight, he is almost at the top of the ridge. He passes the weed-clogged field where he used to play ball and he remembers the smell of wet grass through his catcher's mask, how good he was at calling a game, at being a backstop, and he thinks how he could still do that, he's still strong, and maybe that's the thing he needs, the thing that will kick him back into the motor of this town, and it's then that he catches the first one in his peripherals.

Behind Amick's Quonset about a half-mile ahead, a flame the size of a helicopter rips apart the sky. Ray doesn't breathe or blink. It's near dark but the valley floor is too bright. Pretty quick, a massive cloud of black smoke comes at him.

Someone is attacking. Tall palm trees off the road. He hits the gas and hauls toward the smoke. Overhead, the whir of rotors. He flies around the S-curve past a few of Amick's sheep, before he actually forms a thought. No terrorist ever heard of this place. There's no helicopter. The palms are cottonwoods. He lets off the pedal. What the fuck?

Another cloud of flame, and smoke erupts outside his window. He grabs the mic and turns the radio up, way up.

"PD3 to Dispatch. PD3 to Dispatch." A loud hiss comes off the gully, back in the deep beyond Dry Hollow. There are houses all over the place. Those people have got to be scared to death.

"John, there's fireballs in the sky." Ray swings onto the unnamed gravel artery that links a couple ranchettes and hay farms and gas wells. The smoke is a giant mass, screening electric lines and forest. "I'm rolling out to investigate." The dirt spins at his tires and dust fills the car. He keeps the window down, keeps his eye on the flame burning a hole in the sky.

"Negative, Zebra." John is quick back. "The law makes all possible domestics fast calls. You know that. You hit Dunbars' and check back in."

"That's a bad call, John." He learned this lesson a million miles away. John hasn't ever been farther away than Wyoming. "I'm going in."

"I'm in touch with Fire on this and they're on it. PD3, do not go there."

Sometimes breaking the rules is the only way things go right. He shuts off the radio. John'll thank him later.

Trailer-sized fireballs burp from a big pit in front of a gas well. There is heat and smoke and mess. The rural night smells of airports and long-haul trucks. A crowd of folks across the road from the well looks up, heads back, black spots against a wall of flame. Ranchers, teenage potheads, his seventh-grade teacher, a checker from Don's Market. On every face is a combination of fear and stupid wonder. The only thing between them and fire is a barbed-wire fence, the road, and clumps of sagebrush.

His heart flaps its fucking wings. He's got to get them the hell out of here. Now.

Before he can reach into the car and radio for backup, a woman wearing a pink sweatsuit and silver cowboy boots hustles across the road.

"Stark, what the heck is this about?" Shorty Lee has always been a real bee in cheesecake. Pete Johnson and Jim Boyce crowd around. "We've been calling that dang gas commission for ten minutes and all we get is recording."

"You feel that shaking, Ray? Before this thing blew?" Johnson straddles his four-wheeler, his eyes flinty. "Lottie and I landed on the kitchen floor."

"Shit, I thought it was a goddamn earthquake before I remembered, we don't get earthquakes around here." Boyce leans over to shake hands. "Glad you're here, Stark. I got to get back and check on Nancy, she's all banged up."

What Ray knows about gas wells and what can go wrong is nothing. He has zero training on this type of thing.

"It smells like goddamn Oklahoma around here." Shorty takes a long drag on her cigarette. Exhales and spits. "God dammit, will you look at that. It's still going."

Behind the fireballs and a screen of smoke, the rig pushes pipe into the ground. Two guys with hard hats, too far away to see well, run around the derrick, one of them pointing up at the scaffolding.

"The tanks over there by the derrick got condensate or diesel in them." Johnson nods at a stack of crap near the tanks. "We got no clue what's in them bags of chemicals." He's straddling his four-wheeler, his gimme cap casting shadow across his face.

"And Stark, I ain't seen no one from Amick's place." Shorty shakes her finger at him. "They got them two young kids, you know."

"I'll make sure everyone's safe." Ray wipes a lake of sweat from his forehead. "It'll be all right."

Ray punches the button for the loud speaker with a shaking hand. He clears his throat, coughs.

"You are strongly encouraged to evacuate the area. Get yourselves and your families south of O road on Dry Hollow. Help is on the way."

Help isn't on the way fast enough. Far as he knows, the thing could blow at any minute. He jogs across the road to the rig, sticks his boot on the steel gate, and hoists his skinny ass over. Rocks the size of grenades fly out of the well bore, and pipes clang through the blare. They land in a rough arc three feet away. The wires blur and he swallows hard, but his teeth shake; they won't quit shaking.

Keep it solid, Ray. Keep it solid.

"Where's your safety officer?" he yells at a kid who is up on a ladder near the well.

"On his way." The pad rat looks like someone caught in his first sandstorm. He jumps down off a ladder and falls on his ass. Ray yells over the roar of the fire, telling the guy to clear out, and the kid shakes his head no. Ray's Glock is warm at his side. He won't be the reason for another fool death. Again he tells the kid to leave. Again the kid won't go.

Something explodes on the rig like a street grenade in Sadr. The taste of puke fills his mouth. His jaw gets tight like he's going to flatten the entire fucking scene between his molars. The roughneck isn't safe. He isn't working to make it safe.

"You got to come with me." The gun is out of Ray's holster, not pointed at the kid, not really.

"Officer, what are you doing?" The guy steps back a few paces and trips. "Seriously, I'm just a grunt around here."

Ray wants to break the kid's fucking arm. He points the Glock at him then. Tells him to get on the ground, and he might be yelling a little too. He's just trying to keep the peace around here and no one is helping. He locks his eyes on the kid and stares him down.

"What the heck is going on, Ray?" Ty appears out of no place, sprinting across the rutted mud of the well pad. Ray doesn't bother to lower the gun. Ty stares at him for a second and then just stands at his side. Ty offers his hand up to the roughneck and smiles, like it's pancake breakfast on Fourth of July. Ray watches Ty talk to the kid, feeling like he's on the other side of a closed window. Slowly, he comes back, Ty's hand on his arm. The Glock is too heavy; it clatters on the dirt pad. Ty whispers that he should get out of there and for once, Ray follows orders. The heat of the fire burns the backs of his knees as he runs to his car.

Ray drives a half-mile from the well, rolls onto the shoulder of Dry Hollow, and cuts the engine. He makes short work of what's left in the flask but his head is still full of wasps. He never wants to move from this seat in this car on this shoulder of this road. His muscles ache like he's been in a bar fight and he knows now that he's had an episode and that he's got to get quiet, get down with himself, stay away from people. The fire flicks across his side mirror. He stares long enough that the glow blurs to simple shapes. Eyes shut, the fire burns in there too.

It's gotten late, that time of night where the sun escapes to someplace better. He bangs his head against the steering wheel, hard, three times. He pushes his fingers against his closed eyelids. He never figured on being the asshole.

Then he remembers the Dunbars.

He starts the car, a failure in uniform, driving south.

When the road turns to dirt he's close, and soon enough he's past the old rusted combine and tractors, past the creek where he learned to swim, until he is there. *The pretty little place down below*, Gramps used to call it, back when he and Bill Dunbar ran the two ranches as if they were the same place. Back when Gramps was alive and Bill was alive and that Iraqi kid was alive.

He rings the bell. He knocks. The poplars blow at his back. The mountains above make a white outline against the black sky. He rings again. The night crowds in on him; he shuts his eyes for a minute. Everyone everywhere is basically the same. They all want saving; they just need to know they won't need saving from you.

He's about to clear a perimeter of the house, to see about another way in, to do one thing right tonight, when the door opens an inch and an eye so light it's almost gray, an eye he knows well, looks him over.

"Ray Stark?" She opens the door another half-foot.

"Evening, Sue. Good to see you're all right."

She holds onto the doorframe like she needs it to stand. Pink lipstick is like a gash across her mouth. The tube top is a strange choice for March, but it'd be strange on Sue in August: she's gotten too skinny. Her arms dangle from her shoulders; her cheeks are hollows. She looks as old as he feels.

"I'm real sorry to barge in like this. They sent me up here to make sure you were all OK," he says, apologizing.

"Ray." Her eyes dart from his face to his shoes to the night outside. She bites her lip. "I don't know."

Camila used to say Susan had laughing eyes.

Camila used to say, *Susan don't take crap from any of them.*

There's a long pause while Susan sways from side to side. Her eyes do not smile. They don't seem to take anything in.

"You OK, Sue? Anything you need help with?"

"Good luck with that." She laughs, loud in his face, and this—more than the rest of it—gives him a start.

"Where's Jackie?"

"I'm fine."

He is trying to think what to say, how to make sense of what happened to the girl who was good equally at keg stands and grades, who used to make him laugh, make him feel listened to, who was always way too good for him, who left Silt, saying she'd never be back.

She turns into the hall and gestures for him to follow.

The wood paneling in the hall is cracked and faded. The living room where Susan leads him is cold and musty: nothing but a yellow TV tray in front of a tired couch, a television rested on an apple crate, a dog bed in the corner by the woodstove. He'd heard Susan had been back in Silt for months; she hadn't exactly brought a feminine touch to the place.

Susan curls up on the old couch like a cat. She keeps twisting a big watch on her wrist, around and around.

"Those cows take too long."

"Is Jackie out with the cows?"

Susan stares at the wall, as if thinking wore her out. "Mac and cheese sounds good. Do I seem strange to you?"

"Oh Sue, I could ask you the same thing." He tucks a blanket over her shoulders. "Let me go check the fields."

From the front porch he hears what he didn't before: a cow bellowing, a dog barking. He stops thinking and jogs toward sound. He's got wind in his shirt.

Past the hilltop, the Maglite beam catches the outline of a cow twenty feet away and he slows down. Ray hollers at her, tries to run her off. She doesn't move. He yells and pinwheels his arms until finally she moves off a ways, far enough. There's a lump. Muddy boots flopped on the ground.

Never losing sight of the cow, never turning his back on her, he runs to Jackie's side. Her body's twisted, her left arm draped across her chest. She's pale, like she's got milk in her veins. Her breathing, quick and shallow, makes frost smoke into the night. He should've been there sooner. He should've been a lot of things.

"Howdy partner." He drops into the mud and snow. In the years since he's seen her, she's lost all softness, her body tall and straight. Her face, which set out to be pretty, has ended up caught on its hard edges. "Can you hear me, Jackie?"

With his mouth next to her ear he can smell the mud, and something else, something sweet. He taps her left shoulder. Circles of pink pockmark the snow under her hand. He taps again, harder. Her pulse is wild, her skin clammy. She moans. She blinks. Behind her, across the snowy field, there's a streak of mud maybe twenty feet long, a handprint in the ground by her head. She'd tried to drag herself someplace.

"Shit. Looks like you were made tough like your dad."

"Not tough as the cow." Her words are slurred and slow, but they are words, and they sound like more than he deserves. He drapes his crappy thin uniform jacket across her body and tells the dog to stay. She opens her eyes, her face breaking apart. "She died."

"You're going to be OK. I'll be right back."

He runs. Across the field he skids on the snow but doesn't fall and then he keeps at it, fast as he can, and he hits the hill and slips again and this time he stumbles and lands forward on his bad knee but he pushes off the ground with both hands and takes off again. His mind is like one of those metal cages that the lottery people use to spin the balls around. There's the hawk making a dip toward the river and the feel of Ty standing beside him and then there's Camila's heart-shaped ass. He's going to start being better about things, like lifting weights every day, and maybe he really should try a shrink at the VA like Camila's been nagging at him to do. There's the car with the door still open but he doesn't even try the mic because cell phones have never worked up here and so that might not work either and he just can't waste another second, and then he's at the gate and into the house, not bothering to knock, and to the kitchen and on the phone.

John rips into him. Says Sheriff wants to see him as soon as possible but Ray doesn't hear the rest of it because he's trying to tell him the mess of the now, so he just keeps covering up John's words with his own until John stops for breath and Ray can explain. It's too much time wasted with talk but John says he'll get people out and Ray hangs up knowing it'll happen. He turns around and Susan is there, inches away, hand over her mouth, rocking back and forth, her cheeks full of air.

No one likes bad news delivered on a tray of bullshit. No one deserves to be alone and afraid.

"You heard what I told John?"

She nods and spins and runs into the hall. Ray pauses, but then heads to the door, heading back to Jackie, when she comes out of a bedroom with a blanket.

"Come up there with me? Hold her hand?"

"I'll make coffee." She hands him the blanket. "I know how to do that."

When he reaches Jackie, she's rolled onto her left shoulder, her forehead in the mud. The dog licks at her face, whimpering. Her breathing has lost its pace. Smoke from the rig fire rolls up onto the mesa, and he can't risk a trigger, can't risk anything else. He sits down cross-legged with his back to the fire, his knees close to her forehead, and carefully rolls her onto her back and covers her with the blanket.

"I'm here now. I ain't going again." She's shaking and her pulse is way too fast. She doesn't open her eyes. Her cheeks and forehead are unlined, unscarred, a face vulnerable to life. He looks at her and goes cold with dread. Monica in a ditch, Lilly hit by a car, hurt like Jackie, worse than Jackie, and he, unable to help.

Out of his own fear, or hopelessness or panic, or maybe to offer proof that she isn't totally alone, Ray starts to talk. He tells her what he remembers about her dad, how he was a class A rancher, the type made of barbed wire and leather. *No one runs land and cattle like Bill Dunbar*, Gramps would say. And Gramps, he tells her, never praised easy. She doesn't answer, doesn't say a thing. Cold seeps into his skin; he is shivering now but it's not from the cold. He feels water sting his eyes. He keeps talking.

He tells her what he remembers about the pond on his grandpa's land where they used to fish. About the time he found her pulling porcupine quills out of his dog. He tells her the stars he sees in the sky: there's the big dip, there's the little one, there's Orion's Belt. He talks about his kids. How Lilly is making up her own jokes now and how they're terrible: why did the toothbrush want to brush the teeth? To clean them. Why did the toothbrush want to clean them? To make them healthy. He tells her how Monica is so quiet, how she's shy around him, how he doesn't know how to reach her. He tells her he has no idea how to be a good dad but that he really does want to know. That he hopes someday he'll know more than he does now. He goes on and on; more words come out of his mouth than he would've guessed he knew, until eventually, at last, there are sirens, and then a light jumps across the field. He wipes his eyes dry, glad for help, ashamed to be glad.

Delores Holt runs up on those short legs with a cervical collar under her arm and a backboard. She checks vitals in her calm, steady way and then on three, they're lifting the litter. Jackie's eyes shut.

"Honey, you see Susan tonight?" Delores asks Ray as they scramble down the lip of the slope. She stares toward the house like she's listening for a pulse. "She don't make it to town much these days and I been wondering. My mom was tight with their people. Crazy don't run in that family, it gallops."

Small towns breed two different kinds of folks. There are those who don't feel safe unless they know their neighbors' business, like their tooth rot or if they go to the county dump more than twice a year. Then there's the other kind, who can only stand living so closely knitted together if they keep to themselves.

"I don't know much about that," Ray says. Gramps was in the second camp. "You know how it is around here—everyone got their own special brand of crazy."

"True." Delores grins as they reach the ambulance. "You did good tonight, honey."

At that Jackie blinks. She tries to say something and Delores gives her a hard stare. Ray leans in close and then he gets it.

"Don't worry." He pats her arm as they slide her into the back of the can. "I'll look in on Sue."

The bottoms of Jackie's boots are small and caked in dirty snow. Before the dog can jump in with her, Delores has the bread door shut and they take off, the red lights flick on, the tires kicking mud.

8

SUSAN SNEAKS INTO JACKIE'S room as quiet as death, but no, that's a terrible metaphor. She walks over to the edge of the bed, a fold-out couch really, wedged between two four-drawer filing cabinets in what was not so long ago Dad's office, and stares at her sister sleeping. Ten days since the accident, Jackie's cheeks are waxy, her cheekbones like mountains that have lost their glaciers. They say to Susan, look what you have done. Asleep, Jackie looks younger, less most-likely-to-succeed.

After Mama died, Susan would crawl under Jackie's sheets and hold her little sister's cold feet between her own. To stop Jackie's crying, Susan read books. Entire chapters from *Little House in the Big Woods*. Nancy Drew. As many pages as Jackie wanted. Sometimes Susan made up stories about two pioneer sisters on the Oregon Trail. Dad was always out with the cows. In the mornings before school, Susan would brush the tangles from Jackie's long hair just like their mama had. She'd pack them both a lunch, made sure they had a piece of fruit.

Jackie decided to be a doctor around then and Dad went all crazy for it. *Dr. Dunbar, come clean my wound*, he'd holler from the bathroom when he cut himself shaving. And Jackie'd slide down the hall in socks to fix him up with hydrogen peroxide and a Band-Aid. In those moments, it was clear that Dad favored his younger daughter; in those moments, Susan understood why. Being capable has always been the key to love. Susan grabs a broom from the kitchen and comes back to sweep under the bed, finding dust balls and tissue.

"Susie." Jackie opens one eye. Frowns. "What are you doing?"

"It's dirty."

"Please stop doing that."

"OK." Susan pinches the skin of her inner upper arm until the pain goes away. Jackie shuts her eyes again, her frown as wide as the mesa. Another terrible metaphor.

"Did Pete come by yet to feed out?"

"Yes. I was going to tell him that I would do it but then I got worried I might do it wrong." The dust is a shroud. The broom pushes it around but never takes it away. Susan sweeps, watching the dust fly.

"Stop sweeping." Jackie says it the way she talks to the dog. "Please."

"Fine." Susan sets down the broom, lets it clatter against the wall. And then, knowing what Jackie misses most, "I'm going outside for a walk."

The ditch road is a mess. Snow. Cow pies. Mud. Susan might trip and fall off the narrow path and into the brown ice-water. She takes another careful step. Chicken follows her; he doesn't trust her to walk alone.

She stops to rest. She is panting. She makes herself walk to the side of the mesa, to stare again at the proof of her failure. The coyotes have made ribbons of the dead calf's skin. Guts hang from its belly. She'd dragged it here, almost to the mesa's edge, to let nature take care of things. By summer, the carcass will be nothing more than a pile of bleached bones. Its hair looks so soft near the ears. Its little hoof sticks out like it's ready to walk.

She sits down. The ground is hard; right away the cold seeps through her jeans and thin underpants. She is like a hose with too little pressure, no way to direct the flow. It wasn't always this way.

From here, she can see the ranch as it used to be. All those hundreds of cows in the upper fields like flecks of pepper in a salad. Summers, the clover turned scarlet. The willows crowding the ditch smelled of wet, of relief. Push the cows through a gate and the dust, a mark of accomplishment, rose and drifted.

Everyone worked, all of them, almost all of the time. Mama, off in the summers from teaching at the high school, used to haul bales and move handline, strong as any man. Susan can't remember her complaining about the long days, about the work. *Your mother had the best laugh I ever heard*, Dad always said that, but Susan can no longer remember what it sounded like. And she can't help it—it's not that she wants to think about it, but there it is, the hard turn to the right just before the overpass, her and Mama in the Dodge, on the way home from church, just before everything went wrong the first time.

The radio had been on. *Shh Susan, just a second, he just said something about a late cold snap*. If she hadn't been talking, would it have mattered? And she can't remember what Mama was wearing, or did she have her glasses on, and was she very annoyed with her in that moment, the last moment before she died? In sixteen years she never asked Dad, and now it is too late for that too.

"I don't know what to do, buddy. What should I do?"

Chicken noses one of the cow pies toward her.

"Leave it alone."

He whines and paws at her until fine, OK, she gets up.

One black rubber boot steps toward the edge of the mesa. She pulls it back. Time to go home. Each step takes care. There's a rock. A fallen tree. Poison ivy. She shivers. She is a giant stick bug. Her coat is too big. Nothing fits right. Even the fat on her feet has melted away. She tried when Ray came. She boiled water. But he could tell it was her fault. Anyone could.

Life is never going to just happen to you, Susie, Dad used to say when he saw another report card. All her A's lined up like perfect stitches in a wound. *You go make the Dunbar name something people talk about*. He told her that before he stopped talking.

He'd said the same exact thing six years ago, the day she left for Wyoming with twenty new reporter's notebooks in her bag and a cheap gold ring on her finger. She stepped into Kelly's truck as if life would roll out a red carpet, and all she had to do was run down it, smiling and thanking everyone for the opportunity.

Just a few more steps to the gate, to Jackie inside. *The only way to get there is to put one foot in front of the other*. Dad wasn't one for metaphor, but he did say that. She stares at her boots. They say, go make something of the day.

Inside Don's Market, the vegetables cling to a small corner of real estate across from the end caps of cloth flowers and chocolate bars. Susan stands in front of the lettuce, seeing not the lettuce but the small sticker on the price tag that reads San Joaquin Valley. Perfectly good soil all around, and the produce here has traveled farther than most people in Silt ever do in their entire lives.

The grocery cart is stuck; the wheels aren't working. She walks backward and yanks the cart. A forward push, and no, that's still not right. She bends over until she is eye to eye with the wheels. They have probably never once been washed. Oh well. She stands up. She's almost done shopping anyway.

Mama used to make meals of all the food groups. They ate together every night. Grain, vegetable, fruit, meat, dairy. She should get some bread. Milk. She should have made a list.

"Susan Dunbar, how are you?"

Susan turns toward the deep familiar voice. The voice she's been avoiding. Next to the phone in the kitchen are several notes from Jackie that all say the same thing: *Camila called again*.

"Hi Mila." The aisles are so narrow in Don's Market. Like the spaghetti sauce might fall on them any second now. Ray would have talked. Camila must have heard how weird Susan was that night. Camila has always used gossip as currency, in trade for acceptance; she will have told the entire town. Try to smile.

"How's Jackie?"

"She's home now," says Susan. She touches the blue sheet of paper in her pocket. Just knowing it's there helps a little. "I'm taking care of her."

There's no reason for this to sound convincing. Her black rubber boots stare up at her from the polished floor. They tell her, you have no reason to wear anything nice. They say, you are lying.

"I've been worried about you," says Camila, who is staring at Susan's hair.

Her dirty hair is beside the point. The point has proven pointless. Try a pointed question.

"How are your girls?"

It works. The train switches tracks and there's Camila, off into the mountain of herself. Monica is great at math but isn't used to Ray being home. Lilly looks so much like Ray, you have to see her, it's really been too long. She goes on and on about her part-time job in the lawyer's office in Glenwood, about how well her mother is, about the new color she and Ray painted their bedroom.

She hasn't changed at all. Still the big hair and the eyeliner over the top lid, the same almond skin that Doc Pitkin referred to once as Mexican. She is still beautiful. More beautiful than Susan. Not that it matters. Not that it ever did, despite all those men at the restaurant who asked for Camila's section.

"You never call me back," says Camila.

"I'm sorry. It's just been so busy."

Camila looks at her like she knows everything. Things Ray would have no idea about. She was always this way.

"I just haven't felt like talking," says Susan.

"Well maybe I have. You ever think of that?"

"I'm sorry."

Susan touches her toes to the floor, one foot, the other, breathe, don't look down. She can't feel her feet. Don't look down. Camila pulls her in for a hug. She smells like she always has, like lavender hair gel.

"I'm coming to visit. You can't say no."

"We're really OK."

Camila looks at Susan's grocery cart. A box of Peeps. One potato. Mac and cheese from the deli in a Styrofoam box. "You can tell me if it isn't."

Susan nods.

"See you soon," says Camila.

The dairy case is too far away; she can't make it. Susan abandons her cart by the spaghetti and walks quickly out the sliding glass doors in the front. Back in the truck, she studies the crumpled blue paper, the list she made after her walk.

Stop thinking about Wyoming.
Make sure Jackie eats.
Put on lipstick and/or a clean shirt every day.
Listen to those relaxation tapes every morning.
Read the *Sentinel* at the library.
Finish *Anna Karenina.*

Dad would say, *Good girl, I love a list.* Kelly would say, *I swear, you'd forget to breathe if you didn't write it down.*

9

"Eat this." Camila, wearing a tight pink cardigan, hovers beside the bed. "I pureed my enchiladas so they'd be easy to eat. Your daddy's favorite."

The green mush makes Jackie's belly spasm. Her head spins. Pain tugs her under. She shuts her eyes and the room flips upside down. She is a paper doll, blowing in a tornado, which doesn't make sense, which sounds like something Susan might say. She opens her eyes and counts to ten. Then she counts to twenty. Chicken whines from the floor beside her; he has been standing guard on her all day.

Pain is always in the brain. Pain is always in the brain.

The Vicodin is right there beside her in bed, but she'll need water and then she'll need a trip to the bathroom, which is seventeen steps away. It might as well be Denver. She holds her breath, tries to be still. When she opens her eyes Camila is still there, holding the bowl and spoon. "Eat, Jackita. It'll help your spleen."

"Spleens don't grow back." She could cry or laugh but she's learned about the peril of emotion; it makes the hurt worse. "Listen, I'm fine. Just leave it there."

Her spleen is gone. For the rest of her life, she's vulnerable to sepsis and meningitis. She has three broken ribs; her legs and arms are covered in contusions. Everyone keeps saying how lucky she is, how much worse it could've been. She looks away from Camila, away from the bright light flooding through the window. Out there, snow is melting and new calves are being born. Three hundred and eleven cows on the ground, needing feed, needing care. And one small carcass that there is no reason to think about.

"Was Pete or Amick able to help us feed out yet? Any new calves dropped?" Beneath her broken ribs, fear rises in her chest like a real living thing that throbs and thrashes around. Their neighbors have their own ranches to worry after, their own calves to birth. They can't keep doing double duty. "Is Susan eating? Is she taking her meds?"

"You rest, honey. You don't worry." Camila pushes the hair from Jackie's face and moves a cool washcloth across her forehead. "Tim Layton called again. That's interesting."

Jackie shrugs. At the moment, to care or not care is a thing she can control. Whether to share her personal life with Camila is another.

"Was it fun?" Camila raises an eyebrow.

"I guess."

"I could handle something fun about now," Camila says. When Jackie won't meet her eye, she digs into a big red purse, pulling candies, a tampon, and tweezers onto the bed. With a handiwipe from her purse, she wipes the doorknob, then the TV tray beside the pullout couch. As she cleans, she rags on Ray, how checked out he is, how he could try more, drink less. She goes on and on.

Jackie can think of nothing but certain numbers. The insurance deductible, the inheritance taxes, the monthly payments on the second mortgage her dad took out, the max on her Visa.

Her future medical salary was meant to keep the ranch afloat. The "J. Dunbar subsidy," Dad called it, when she proposed the idea at some point in high school. Never has that plan seemed more out of reach. She slips toward thoughts of medical school, of her friends there, of rotations. Stop. If only there was a stent she could put around the part of her brain that remembers Denver. There's no use thinking about what she might be doing.

She adjusts her hip, a fraction of an inch, and her stomach seizes with a knife-sharp pain. Sweat pools at her back. Her dad must've suffered terribly at the end, worse than this, and there's no chance he would've talked about it, complained. There was the time he hammered his thumbnail, the time he fell off the tractor and landed on his back. There was a regular occurrence of sunburns, rope burns and snake bites, sprains and gashes. Not once did she ever see him do more than wince.

Pain is always in the brain.

"Can you say that again?"

"I was saying how yesterday, I told him about how Pete and Lottie Johnson can light their lemonade on fire and Ray had no response."

"Camila, I'm pretty tired."

"Ray says we should mind our own business, that what's happening to the Johnsons isn't our problem."

"What are you talking about?"

"There's methane in their well. Tell me that doesn't have to do with all this drilling."

Camila crossed the desert when she was twelve after a garment factory moved to her town and ruined all the ranchers' water. There were no protests; the drug cartels owned the factory. Jackie can't count how many times she has heard Camila go on about the responsibility of freedom. The next Dolores Huerta, people called Camila, until Ray got her pregnant and moved her into his mom's house.

"Ray sits on the couch with his beer all day. What am I going to do with him for three months?"

Jackie had heard all about it, from Delores, from Pete, from Susan. How Ray had pulled a gun on someone the night of the flare-ups, how he was somehow late getting to the ranch, how the department was doing an inquiry and had put Ray on forced leave. It was hard to believe.

In the bits and pieces of what she can remember, Ray had put his coat across her shaking body with great care. His words had been steady and kind. They'd been all that kept her there on the ground, away from the echo of her brain.

"Jackita. I have an idea." Camila puts her hands on her hips. "Ray can come up here to work, to help with the ranch, until you're better."

"No. That's too much. I'll be out of here in just a few days." With enough meds on board she'll ride the four-wheeler, and with Susan's help she'll mend fences, and somehow they'll get the irrigation in place and get on the tractor to break up manure for growing season. Pain is only in the brain.

"Cut the crap. Look at you. And your sister?" She looks at the bedroom door and lowers her voice. "Yesterday, she left the gate open and a whole bunch of cows got onto the road. They wandered all the way over to Boyce's and he brought them home but anything could have happened. With all those new gas trucks on the road. Can you imagine?"

A dam breaks inside her chest. She swallows hard. As a general principle, help is not the problem. The problem is what comes from needing help: the waiting for someone to be mad that Jackie hasn't been sufficiently appreciative, the worry over what is owed. If she needs someone, really relies on them, they'll tire of her in no time.

"But we can't pay him anything."

"He's on paid leave. Please. It would be a favor to me."

Jackie stares at the ceiling and sighs. As a teenage mother, Camila managed to earn her GED and take night classes to become a paralegal. When people called her a whore, she joined the church choir and got herself elected treasurer of the chamber of commerce. Camila has been bossing Jackie around since she was nine. There is no way to say no.

"You are sweating, Jackita. Open your mouth. Take this."

10

RAY DRIVES THE TRACTOR through Dunbars' gate, over tracks made deep from years of use. His head feels like it's bent sideways. The night before, he'd stayed up drinking in his truck, parked in the driveway, away from everyone. It didn't help. He ought to re-enlist. Get the fuck out of here.

He idles the tractor and jumps down. The cows press round back, grabbing bites off the hay bales.

"Hold on." He swings the wide metal gate closed, and as he gets the wire up and over the post it pinches his finger. "Shit." His body is slow; it's been too long since he fed out. "You're stuck with me today, ladies."

Get your shit together, Stark, Sheriff had told him when he served up the probation. His face burns remembering how Sheriff wouldn't meet his eye when he turned in his badge. Ray'd left by the back stairs, using the door that the perps use. He's been avoiding the diner, the Skyline, any place he might run into another person with a look on their face that makes it clear, Ray Stark is the butt of everyone's favorite joke.

When Camila told him, never asked him but told him, to hustle his ass on up here in the morning, she talked long about neighborly duty, about Jesus, but he's been married to that woman long enough to know when an idea serves her purpose more than God's.

It's not that he minds helping out. But only if he does right, and he wouldn't bet on himself this morning, not one penny down. And no matter that Jackie and half the county feed cows alone, it isn't easy work.

He'd been the first to get out to old Jonathan Pyle after his neighbor found the dead-ended tractor, engine still running, in a ravine near the creek. Center of his body was crushed like a beer can. He must've tripped, a piece of shirt got caught on something and that was it. The big rear tire had run him right down. That's the way it'll probably go: live through war and then die at home under a fucking tractor.

Camila won't think any of that through; she never thinks it through from his side. How it might be for him to be doing all this for the first time since his gramps died and his dad, living someplace in Pennsylvania, without asking Ray, leased the land to some hobby farmer from Boulder. In the cool morning he turns the question over in his mind again: is she still in love with him? If she were, it seems she'd want to have more sex, that she'd care for him in the way she used to. All he's ever wanted is to be good to her. She used to let him take care of her, to wrap her up on his lap. She used to look at him, really look. And caught in her gaze, life was just fine, better than fine.

Here goes fuck-all. He wraps the bungee from the steering wheel to the hood and sets a dead slow gear. Then he jumps. He stumbles and rolls onto his shoulder and he lies there like a goddamn idiot, staring up at the wide blue sky. Cows crowd around, snorting. One starts to shit right near his head.

"God dammit."

The tractor is already halfway across the field. He gets there with all the quick he can and hauls himself onto the trailer in back. The pocketknife in his pocket isn't there. He has to get off and go back for it to where he fell and there it is, covered in shit, but he wipes it in the field and gets his ass back on the trailer and finally, he gets to it.

He slices the orange twine that binds the bales. Womp. The flake falls off the end like a thing that can be counted on. There's the sweet dry smell of the clover that grows good in this silty ground. He flakes it off the trailer like he's done so many times, so many years back. Loose bits of hay rise and fall in the wind, blow back in his face. It isn't much to do—it isn't keeping the peace or saving the world—but those cows do get fed.

By the time he's done and gotten back to the stack yard and set the tractor right for the next day, he's sweating like a fucking old man. The blue tarp cracks in the wind; he's climbing up the haystack to pull it tight over the bales when he hears the sound of feet shuffling across the concrete slab.

Susan looks lost under her big sweater and scarf. He climbs down. Camila had told him to get Susan outside with him, *Get that girl away from herself*, but Ray sees fear in her eyes and he doesn't care to push.

"Jackie needs you for something." She stares like something wild and trapped and figuring his intent.

"You bet." He touches her shoulder. "How you doing, Sue?"

She shrugs and starts back to the house. Her red hair flies from her hat. When Monica was a baby she used to grab that red hair, sitting on Susan's hip, Susan dancing them around the trailer kitchen. Monica was a shy thing but Susie made that baby laugh, dipping her and holding her arm out straight. One time he and Mila had joined in, turned up the music. The kitchen was small, and they kept bumping into each other, all of them happy and warm and sure about the world and how it worked.

"I didn't mean to, the other night." She stops by the gate, not looking at him. "I'm sorry."

He starts to ask what the hell she means, but she doesn't give him a chance, just spins on those big-ass boots and walks away.

He enters into the bedroom like he might a courthouse or a church. Jackie sits up in bed; a poster of Colorado native trout is tacked to the wall. She's staring out the window, a book in her lap. Her dog jumps up to sniff at him, and Ray gives him a good rub. She looks better than she did at the hospital, still pale but better. He can smell himself, his stink of sweat and liquor, and he keeps by the door until she tells him to get over and sit down in the plain wooden chair. He takes off his hat.

"I didn't kill any cows this morning," he says. "I guess that's a start."

"Well, you're already doing better than me."

"I didn't mean it that way. You took that trouble from the cow as good as any man twice your size."

"You're a bad liar."

"I'm not trying to lie."

Her look is soft and she tells him to fish into the coat on the back of the door and bring what's in the front right pocket. He finds the fifty and hands it to her.

"I know it's not much, but please take it." She sounds annoyed.

"Don't mind about all that." He steps back from the bed, from the money.

"If it wasn't for you, I might still be up in that field."

"Just doing my job. Not even that well, to be honest."

"Give me a break. You saved my life, Ray." Her stare is fierce. "And now you're up here helping us. It's too much."

"End of season, we'll worry about making it right."

She glares at him, and he knows stubborn women enough to bow his head. He pats her hand. "I know you're good for it."

He spends the rest of the day mending fences. Every little bit, he stops to notice the line of juniper posts running straight as buttons down a shirt and he takes it as a sign that he might, maybe, be worth more than a bent fucking penny.

11

SUSAN GOES OUT IN the white dawn, hunting sign. There are muddy footprints. There is Ray's car. There is the near-empty fifth behind the shed.

A canopy of wings overhead pierces the sky. Head back, she stares up.

Quickquickquickquickquick. Her heartbeat pulses to match the ancient staccato sound. Nothing else matters. She holds her breath, shuts her eyes tight. Thank you. Then they are gone, heading north to Wyoming and beyond.

"Those sandhills are beauts." Ray's voice startles her.

"I was looking for you," she stutters, "but I couldn't find you."

"What's doing?"

Look him in the eye. Ray Stark and his sad eyes. Ask him. Now.

He will bite his lip and spit. He will tell her to try and rest. He will say that Jackie's the one who needs help.

She is about to offer, she's working up to it, but maybe she has been standing there not talking for too long—Kelly says this happens—because Ray jumps in first, says he has to get down to the lower field.

"I haven't been down to the lower field in a while."

It isn't what she meant to say.

"There's a doe down there, stuck on the fence," he says. "I'm gonna see if I can spring her, but hell, I haven't done this in a long time."

It's her fault. He can see that right away. Her feet melt into the ground.

"Come along?" he asks.

She nods. Yesyesyesyesyes. Years ago, she had waited months for him to ask her that question.

They load tools into the truck. Ray grabs the Ruger from the mudroom, just in case, which makes her stomach whirl around. Dad taught her how to shoot that gun when she was eight: Put your feet apart. Steady your body. Never lock your elbows. Find your aim. And always, always, keep your eyes open.

Dad had close relations with his weapons; the Ruger, forty years old, a gift from his own dad, was relied on and cared for and babied. Some Sunday afternoons, he would disassemble the gun on the kitchen table. From a tackle box would come a little wire brush, soft shammy patching, bluing, and an eye-dropper bottle of oil. He'd work the oil down into the hammer, rock it back and forth with his thumb, squeeze the trigger and rock back again, and then he would hold it to his ear and rock it back and forth until he heard a clear deep click, a beautiful click, the sound of a blackbird's warble. He'd mess with that gun for more than an hour; she wasn't expected to ask questions, to do anything more than watch.

She will never shoot that gun again.

Ray always has known how to ask a question and he tries to get her talking, but she doubles back on him.

"No, you tell me how *you* are."

"I'm OK, I guess." He keeps tapping the steering wheel with his middle finger and rubbing his hand through his stubble. "It's strange not working for the sheriff. I guess it's got me a little sideways."

"I know what that's like."

But it's like he doesn't hear her. He points.

"There she is. Dumb fucking luck."

The top strands of barbed wire trap the doe's hooves like they're caught in a twist tie. The animal doesn't move at the sound of the four-wheeler. She hangs from the trap, her face in the mud. Her body is splayed against the fence.

They stop and get out, quiet. Susan crouches beside the car but Ray slides in close to the doe.

"Easy, girl. Easy," Ray whispers as he approaches. The doe doesn't stir, doesn't look at him. All the skittish in her drained away.

Her cousins and aunts and sisters and maybe even her babies, all of them would've seen her there and not been able to do a thing. Every night there'd been near a hundred deer coming down from the snow-clogged mountains to feed on pasture. The doe would've seen them, smelled them, and watched them go.

With the long pole, Ray tries to pry the wire below her hooves up and over. It won't give. He tries again. Again it doesn't work.

"Shit." He throws the pry bar down.

Susan looks at the truck but her boots won't move. Go. Jackie would get the gun. Jackie was always a better shot. This is penance. This is what you get. The doe's skinny chest heaves, defeated, already done.

"You want the Ruger," she says. It's not a question; it's defeat.

"Maybe."

He takes wire snips from his pocket and, talking soft the whole time, easing up on the doe, he makes a cut in the fence. And just like that, the doe spins onto her side and hits the ground with a thud. She breathes mud.

Ray circles back to Susan and crouches beside her. She can feel him staring at her but she won't look at him. She is focused on the doe. Get up. Get up.

And then the animal tucks those trembling legs under her and pops up on all fours. She looks around and stares at them like she knows she's prey, and bounces off into the woods, her white butt rising and falling.

"Well that's something," says Ray. "See that, Sue? It ain't all bad. You OK?"

"I'm so sorry, Ray." She looks at the cuff of his jacket, at the broken fence, the edge of the woods. "About the other night. I'm so ashamed."

"Sue? You going to tell me what you're talking about?"

She looks at him then, really looks. She had decided all those years ago when he didn't pick her that he wasn't worth her time. She had been wrong. When Camila was pregnant, the only thing she could keep down for those early months were smoothies, and Ray made her one every day. He helped his gramps out on the ranch when his dad left. His mom had early dementia and was sent to an institution in Junction, and Ray didn't talk about it but it was another thing to appreciate about him, that he knew something about loss. The guy can fix anything, make anything better. There is a yellow dot in his blue eyes like the sun on water.

"It's my fault, about Jackie." She whispers it into his canvas coat. "I was so out of it. I should've known something was wrong."

"You didn't set that cow running toward your sister. You're all right." He throws his arm around her. He smells like cigarettes and hay, like her dad used to smell.

"I should be helping. This is my land. Will you let me help?"

"Of course. I need all the help I can get."

The next morning, Susan walks behind Ray, fence staples in her pockets. His footfalls touch the ground like flint against rock. He's wearing the right clothes, flannel shirt, wide-brimmed hat, leather gloves. She forgot her hat; her sweater is too heavy. She tries to step inside his footprints but they're too far apart.

After an hour of moving along fence line in the lower field, mending, the house disappears from view. The knife in her pocket, her dad's old pocketknife, knocks against her thigh with every step: keep going, keep going. Chicken runs ahead, flushing swallows from the poplars, a blur of color in flight. The sun rises bright in a blue sky. The air is cool. The baby calves wobble in their shiny Pantene-brown coats. Snowmelt floods the ditch.

"It's spring and we're sprung." The exclamation point in her voice is too much. It wasn't as clever out loud as it sounded in her head.

"Whatever you say, Sue." Ray squints at some rusted wire, his body collapsed to the task. "Will you string this out while I set this post?"

"Don't you love being outside?"

"It's better than a hole in the head."

Susan pinches the skin on the side of her neck. If she had ever learned a prayer, she would say it now.

He asks for the fence staples and he asks for stringing wire and he doesn't say anything else for forty-five minutes. This isn't anything to take personally. Not really.

Except that she remembers Ray, a ghost of his younger self, when he was young and skinny and sunburnt, standing on the back of a trailer in this same field, haying with the rest of them. His smile used to creep into his face like a surprise. There was something solid, calm in him, that put people at ease. Before heading back to town, he used to kiss his gramps on the cheek, a rare gesture of love between men. She had thought she was cooler than him. It wasn't until later, when it was too late, that it was clear she'd been wrong.

At the edge of the upper field, where the land is too hardpan at the surface to dig a post hole, an old rock jack has tipped over, the bottom support torn off. Ray kicks the bottom cross piece and spits. There's a crosshatch of wrinkles by his eyes. He looks out across the field, his features hard; if he sees ghosts on this land, they aren't friendly.

"You all got timbers in the barn?"

"I loaded a few up in the back of the rig before we left."

He looks up, a smile tip-toeing in his eyes.

"Good thought, Sue."

They talk about what lumber and nails can be salvaged and about the merits of narrowing the angle and should they fix what's been done or rebuild it entirely of a new design. They decide to keep it, to resemble the way of her dad. Ray's just being polite, including her in all this discussion, but it means everything to her.

"You miss working with your grandpa?" she asks. "Seemed like you liked working up here."

"Long time ago." He bends to his knees and begins to take off the old wire. His voice is tired. "We work hard, might get this done by lunch."

They pull out rocks the size of gravestones. Sweat pours out of Susan. It's hot dusty work with them both on their knees looping new wire, rebuilding. Chicken runs between them and around them, his tail high. The time passes quickly, the two of them working together steadily, and in a little over an hour, they're done. They stand back admiring their work, and only then does Susan realize: she hasn't thought about Kelly, about Wyoming, all morning.

"That looks all right," says Ray.

"It'll hunt."

And then it happens. The smile creeps into his face, floods it, a gift. And she laughs and then he laughs too.

"This is the best day I've had in a long time."

"Girl, you got to get out more."

"I know." But she doesn't stop smiling. A thousand blue birds fly across the sky. She would give anything to hold onto this moment, to cast it in galvanized steel. Her hand finds the knife in her pocket and pulls it out, the sun bright against the blade.

"I want you to have this." She holds it out to him.

"I can't take that."

"My dad always liked you."

"Sue."

"Please, Ray. You're helping us so much. It'd mean something to me."

Ray picks up the bone handle and admires the silver inlay. It's solidly made in the way of old things.

"They don't make men like your dad anymore."

"I wouldn't say that."

He holds her eye and nods, puts the knife into his jean pocket. The sun warms her back and the smell of sage rises from the ground to meet them.

12

After a week, it's clear that Ray Stark can show up mostly on time, that he's still a nice guy. Their conversations about the herd are the best part of Jackie's day. But whether or not he's competent is hard to size from her bedroom window. That morning he'd told her that he looked forward to mending fences. No one thinks that.

Using an old mop handle as a cane, Jackie manages the hallway, the door, the porch steps, one, one thousand, two, two thousand, breathe, move, breathe, move.

Susan stands in front of the truck's passenger door, her hands on her hips. Their dad's old hat is too big for her, the felt brim almost to her eyebrows. Her face a scowl.

"The ditch road is too bumpy."

They have been over this. Jackie needs to check the work; Dad would check the work. A person can lose everything on a slapdash style. Their dad had told her this, repeatedly, especially when looking at her math homework. Too often she would understand the concept but forget to carry the one, forget to check her work. And so an A minus would slide to a B. It had offended her that mastery of concept should be diminished by a simple sloppy mistake. Her dad, usually so quiet, usually so hard to read, had made himself and his disappointment absolutely clear: you have got to take more care. Jackie looks down at her bruised body and cringes.

"Come on. Load up, Chicken. We only have forty-five minutes before dark."

Chicken's tail wags and he jumps onto the back like his bones were made of springs.

"Ray's doing a great job; everything's going good."

"I have to get out there. I have to see it for myself."

"But I've been out there with him. I've seen it."

If Jackie watches another news show, if she sits up in the old bed trying and failing to read through the stack of medical journal articles for her research proposal, if she snaps at Susan and then feels bad for snapping, if she thinks again about her dad and the mysteries of his life, if she does any of this for another minute she will officially be worthless. She needs to smell the sky and see the grass. "Sue. Please."

Susan won't budge until Jackie promises to tell if it hurts too badly and consents to only visit the near field. Two minutes into the drive Jackie is pushing up her sleeves, the sweat rising with each bump in the road, and the road is made of bumps, and the old truck spews exhaust. Her ribs are cracking deeper. The stiches in her belly pulling at the seam. Pain is only in the brain. She has no choice.

"You're pale." Susan tries to sound like someone with medical training.

"I'm fine." Jackie holds onto her sides to try and keep her ribs from bouncing. "Watch the road; you're too close to the ditch."

The willow branches are redding up in knots. Red Indian paintbrush and blue larkspur pop on the hillside above the ditch. The first wildflowers of the season. If Jackie focuses on them, their bits of color, the pain is not as bad. It gives back, this place. Her body softens and she looks hard out the window, hard enough to imprint each section so that she can remember it later when she is alone in her room.

Susan talks about how she's been mending fences and feeding out in the morning, like she invented the idea of hard work.

"That's great, Susan."

Brown meltwater flows fast through the irrigation ditch, coming down off Mount Baldy. The level might hold off a drought if there is one this summer. From this vantage, the fields are lush with the leavings of winter. The alfalfa is coming in green. A new calf runs and bucks; in just days on earth, its balance is already perfect.

Susan drives up close to the juniper staves, strung with strands of barbed wire. The posts Ray replaced, the ones that had gone to rot or were knocked clean by elk, run straight. A sign of planning and workmanship; a statement of time invested.

"It looks right, doesn't it?" Susan turns to smile, the smack of I-told-you-so smeared across her mouth.

"Keep going; let's see to the rock jack."

Everything looks fine. Except her idea of fine and her dad's idea of fine might not be the same. There is the distinct possibility that she may not know enough to know what's wrong, what needs to be done.

Jackie stares at the side of Susan's face and wishes her friend Jean were sitting beside her on the seat instead. Her funny and thoughtful roommate in Denver would understand this feeling. She would know the right thing to say.

They had met the first week of medical school, staring at each other over a dead body. Anatomy class. Jackie can't remember exactly what Jean said that day, or on any of the subsequent hundreds of days they spent together. It was more a tone feeling. She was the first friend Jackie had ever had where they had the kind of conversations that tangented and maneuvered through one exciting, endless subject after the next. The kind of conversations where the sort of person that Jackie had always wanted to be, hoped to be, seemed like a possibility. But now Jean is in Denver, living a life that could not be more different from the one happening here in this old, barely functioning truck.

The sun, tucked behind a thick cloud, casts a flat light. There is no shadow, just the gray world. Jackie leans her head against the cold window and stares outside, longing to see her father's long legs walk across the fields toward them.

"Remember how if Dad found a nail in the rig after you'd been mending, he'd bring it home and lay it on your dinner plate?" Jackie says. "He wouldn't throw away one lousy nail."

"Those old horseshoe nails in the Folgers cans in the shed. I remember. The staples Ray uses are way easier."

Dad's hands were always red, like they'd been boiled. The rough of them as they threaded her hair.

"I hated mending fences." Jackie stares at her fingernails, wide and short like his. Digging post holes, her teenage self used to dream about when she could drive away from this place. Being a doctor seemed like a noble enough cause that even Dad could get behind it. "'Looks like an old lady made this fence.' Remember how he'd say that?"

"Even when we did a good job, he never said so."

"He was genetically incapable of giving a compliment," says Jackie.

"Remember that hike we'd always take up to Mount Baldy after haying season? I think that was the only full day he'd take off all year."

"I can't believe he's gone." Jackie looks across the seat at Susan's familiar profile.

"I know. Me too." Susan stares out at the sky, her fingers anxiously tapping the steering wheel.

Jackie puts her hand over Susan's hand, feels the thrum of her sister, and waits until her fingers still. Night starts its slide down off the mesa to settle on the clover. Jackie stares out the window at the perfect row of fence posts and the wind in the fields, moving anywhere it wants, and she wants to punch the glass, which of course is something she would never do.

"Let's go home," says Jackie. Her fist slackens; her jaw relaxes. The dark sky falls around them. "I've seen enough."

In the morning Jackie climbs into the tub, steam rising, and lets her bones float. The water comes direct from the creek, run through some carbon filter Dad rigged in the pump house. It smells of sweet and loam, the smell of something that never needs fixing.

She closes her eyes, breathes in the smell of outside. Ray will push the cows across the snow-free fields to drink the creek. In the three weeks since her accident, with the help of the neighbors and between Ray and Sue, the rest of the babies got born without incident. The animals will be huddled close now, their separate shapes merged into one. She takes the memory of the gruff of their breath and the lap of them drinking and tucks it into herself. A part of her own sound.

This morning she had pulled a thin brown thread out of her belly button. She'd thrown the suture thread onto the floor and tried and failed to avoid looking at it. She still can't walk more than two hundred feet at a time. Then she needs a glass of water. And a nap. It hurts like hell to cough or sneeze. She tries to study, she reads and rereads paragraphs, but she can't concentrate. She has never been so useless in her entire life.

The first female doctor she ever saw was the lady with the white coat, a rose embroidered on the pocket, who patched up Susan's cuts after the accident. Mama was in the morgue, but Jackie didn't know that yet, just that something bad had happened, was happening. The doctor, an ER doc she must have been, was unsurprised, full of calm and kindness. Her eyes were the color of blueberries. Jackie went home and made a stethoscope out of a ribbon and a button, put it around her neck and tucked it under her shirt. She wore it for the rest of third grade. Throughout high school and college, she had been sure that if she worked hard enough, if she joined science club and the mathletes, if she studied more than anyone else, she could be just like that lady doctor with the blueberry eyes.

Jackie rubs the oatmeal soap into the hollow under her arms. She's lost too much weight; her ribs jut out, in a perfect example of a deconditioned patient. The contusions on her legs have faded from purple and blue to an ugly yellow with blurry crescents of brown, hoof-sized, across her abdomen, arms, and chest. At the costochondral junction, she presses into cartilage until there is a dull, painful ache.

She makes a fist and raises her arm over her head, one side and then the next. She'll walk the hallway twenty-five times today. She'll eat every two hours. She visualizes herself running.

Eyes squeezed, she ducks underwater. Susan went to town; the house is empty. Her fingers find the coarse hair between her legs and she presses into herself, longing for relief in the quicksand of circling. She arches her back so her mouth finds the surface. But her body doesn't give. She presses harder into herself, but there is nothing. She gives up, disgusted. The water has gone cold.

She is drying off when she hears the knocking, and then Tim's voice, calling her name.

When she finally gets dressed, gets down the hall, and opens the door, Tim is on the front porch, holding an aluminum casserole dish with a CD on top. He looks nice in his jeans; she reminds herself that she doesn't need any of that right now.

"This is lasagna and this is the best new band in the West." He holds out his offerings, an odd apologetic smile on his face.

"Thanks. How nice." The dish is heavy and it strains her ribs to hold it. She sets it down inside, out of sight.

"Nice to see you." He awkwardly sets his hand on her arm and squeezes it. "You look good."

She looks down at the orange T-shirt, knit skirt, and leggings she has been wearing for days. "You're insane."

"Well, you look better than you deserve."

"Amazing what a person can do without a spleen."

"I'm really glad you're OK." His eyes are soft.

"I should've called you back."

"I understand. Can I come in? Coffee?"

Does coffee mean coffee, in a cup? Or is it something else? Something else, even if it's just conversation, is something she's not at all capable of at the moment. Her body aches all over.

Her dad must've felt like this and been beset with all manner of visitors and she hadn't been there to fend them off.

"I'm not good company right now, Tim." She tries to smile, to act normal, to pretend that she doesn't need to sit down. "I know I said this before, last time you were here, but how about a rain check? I really do mean it this time."

His smile turns strange; he shifts his feet.

"There's something I need to talk to you about." He looks behind him and then past the house. His right eye twitches. "I meant to bring it up when I was here a couple weeks ago, but then it wasn't the right time."

She holds herself perfectly still. He has herpes. He's married.

"Go on."

Tim takes a big breath. "My company wants to drill some exploratory wells on your lower field. We expect that you're sitting on a mega amount of natural gas."

The white envelope he takes from his back pocket is thick. Tim talks about the Mancos Shale formation versus the Mesa Verde. He uses the word strata. He says something about $50,000.

"But if they find gas, which they probably will since Johnson's wells have always been big producers, you get a percentage." Tim's face is lit up; he's using his hands. "Could be tens of thousands of dollars over the life of the wells. Could be more."

The envelope is too heavy; she drops it onto the front step.

"I don't know what to say."

"Say yes." He picks up the envelope, brushes it off, and hands it back. "We'd want to punch that first well pretty soon, maybe early summer."

She opens the envelope and reads the contract, quickly, skimming for the pertinent details. Her heart slows and the land around her seems to disappear. There is just the concrete stairs and Tim framed in the door. Good news, at very long last. Her eyes pool with tears and she presses her fingers against her eyelids, damming up the water.

"You could've just brought enchiladas like everyone else."

"Just doing my job."

"Thank you. This is a big deal."

"I don't want this to be weird after what happened the other day. That was fun." There's a freckle just north of his lip. Thousands of cells could fit in a dot that size. "You're fun."

Smart, *stubborn*, *brave*, these are the correct adjectives to describe her. Never has anyone described her as fun. She sways, just slightly, but enough for him to notice and he reaches out to steady her. With his other hand he touches her cheek. His touch rolls through her arms and legs and she stiffens. Any tenderness puts her at risk to all pain. The sound of the cow as it ran over her chest. The moment when she was too tired to drag herself any farther across the field.

"Listen, I'm grateful for this." She nods at the contract. "Really I am, but it's not a good idea for something to happen between us again. I mean, I just got out of the hospital. My skin looks like Rainbow Sherbet."

"I've been thinking about you."

"There's no reason for that."

"I'm not so sure. I'd like to get to know you again."

"Come on. You just want to fool around."

He smiles and shrugs. "Nothing wrong with that. What is it you want?"

The question fills the entire sky. She sighs. "Probably nothing. Probably too much."

"Can I give you a hug?"

"Don't hold too tight." She stands there, arms pinned to her sides. "My ribs." Her words muffle against his shirt. They stand that way for a long time.

13

SUSAN ALMOST HITS THEM with the front door. Jackie jumps out of the arms of a short guy, average-looking in every way. Jackie introduces him, expects Susan to remember him from high school. Jackie's cheeks are red. Then she hands Susan a white envelope.

"Tim just solved our money problems."

Limitation of Forfeiture. Shut-in Payments. Surface Rights. All lessee this and lessor that. Jackie keeps talking and Tim Layton, landman, keeps talking. And Susan reads and reads and doesn't understand a damn thing except that she wants to take Dad's Ruger from the red holster in the hallway and point it at them both.

Granny, straight-backed on her white horse Pinky, used to trot off across the lower fields into the woods to hunt mushrooms. Jackie walking through waist-high clover. The scratch of it threading Susan's fingers as she followed. There is Dad at the kitchen table, oxygen tank by his side, telling Jon Amick not to sign a lease. *Those wells make the land less yours.* Telling him not to double down on a bad bet. Jackie was busy at medical school; she doesn't know.

Tim Layton is talking about how the lease money is keeping ranchers afloat all over the valley when Susan interrupts him.

"I don't know anything about you or your company. Do you work up in the Jonah Field?"

"We don't work in Wyoming." He looks way too nervous for a guy who has given this spiel many, many times.

"Susie, this is a lot of money," says Jackie, talking slow as if English wasn't Susan's first language.

Jackie always thinks she's right. She always thinks she knows. She might not be the type to lose her wallet but she misses things all the time. People who don't make mistakes are not trampled by a cow.

"What about the fire the other night down Dry Hollow? I heard one of Amick's wells blew up. A kickdown, they're calling it. They could've died. How do we know that wouldn't happen here?"

Tim Layton talks very fast, explaining how the fire wasn't as big a deal as it might seem. Something about the percussion being louder than normal. Something about the pressure building up higher when a choke was plugged, so they had to flare the gas longer.

A good reporter always carries a pen. Where is a pen? She needs to write all of this down.

"That kind of thing rarely happens, and in a way it's good news," he says, jazz hands at the ready. "Means there's so much gas in the seam, it's eager to flow out. But that was wasted money. You'll want to get in on things before it's all gone."

"What about Tina Krest's goats? Three of them were born stills the day after that kick. Kickdown. Whatever."

"That wouldn't have anything to do with us."

"And the things I saw in Wyoming, the crap in the air and the kids with nosebleeds, the traffic and the noise, that doesn't have anything to do with you either?"

"Listen, I get your concerns. I mean let's be honest, extractive industries always have some things associated with them. Your cows crap near the rivers and that makes it tough for the fish. Logging changes the forest ecology. That doesn't mean we shouldn't ranch or log. Honestly, I appreciate that you care about the environment. I believe this company cares too. We just won an award for stewardship."

There are more questions to ask, more fine print to go over but this Tim, this classic example of a male human, has to explain it all to Susan.

"You have to think of it this way, Sue. You're a rancher. My family is in forestry. We all work the land, we all take our living from it. Our great-grandparents understood this; it's why they moved to the West. Cross my heart, I really believe they'd be proud of us for helping develop homegrown sources of energy."

The guy keeps talking, unaware that a conversation should involve both parties.

"Let's have dinner," says Jackie, her face red. She tries to steer Susan into the kitchen. "I'll heat up this lasagna Tim brought."

"I ate in town."

Susan shoves the contract under her shirt and leaves them to whatever it is they think they're doing.

A few days later, Susan and Ray are driving into town, him for baling wire, her to get milk, to get away from her sister. She and Jackie have gone rounds about the gas deal and the more they talk, the less Susan feels heard.

"How's your home life?" she asks.

"Whoa there, Sue, don't hold back." Ray turns up the hip-hop on the radio.

"Well I don't want to talk about the gas deal anymore."

"That's all I got to pick from? Marriage or the gas deal?"

"I'm curious. You seem like the kind of guy who could make marriage easy."

"You'd best ask Camila about all that." He leans his head back against the headrest. "Actually, don't. You ever think about dating again?"

"Oh, God. Not really. I mean I'm basically middle-aged."

"You sure aren't planning to live very long then."

"I feel old."

"I know what you mean."

It's quiet between them while the music pours into the car. Raindrops fall onto the windshield but she's dry and warm inside. She focuses on the contrast of that, on the thin glass of the window that makes the difference between discomfort and ease. Grace can be afforded in the smallest places.

"Plenty of men around here." Ray looks at her sidewise and shrugs.

"I mean, maybe, if someone asked me out. But isn't everyone in this town married or drunk or both?"

Ray laughs. She said something funny. She used to be funny. She once made Jackie pee from something she said, but she can't remember now what it was.

"What about Ken Fontaine?"

"Oh, Ray. He's old. I saw him at Don's last week and he had suppositories in his cart. He didn't even try to hide them."

"Good point. And he does complain. He cornered me to talk about his ingrown toenails for a fucking long time. Doug Magee's single. He owns a house. Got a manager job at Dumo's. And he's good-looking, right?"

"If he hadn't smoked his whole life. And he's so ashamed about being from South Dakota, which is actually kind of interesting. Why does he pause for so long before he answers a question?"

"Well, there's Stu Allen. He's a nice guy. High school quarterback. Owns a business."

"He never talks to me. And anyways, he has a stomach like pudding."

"I think his meds make him fat. He overdosed on lithium a couple years back. Only reason he's not dead is Jack Casey went over to buy a cord and found him passed out in the bathroom."

"Sounds perfect for me."

Her throat catches on the sentence. She didn't mean it to be funny but it is, sort of, and she can't help it, she snorts into the window. Ray smiles at her, his eyes big, like he's impressed she's remembered how to laugh at herself. She can tell he's studying her, thinking things through with his thoughtful mind, and if it were anyone else she might panic a little, but it's Ray.

"Wyatt Olson was back in town for a while."

"He always liked Jackie."

"Well shit, Susie, I guess it's not that promising. But you'll find someone good one of these days."

"Do you really believe that?"

"Sure. You're a good one."

She doesn't know what to say. He doesn't mean it. But even so. How nice. The nicest thing anyone has said in a long time.

Her eyes burn. The fields out the window blur. She hasn't cried in weeks. Exactly seven weeks.

"Thanks, Ray."

He starts to talk about the ranch and what he wants to do later in the upper field and his grammar is terrible, full of all the ruralisms she worked so hard to purge from her speech when she got to college. The bent language made her ashamed, made her feel like she didn't belong, but the way Ray sounds is honest. It makes her unafraid to trust him. The rain falls lightly outside the warm car and it makes the green of the fields pop, and she's noticing all that when she sees a brown paper bag in the middle of the road and Ray hits the gas.

"Holy fuck. Get down. Get down." He's yelling, while she is thrown back against the headrest.

"Stop. Ray, stop."

His face is red and his jaw is clenched and they're going close to 60. Susan braces her body with her feet on the floor.

"Ray, what's going on? Slow down. Stop."

Finally he does. Pulls over. His hands shake. And he shuts his eyes.

"What was it?"

"Damn, Sue. I'm sorry. I got confused. The war. I don't know."

"It's OK." She puts her hand on his shoulder. "I understand."

And maybe she does.

"Want to talk about it?" she asks.

"Nope. But thanks."

People used to tell her things just because she asked. Personal, hard things. And she used to think the listening helped. But maybe it was the writing it down, the publishing, that mattered.

Ray rests his head on the wheel and doesn't move. She wants to ask if he's breathing, but that's stupid. Of course he is.

"Ray?"

"Sorry, Sue. I just need a minute."

"Do you want me to drive?"

"Well. That sounds good."

The rest of the way into town, Ray looks out the window, chewing on his thoughts. Poor guy. Nice guy. Not everyone gets the same share of hurt in this world. Watch the big turn. Ease on the gas. She puts her hand on his arm and pats it.

"We're almost there, Ray. You don't need to worry."

Late that night, in the dark, she walks outside to feel the stillness all around. In the front, near the rotting chicken coop, is an old garden bed long gone to bindweed. Her mom used to sit on the railroad tie, a cigarette in her mouth, a pile of dead weeds at her side. She'd had a deep voice for a woman and she was strict—not in an unkind way, just the type with expectation.

Susan thinks about Ray being so scared but still getting out of bed in the morning. *You're a good one. You're a good one. You're a good one.* The noise in her head quiets down, settles into a quiet place. She bends to the bindweed and pulls. It's cold, even with the wool blanket wrapped over her shoulders, but she doesn't stop until the bed is clean, ready for seeding.

Mama would be pleased. Susan sits on the old railroad tie and stares up at the stars. They look closer than they did in Wyoming. They look just the way they should. Kelly never thought she was a good one. He never really wanted kids, or her, just an idea of something he didn't expect to be hard. They would never have made each other happy. How much better to be here, without Kelly, than bound to a life set to rot.

14

LATE AT NIGHT, THE girls long asleep, Camila and Ray sit up in their bed, both of them leaning against the wall, writing. Ray kicks off his jeans and makes a mental list of what needs to be done at Dunbars the next day.

Skunk in pipe/gate, lower field/Una's tits.

If Camila asked, he'd tell her his hands are finally toughening up, his back feeling strong. If she looked at him, she'd see the strength in his bare legs, the new edge to his abs. He hasn't had any liquor for more than a week, which he'd expect to please her but has caught no praise. For the third time, he looks at his wife, hoping she'll look up too.

Camila has on an old T-shirt he got at a National Guard thing in Meeker; it's huge on her. There was a time she didn't wear a single thing to bed. He puts his hand on her leg.

"You should bring the girls up to Dunbars' this week. They'd love to see the calves. We got another nine last week."

She doesn't look up from the yellow legal pad in her lap. "That's nice, honey."

"I didn't know how much I missed working with my hands."

"Hmmm." She scowls and writes something down; she crosses her legs in a way that knocks his hand off.

"How's your thing going?"

"I helped get Roberts elected. When you were gone, I went door to door for him, dragging the girls with me in the cold." Her face is tighter than a wood screw in summer. "He needs to pay attention to us now."

"What are you on about, baby?" He strokes her leg.

"The governor. I called his office to tell them about this gas well kick. And all the problems we're dealing with, how the gas companies threaten the fabric of our town. His aide said she'll look into it. I want to follow up with an email and I'm just working out the details."

"Baby, the governor doesn't care what happens in Silt. We're three hundred miles from Denver; might as well be Alaska."

"Well he can't care until he knows about it." Here she goes. "At the chamber meeting last night, Amick was there. He talked about how the night you lost your job—"

"I didn't lose my job. I keep telling you. It's just a few months' probation."

"Since that night the well blew up, the foundation of his house is cracked. And the walkway is crooked." She's finally looking at him now, counting on her hands. "And people say they're having headaches and their eyes burn at night with the flares and some of them throw up and can't sleep."

Ray hasn't ever been able to keep up with Mila when she gets on her high horse. This is stupid. He pulls off his sweatshirt and T-shirt and socks, hoping for a sorry second she might see his naked body and stop talking.

"Let me tell you, Ray. Ever since Deb Cowan got a well, she has a burn in her *biscoche* like a bladder infection, except Doc Pitkin of course says she doesn't have one."

"You don't know that any of this has got to do with any of the rest of it." He throws his mud-caked jeans into the hamper; his pocketknife falls on the floor. "People see a big company and they see a chance to get free shit. This whole thing is going to blow over in a few weeks; it'll turn out to be nothing."

"How can you not be worried?"

"Look, Camila, it's not going to go down here like it did in Las Flores. This isn't Mexico. We aren't going to have to leave."

Camila, her eyes flat, pulls the covers up to her chin and drops back into the hard place inside herself, shaped by a fear of change that is heavy and guarded. Ray has gotten lost many times while trying to find the gate to the inner workings of his wife.

"What is that?" Camila points at the knife.

"Susan gave it to me; some kind of thank-you, I guess." He sets the knife on the dresser, behind a framed picture they took at the mall before he shipped off. "Want tea or anything?"

She studies him, her lips pressed together into a thin flat line. She stares like she knows that he is never without Bill Dunbar's knife, that the feel of the metal against his leg makes him steady.

"You are working up there a lot, Papito."

"You're the one who told me to give them a hand."

"We're lucky, not like those Dunbar girls. They're single. They don't have families. I feel sorry for them."

He studies the picture on the dresser. Lilly's on Camila's lap, her cheeks still chubby, and Monica, his big girl in braids, leans against his chest. He's got his arm around the back of Camila's chair, he's touching her shoulder and they're all tight and close. He tries to remember how it was back then, when what was between them didn't drag like a limping dog.

She has been at him all the time for the littlest crap. That morning he'd lost track of his keys again, and she was mad about that. And she was already mad that he forgot to call Sheriff back to set up a meeting. Which isn't a big deal. Sheriff doesn't return calls for days.

"I'm tired, Mila." He gets into the bed and shuts off the light.

It's quiet for a while and he is almost asleep when she rolls over, touching his arm. "You yelled in your sleep again last night. Something about Marcus. Who is that, honey?"

"Just a guy I used to know."

"You can tell me about it. You never tell me anything about your time over there."

"Leave it, Mila." Her hand weighs a thousand pounds and even though it's on his shoulder, not his throat, he can't breathe.

"I just want to understand."

"You can't."

It's quiet again for a while and he is working on sleep, working to ignore Marcus Wilson and the rest of it, but Camila doesn't ever know when to let a thing drop.

"You're saying all these people up Dry Hollow Road are making this up?"

"Maybe," he sighs. "I don't know. I overreacted; not everyone needs to."

"This isn't overreacting, Ray. Three days after the kick, two of Tina's goats had stillborns. And Johnson's lost a baby cow the next day."

"We got enough problems of our own right now."

"What do you mean?"

"You can't do anything about this, Mila. It's not your problem to fix."

"Things don't work out just because you want them to, Ray."

"I know."

How anyone ever stays married is a fucking mystery.

"I don't know how you were ever a soldier."

"What?"

"Baby, I know all of it, the war, it's hard on you. But you don't share anything. Why am I the bad one because I say how I feel? Because I fight for things to be better? You. You've dropped out of this family, this town, your life."

"This is shit." His feet hit the floor before his mouth makes it worse. "You're out of line." The pillow is a better thing to punch, and he does. And he is already out the bedroom door, he can already taste the whiskey, when she says it. *Don't go*.

For a long time, he sits in the parked truck, staring at his dark house. Inside the garage is Camila's used Kia, payment due end of the week. The backyard, a snarl of weeds and broken things, looks like shit. The shingles on the roof are curled and cracked in spots. This is his job, to handle such things. The loneliness of adulthood is like dirt under his fingernails. He carries it with him, embarrassed by it, a constant job of digging it away.

The JD doesn't help; neither does Eazy-E, turned up as loud as the old tape player will go. He's cold, wearing only his boxers, a sweatshirt, and a hat. His bare feet touch the rubber floor mat and he's safe, he shouldn't need to tell himself that, but so much went wrong that he never planned on and why should he get to feel safe, no one made him that special. His mom, with her long days sitting quiet in bed with the curtains drawn—she could've told him that.

He tries but fails to not drag out certain memories. Eventually, he gets out of the truck and into the house. He stops at the kids' bedroom door and listens. Gently he opens the door. He visits each girl's bed, pulling Lilly's covers back over her sprawled body, setting Monica's book onto the floor. He lies down on the floor between their beds and listens to the air coming and going from their bodies. He takes a breath every time they do. After a long time, he falls asleep.

15

Tim takes it slow and lets Jackie keep pace on the wide, worn trail. It's a warm April afternoon and the runoff has mostly slipped through. Beside them, Clear Creek runs silver. She stops, her ribs aching, out of breath. Tim's lightweight waders swish as he walks ahead, in his short vest and cylinder case, all of it straight from the Orvis catalog.

"Did the guy who sold you those $800 waders tell you that they don't actually catch the fish for you?"

He looks over his shoulder, slack-jawed, and points his finger at her dad's old cotton fishing vest with a slow smile.

"It's not about how many fish we catch, Jack. It's about being here."

"It's totally about how many fish we catch. Let me clarify—it's about how many more fish I catch than you."

"Jackie Dunbar, you are going to miss the forest and the trees. What? What's funny?"

"I think you mean the forest *for* the trees."

"No, miss smarty-pants, I mean what I said. Look at this place."

Midges buzz and dive above the surface. Twenty miles north of Silt, back up in the mountains, where the road turns from cement to dirt and narrows to trail, everything is left to its own devices, a relief in country where land is meant for hard use. Things are leafing out. There is more air here. For the first time since her accident, she feels like she can breathe.

Her dad used to say he fished to commune with the bugs, but he always made sure he caught the biggest fish on the river, the most fish, and that he returned with the best story. He put a rod in her hand when she was five. He loved it here.

Jackie and Tim break away from the trail and through the willows to a place where the creek is no wider than ten feet across, held by the twin edges of a sloped hillside. In her old canvas shoes, blown out at the sides, she steps sockless into the current. Water slips past her calves, quick and cold. Sun falls through the new green leaves on the aspens and scatters the trail with bits of light. Wind raises goose bumps on her bare legs.

She looks down at herself, at the contusions that have faded to a light yellow below the frayed edge of her cutoffs. She is weak, possibly too weak to be at leisure in the late afternoon.

"We shouldn't stay too long," she says.

"Will you do yourself a favor?" Tim stands beside her and stares at the nail knot he's tying to connect his tippet and leader. His big fingers are clumsy; he'd make a terrible surgeon. "Can you try to enjoy yourself for just a few hours?"

She tilts her head and raises an eyebrow at him. At no time in medical school has she met anyone like him. "You're like a gateway drug to indolence."

"Be nice, Dunbar. You're alone in the woods with me and you're basically a gimp. You walk any slower on the way in and I thought I might have to carry you."

"Like you could carry me."

"I'd do what it takes."

He licks his lips, grins, and turns to wade into the creek. His compact body moves in tandem with his rod, and he is such a surprising thing of beauty to watch that she forgets to be a smart-ass. He casts and his line makes a clean arc across the water, landing exactly where it should, behind a large boulder. For a few minutes there is only the sound of his line whipping the air and the white noise of the creek and the buzz of insects weaving above the water.

Be the fly. That's what Dad used to say.

She casts away from the sunlit water into shadow, where fish hide in the weeds and feed. The sharp pain in her chest when she raises her arms doesn't hold her back. For a string of perfect moments, she thinks of nothing but trying to keep her wrist straight, to forget about her thumb. She reels in. She casts. It's almost as if she were actually the fly, floating on the river, held between water and sky. Her laughter skids across the air.

"Hey, Dunbar, you're scaring the fish," Tim whispers over his shoulder. "Hush up."

She smiles and gives him the finger and wades deeper into the water.

She had never let her dad meet Tim, never even let him know she had a boyfriend. She had seen how it had gone with Susan, the frozen forced smile he gave to the boys who showed up at the door, the sarcastic comments he'd make later. Jackie learned to duck such encounters. Her dad, she was sure then, wouldn't be too crazy about Tim, with his easy life in town and easy smile, his popularity, all his friends. But now she reconsiders. Her dad might have seen the earnestness in Tim. He, like Susan, was perceptive in this way, in a way that Jackie is not. He might've sensed, without being told, that Tim was weighted by a longing to be his own man. She glances downstream at Tim, at his fancy gear and strong cast and feels oddly proud of the person he has become.

At dusk they sit on the hillside above the creek and trade the glass pipe back and forth. The valley splays out below them and the ridges and green and red grow soft in the fading light. The fire burns her throat but she manages not to cough, not to look like the prude she truly is. There's a lightness behind her ears.

"You don't look like someone who doesn't smoke pot," says Tim, looking at her admiringly.

"This isn't me."

"If you say so." Tim takes the pipe, cashes it, and tucks it into the open flap of his backpack, a mess of orange Twix wrappers, lip balm, and the unmistakable blue edge of an unwrapped condom. Jackie is staring at all that, distracted. Tim had brought a portable radio and the song pulses into the sky. She feels inside the music, her body hopping across the lyrics, as if she were physically propelling the notes forward. The night air settles on her skin like something alive, which maybe it actually is, she stops to wonder at that, when Tim is suddenly close, his mouth on hers, his tongue jostling against her teeth. Again, like before at the house, the closeness towers over her.

She pulls away and reaches to turn down the radio. And again she stares at the condom and wonders at what exactly Tim had been planning and what had she been planning herself. She wonders at how she hadn't really thought it all through. A wide puzzled smile sits on her face. It has been such a long time since she has felt capable of letting anything go. She lies back onto the scrub of the hill and watches the bats swerve and dive, hunting without sight.

"Did I ever tell you about the first time I tried to wear a condom?" Tim lies on his belly beside her, the length of their bodies touching. He is up on his forearms as if at a slumber party.

Jackie shakes her head no.

"I'm like 10, maybe 11, and all I know about condoms is that they're sexy, right? I've heard Barry, my older cousin, talking about them and so one Sunday at family dinner I take one from his underwear drawer. That night after everyone has gone to bed, I get the condom on my dick and then I do what I think they're made for." He grins. "I pee in it."

She turns to stare at him. "Shut up."

"That's what I thought you were supposed to do. I pee in it and it gets huge, like a massive water balloon, and I panic a little because how am I supposed to get the thing off without getting pee everywhere." Tim laughs. "Finally, I just take it off and of course there's piss all over my legs and the floor. I tie it in a big knot and throw it away. I couldn't understand what the big deal was."

Laughter slips easily from Jackie's body. She can picture a young Tim, his hair a mullet, the roundness of his face. "You really know how to put a girl in the mood."

"Too much information?" His eye twitches twice.

"No way."

"I over-share when I'm nervous."

"Oh, right. Spare me."

Again, he tries to kiss her, but she is thinking about bats. Little brown bats can eat one hundred fifty mosquitos in fifteen minutes, they pollinate crops, they work hard. She is up there hovering with the bats, watching herself and Tim, their bodies vulnerable, easily bitten by hundreds of mosquitos. Tim slides his hand across her belly and she wonders at the distance from his eyes to his hands, at how a central human instrument for noticing could be so far away from the mechanism for action. Her body is responding to him, she's kissing him back, but her mouth is too close to her eyes, the kissing too pure an expression of optical insight. She pulls away and sits up. "I'm not emotionally available."

Tim laughs nervously. "That sounds like something you read in a magazine."

Jackie startles because it is in fact something she had read somewhere. "I don't know. I'm sorry. I just want to be clear about where I'm at."

"Didn't we have sex like a month ago?"

"Yeah, but you were more of a stranger then."

"I don't get it."

She shrugs and smiles. She tries to make the muscles of her face perform the action that the rest of her body is incapable of.

Tim tilts his head, studying her. "I remember this about you."

"What?"

"How you push people away."

"I do?" She considers the space between them. "I never thought of that."

"Look, Dunbar. I don't need to make out with you, but you got to keep hanging out with me. I can't play another hand of canasta with my mom."

"That's a compliment?"

He reloads the pipe. "We can prove Mill wrong."

"Mill?"

"The philosopher? John Stuart Mill. Heard of him, miss smarty-pants? He said that the highest good in life is what produces the most pleasure."

"Philosophy is crap." Jackie waves away the pipe when Tim offers it to her.

"Like you studied philosophy," he says.

"Well no. Do you have any snacks?"

"See. The pursuit of pleasure," he says.

Jackie rolls her eyes but she also laughs, her body relaxed, her ribs less hindered. The night creeps in close and the hard edges of Tim's face dissolve. She shuts off the radio and there is the creek, the cicadas, her own pounding heartbeat.

The next morning, Jackie practically dances into Susan's room. The memory of fishing the river and of the afternoon that became the night simmers under her skin. She's definitely healing. She can be useful again. She throws open the curtains. Let there be light. Let us be happy. She sends beams of love toward the thin width of Susan's back, huddled under the covers.

"It's cold in here. Scoot over, Chicken." Jackie straddles the old sweet dog and slides between him and her sister.

Wearing a sweatshirt and long johns, Susan adjusts, just slightly, so that the Z of her legs and shoulders presses up against her sister.

"It's so quiet when you're not here," says Susan to the wall.

"I got home late last night. I didn't want to wake you."

It's quiet for a while and Jackie settles in closer to her sister.

"I had a dream we were fishing in Stark's pond," says Susan at last. "Do you remember that place?"

The summer before their mom died, when Jackie was seven and Susan was twelve, they spent the occasional afternoon up there, freed from chores. They rarely caught anything, but they'd swim and play cards and read. They'd complain about how boring it was to live out of town. They wanted to go to the public pool and hang around the baseball field. Now, she sees, it was perfect.

"What was that game you always made us play?" Jackie asks. "You had to pick a number, and then you'd count through all those lists to see if we'd live in an apartment or mansion or something?"

"MASH. I haven't thought about that in forever," says Susan. "You will live in Durango, marry a basketball player, have nine kids, and wear a green wedding dress. We loved that game."

"You loved it. I just wanted to hang out with you."

"Who else was I going to hang out with?"

"I'm sorry I was away yesterday."

"You were with Tim the Landman? He talks like a used car salesman."

Jackie stiffens. Susan is more like their dad than Jackie ever gives her credit.

"So he wants to be liked. There's nothing wrong with that."

"Are you sure he doesn't just want you to sign that gas contract?"

Jackie rolls away from her sister and onto her back. She stares up at the water spot on the ceiling, another thing that needs fixing.

"He doesn't need to convince me. I want to sign. I keep telling you, I don't see another option."

Susan stares at the quilt.

"There's got to be another way. Dad thought so."

"Look at every other rancher on Dry Hollow Road. They've all leased their mineral rights."

"I'll get a job."

"Oh really."

"I could wait tables. I'm smart. I can do lots of things."

"Honey, you've been out of it for weeks. You almost never take your meds. I don't see it."

"Stop calling me honey."

"No amount of work is going to get us as much as that gas deal. There's nothing around here that comes anywhere close."

Susan sits up in the bed and throws off the covers. She pats the pillow and Chicken comes to her side, the two of them together on the edge of the bed.

"You're wrong, you know," says Susan, petting Chicken, not looking at Jackie. "Money and drugs don't solve things, not for the long term. You're being naive where Tim's concerned."

"I'm naive? You're the one who doesn't want to sign a very practical contract that will give us money that we absolutely need, for what reason again?"

"Random terrible things happen to good people and to beautiful places; we're all entirely vulnerable." Susan's voice is measured, quiet. "Life doesn't have some big purpose set out for each of us."

"I wasn't suggesting God has a plan."

"No, you were suggesting you have one."

"Well someone around here needs to." It's not yelling exactly but Chicken gets up, ears perked, and leans against Jackie's legs, herding her into the wall.

Susan looks at Jackie and slides out of bed. "I think I'll take a walk." Susan pulls her boots on over her long johns. "Come on, Chicken."

"Let me get my coat." Jackie jumps up. "I'll come."

"No, don't. I want to be alone."

After Jackie stares at the wall for a few minutes, considering what she might have said differently, she walks outside and stands on the porch, her hair uncombed, her shirt untucked, everything about her slapdash and undisciplined. Don't leave. Stop leaving me. She, Jackie, keeps trying and she keeps getting it wrong. The small black arc of Susan's back gets smaller and smaller until it disappears behind the willows.

16

OUTSIDE, SUSAN WALKS AS fast as she can with no clear direction, glad to have Chicken beside her.

You've been out of it for weeks.

Jackie doesn't know everything. Her little sister. Arrived on her doorstep in Wyoming unannounced, two days after she didn't get into medical school. Stayed in bed crying and smoking Marlboro Lights. Susan took her out for drinks and made her dinner and did her laundry, and eventually she got Jackie laughing. Got her convinced to reapply and she did, and look at her now. Not that she ever said thank you. She didn't even strip the bed. *You didn't strip your sheets*, she imagines saying. Jackie'd probably laugh. Laugh at her.

After her first miscarriage, she had called home, snot-nosed and sad. Dad had spent less than one minute saying he was sorry before asking about the weather up there, the early snow, telling her to make sure she didn't run the heat too high. Jackie had sent a letter: more than 50 percent of all pregnancies end in miscarriage. It's normal, she'd written. It's a good sign you could get pregnant at all. When Susan never responded, Jackie called wanting to know why she was being ignored.

The watch on her wrist shines in the daylight. The band is too large, a man's band that she will never replace. Unlike what she had told Jackie, their dad hadn't actually given it to Susan. She took it from his nightstand while he was comatose. If she wore his watch, she had told herself, he would wake up and ask for it. Of course the jinx failed. But she kept wearing it, hoping it might give her the feeling of being the one he talked about to the neighbors, the one he noticed.

At Divide Creek, sunlight bends around the ocher boulders and infuses the dry air with weight. Jackie would never sit by the creek and just pay attention. She'd need to skip rocks, to try and get three skips and then have the rock hit the bank. Someone please explain how that's not crazy. The creek slides down from the mountains, silver and lush, and she can almost hear her dad say *Look at it long enough, it'll be enough.* She stares hard at the sky and the water and shoves them into the hurt. Chicken brings her a stick and licks her face, noses his snout into her side until she laughs. "All right, you. I get it." She rubs his ears. "Bring me that stick." He does, his tail scribbling odes of joy into the air. It is only when she tosses the stick into the creek that she sees.

The water is wrong. It's like Sprite is coming down from Mount Baldy. Bubbles for as far as she can see, up and down. She looks again. She's never seen anything like it.

17

RAY TAKES A POWDERED donut from the bag and shoves it into his mouth. The fact that there are still things in this country so good and perfect that cost fifty cents is a goddamn miracle. Spring has spread itself throughout the valley and the sagebrush smells strong. The mud makes more work and makes all of it more a mess, but that seems right for a world set on making itself brand new. Up top on the mesa, the rivers will be breaking open; the aspen will be green.

He pushes open the Dunbars' door without knocking; it's gotten to be like that between them. In two months, he'll be a deputy again, which is good, it's something his family can depend on; it's something he can do well again if he can keep himself straight. But he will miss the wind outside, and the heat of the cows in the morning and the feeling he gets from being around the Dunbars.

Jackie's at the kitchen table, a thick medical book in front of her; she hardly looks up when he comes in.

"I didn't know what you gals liked, so I got one of everything." Ray clears his throat and sets the white paper bag near her book.

"Thought I'd clear out that dead skunk in the pipe first thing. And I want to prep handline today. Sue ready to get to it?"

"She's mad at me." Jackie shuts the book and taps her finger against it. "Ray, can I ask your opinion about something?"

Ray shifts his feet. He always feels a little nervous around Jackie, like every day he has to prove himself over again. That someone as smart as Jackie Dunbar has expectation for him is not unflattering—it makes him want to rise to all occasions, to be better than he is—but on the edge of that is a deep fear that he doesn't have what it takes. It's easier with Sue.

"Shoot," he says.

"Do you think life just happens to a person? I mean, don't you think it's totally possible to improve your life?"

"I think it's good to try. It's good to help other people out. But some days the wind blows the right way. Some days it doesn't."

"Sure, but you think we have the capacity to change, right? I mean, isn't that inherent to human nature?"

"I don't know, Jackie." He counts his dead silently to himself. Marcus Wilson. The Iraqi kid driving toward the check point. The woman with the bag of groceries. The little girl on the wrong side of a tank.

Ray takes another powdered donut from the bag and shoves it into his mouth. He chews for a long time, gets some water from the sink. What he believes isn't something he knows how to explain, especially not to someone who has never been married or gone to war. He doesn't know how to say that getting older is about setting down the hope that everything works out if you just try hard enough.

"You ever read your horoscope?" he says, finally.

"You don't believe in that stuff."

"I read it in the paper sometimes; honestly, I read it a lot."

"You have to know some stoned kid fresh out of journalism school writes those."

"I never thought about who writes them." Ray shrugs, the color rising in his face. "Don't you ever want to feel like you're not in charge of everything?"

Jackie stares at him for a second before her face softens.

"All the time."

She smiles and Ray has the feeling that he's passed some sort of test and he nods, ready at last to get outside, when Susan runs into the kitchen, her hair flying, her cheeks red like they've been slapped. "The creek is bubbling." Susan's words are full of air, as she gasps for breath.

Ray and Jackie look at each other.

"Doesn't the creek bubble sometimes in the spring?" Ray asks Jackie. "From the melt?"

"It's not the melt," says Susan. "There were dead frogs. And dead fish swirling in the eddy. Ray, you've got to come. Please, I know something is wrong."

"Don't leave me out of this," says Jackie. "I'm coming too."

When they get to the creek, the bubbles don't stop coming. Just as Sue said, there's a dead frog with a balloon belly, white, like the end of a fingernail. The creek has never done this, not since Ray can remember. Both Sue and Jackie stand at the bank, far apart from one another.

"I'll be right back," he says and jumps in the truck.

He returns with a two-liter Diet Coke bottle he'd fished out of the recycling. He cuts the top third off the bottle and discards the rest. He wades into the creek with the homemade funnel and some matches. With the wide part of the funnel on the water, he lights a match and holds it at the mouth of the bottle. The flame shoots straight up. Ray's hands start to shake. He swears. He starts to sweat, his forehead creased and shiny. He feels like he is drowning though he's only thigh-deep. Then, somehow, he manages to light another match. This one flares up past his head. As quick as it lights, it dies.

18

LATER THAT DAY, AFTER they have left messages for the EPA and the DNR and the Fish and Wildlife people and the county commissioners, after Susan can't wait another minute for someone to call them back, she walks the ditch. The midday sun is high in the sky and heavy with heat. Susan finds that the noise in her brain is quiet for the first time in weeks. She passes rusted barrels and screens and irrigation wheels and truck wheels and dented pipes, all the old equipment piled up for parts. She crosses the upper field, through the gate onto Johnson's, until she finds what she came for.

Behind a string of orange and yellow flags that rope off a sump is a row of well heads and a couple tanks the size of outhouses. A former section of alfalfa, it's been scraped to dirt as if with a giant spatula. The green water has an oil-slick shine. The wells hiss and clang. The windless day gives no relief.

In front of the army-beige tanks is a sign. She reads it twice. Something hollow inside her fills with air. An old feeling, one she used to listen to. She needs a pen. Real reporters always carry a pen.

"What's doin, Sue?"

She spins to see Ray walking toward her, wind-burned and brown. In the weeks since he's been working cattle, his face has lost its puffiness, his hair has grown out; he looks less like a deputy, more like the boy he'd been. She waves, her hand is spastic. She is too excited, too glad to see him. She pins her arms to her sides.

"I was seeding alfalfa in the upper field and saw you leave the gate open; you all right?" He's been tracking her. Worried she's fragile as a leaf.

"I had to see all this." She nods at the mess of well heads.

"Place is the same, you know," he says, nodding beyond the well pad at Grass Mesa and the rough-cut mountains. From the fence line to the hills had been Stark land for all their growing up. "Look past all that and it's still real pretty."

Unthinking, she touches the wool of his work shirt and they stand there hinged to one another, quiet in their own lost thoughts.

Where does one story end and another start? Ray's dad sold this field to Johnson, the day after Ray's grandpa died, without asking Ray his opinion in the matter. Ray, out to spite his pacifist father, joined the guard the next week. And then Johnson leased the mineral rights, and now twelve wells puncture the fields where Ray once rode horses into the wind.

Now there is a sign that Susan can't stop reading.

"You have any pen and paper?"

Ray digs a pencil and a receipt out of his jacket.

Her handwriting is bad. Shaky. She keeps writing.

Danger! Extremely Flammable. Long-term repeated exposure may cause cancer, blood and nervous system damage. Contains benzene. Overexposure may cause eye, skin, or respiratory irritation or damage, and may cause headaches, dizziness, or other adverse nervous system effects or damage, including death.

"My arms are burning." Her T-shirt is thin. Her skin pale. "Ray, are your arms burning?"

Inside the house, she heads straight for the bathroom.

Including death. All the people in town who've died from cancer: Shorty's sister Trish who worked at Why Not Hair, Pastor Charlie, Millie Ramirez, Lydia Allen's mama, and then her daddy three months later, Kim Mobaldi, Sharon Haire, Liz Amos, Uncle Ellis, Dad.

The water is warm and she stands in the shower for a long time. Dad needed help with his bath at the end. His skin sagged. It was ashy and dry, like the skin of an old person. *Make it stop, Susie honey. Give me all of them pills.* He had said this as she drew the curtain around the tub. Needing help was not in his genetic code.

Dad, you've got a fever. You're just loopy from the pain. You don't mean that.

Please.

There are so many things she would do different in life, but that part with him at the end—someone else would've done better. The water pours over her face, her arms. She stares at the showerhead and suddenly it strikes her: this is creek water. The tanks aren't at all far from the creek. Her skin starts to itch. She looks for bubbles but the flow's too strong. She shuts the shower off, steps out with shampoo still in her hair. She scratches until red welts form across her arms, her belly, her thighs. The tile floor is not cold enough to calm her down.

When Jackie calls her name from the hall, when she opens the door and finds Susan wrapped in a towel, hair wet, sitting on the floor, she doesn't ask what's wrong but she sits down and puts her arm around her, Susan's wet hair getting her shirt wet.

"Everything's going to be fine, honey."

"But it's not." Susan pats the wet spot on Jackie's shoulder with her towel. "The water isn't safe."

"Let's try not to be too dramatic. We've called the state and the feds. We're going to get this tested. We'll find out."

Again, the hollow feeling in Susan's gut fills with air, as if it were being blown open by rusted levers and pulleys. This is the feeling of a good lead. *You're Silt's own Erin Brockovich.* Dad said that once. She sits up straight. Tucks her hair behind her ears. If she does some shoe-leather reporting, if the *Sentinel* runs it, if she can start stringing for them again, then maybe, just maybe, everything can be different.

"Jackie, this is a good story."

"What do you mean?"

"I mean, this is news. I can write about this."

"Aren't you way too close to this to be objective?"

"You don't think I can do it."

"Don't make this about me."

"An article opens the door. It's access."

Jackie crosses her arms, her face pinched, listing the reasons Susan should reconsider, but Susan focuses instead on a list of questions. All her thoughts line up along the tracks. There is one, and another, and the next. This is a problem she didn't create; there's a calm in that. This is something she can do.

19

RAY AND THE DUNBARS sit on the bank, a trio of sitting ducks, and watch Benny Fisk from the DNR collect water samples. Fisk wades into the creek in hip waders, a kerchief folded into his top right pocket. Every few minutes, he takes it out to wipe off drops of water that have splashed onto his chest or arms. Several times he says, in response to Susan and Jackie's questions, that he'll "have to run that up the flagpole." Twice he mentions the "limitations of his jurisdiction." When Susan asks his personal opinion, he takes the rubber glove off his right hand and looks at Ray with an arched eyebrow. "My opinion belongs to my boss. Ain't that right, Stark."

Ray makes the corners of his mouth rise. "Well, if that's about all for the day, I guess I'll head." He salutes Fisk, turns, and walks.

"Ray, wait up." Susan catches him on the other side of the willows, her cheerleader legs quick across the rocks. "I've been wanting to ask you something."

His mood lifts upward, above the willows and the scrub oak, up into the wide cloudless afternoon.

"Anything."

"Would you help me interview some of the guys you know who work in the gas patch?"

"Come on, Sue. You don't want to get yourself stuck in the middle of that circus."

"Does that mean you don't want to ask them?"

"A story in the paper's not gonna change anything."

"Oh?"

"You think the state cares about this? Why'd it take them five days to get out here to test the water?"

"Exactly. That's a great question."

"Sue, don't try to be some kind of hero. It won't end well."

"I thought you would understand." In the shade of the oaks, her upturned face is the color of a deep bruise. "Forget I asked."

Quickly, she walks away from him, her shoulders bent and so very small.

"Hold up, Sue. I'm not saying you're not a good reporter."

When she doesn't wait, when he tracks her back to the bank, she's already asking Fisk to tell her exactly what he's sampling, and oh Benny where did you go to college, and how long have you worked as a biologist, and it must be such fulfilling work. Fisk puffs up like a goddamn chub. She doesn't look at Ray, not once.

"Sue, shouldn't we move pipe before dark?"

"No, you head home." She threads her arm into the crook of her sister's elbow. "We wouldn't want you to be late for dinner."

"Are you sure? It won't take me any time at all."

Jackie starts to say something but Susan steps in front of her, her hand grabbing her sister's arm. "I'd hate for Camila to worry."

It isn't the first time he's been dismissed, just the first time she's done it, like some bullshit salute. And everything he's been keeping tamped down inside of himself in the days since he lit the creek on fire, everything he's been working so hard to keep steady, rips loose. He hasn't told any of them how fire brings it all back. He hasn't put that on them. He never would. On his way out, he kicks the gate until his toe is numb. Then he drives to the Skyline. Whiskey. Line it up.

After hours of throwing darts against himself, he's getting in his car to drive all of one mile when Ty, Officer Fucking Friendly, grabs his elbow and tells him he'll give him a ride, that he's had too much. Ray tells him to fuck off. He walks home.

But he isn't ready to go inside. Not yet. He sits on the swing and stares at the pool of yellow light in the girls' bedroom window. And pretty quick, he is staring at the house but it's not what he sees.

Light her up.

She had on a burka and she just kept walking at them, which wasn't normal, especially after they yelled at her to stop. He and his guys didn't have good armor or radio equipment. And the way she held that brown paper bag, like some sort of shield. So command said *light her up*, and they did. Not Jonny with an M4. Not Caleb with a 50-caliber machine gun. Not TJ or Gustavo with a grenade. It was Ski and him at the Mark 19.

Then the dust set down.

In the middle of the road was a piece of bread and body parts the size of marbles.

Her bag had groceries in it. She'd been trying to give them food. They—he and Ski, not Jonny or Fred or Andy, but he and Ski—they'd blown her to pieces.

It'd been months of bullshit sweep missions, driving around waiting to get their own ass blown up. Not one person could say what the fuck they were doing in Iraq. But he was still stupid enough to think his sergeant might care that he, Ray Stark, military police, thought it wrong about the woman with the groceries, that this wasn't the war he'd come to fight.

You goddamn loser.

That's what sergeant called him. Like he reached inside Ray's lungs and squeezed. They'd been on an overpass, looking down on what passes for a street, a goddamn puddle was all it was, that was maybe empty, maybe not.

That attitude jeopardizes your whole squad. You'll kill your guys with talk like that. I hear you talk like that again, your honorable discharge is fucked. Your choice, Stark. Go ahead and do it. Fuck up your own goddamn loser life.

He wouldn't do anything to hurt his guys and not his girls at home neither, so of course he shut up. Took the shit-burning duty sergeant assigned him and kept quiet about it. Every day for a month he'd haul the metal half-barrels away, from under what stood as a john, out to the sand. Thousands of people's shit. Fifty gallons at a time. Sweet and sick. Hit it with diesel and a match and while a big-ass plume of smoke went up, he stirred the pot. Time it took to get done, he was covered in soot, shit soot, the taste of it in his mouth even with a bandana over his face.

Then there was the thing with that kid in Sadr City in the car. The kid he killed. And then there was the dog he shot for drinking from a puddle of human blood.

For the next few months, he collapsed into himself. It was not something a person watching him might notice, not that people watched him much. But he felt like there were two of him from then on. The person with skin, who followed the rules and said very little. And then on the inside was the other part of him, the one who felt nothing, who tasted nothing, who didn't dream, who saw a sunset and thought of apocalypse.

But then Marcus Wilson died. And for days afterward, the grief in him rose above his will to toe the line, and it was then that Ken Singer from the *Washington Post* asked him for a quote. Even though Ray'd been told, *You talk to a reporter, you go to jail.* Even though the smell of shit smoke still stuck to his underwear.

He talked. He talked about the trucks with no armor, about the colonel and the hundred-dollar bills he gave civilians on his daily walks, thousand dollars a day, about the books he stacked in the barrack walls for extra protection. The interview was two hours, longer than he'd ever talked in one sitting.

In the article that ran six weeks later, Singer didn't mention one thing Ray had said. Like it wasn't interesting. Like none of it mattered. His only quote wasn't even something he would ever say. *"This war is a nonexistent national emergency," said Ray Stark, Military Police blah blah blah.*

He didn't go to jail; there was that, at least. Major said if the band was doubled up as personal security detachment to the general, they sure as hell couldn't afford to waste his boots on the ground. Ray got fined a couple thousand dollars and he got demoted and he kept to himself, stopped trying to change anything.

In the cold Colorado air, he is sweating through his wool shirt; his hands shake and he makes a fist. He stares at the window into his kids' room and imagines them asleep. He's so tired. Of himself especially. Of all his ideas about the way life is and isn't going to go.

And there's Sue Dunbar, taking a chance on herself. No reason she shouldn't. She'd come with him years ago to write about wildfires and she nailed the story. Every detail was right. It wasn't that anything at the Forest Service changed particularly, not enough, but there was something about the way she listened that made a person feel like their life mattered.

In the dead quiet of the house, he calls Dunbars'.

"Sue, I'll do it. I'll set you up some interviews."

"You will? You're sure?"

"I'm sorry about what I said before. I'm glad you're writing again. I think you'll do good, better than that."

"You have no idea how much that means to me."

"I'm real glad, Sue. See you tomorrow."

Camila stands in the doorway, watching him, even her eyes listening.

20

ON THE FIRST EVENING Jackie feels good enough to move handline, a day that smells of sage and loam, the smell of every spring, she sends Ray and Sue to move pipe in the field below, eager to test her capacity for working alone.

She drags the first pipe sixty feet. Slowly. Chicken does what he can to help, which is to bark at imaginary coyotes and to sniff his own ass. The aluminum is cold to the touch, the sprinkler heads tricky to keep upright. Every muscle in her body appears to have atrophied. Her heart pounds. Sweat beads. But one pipe becomes four, and then seven. She can do the work. She celebrates by keeping at it. She moves across the field, feeling the soft give of the land beneath her feet. She breathes in the smell of wet soil and the promise that the work will create something bigger and more important than herself. It isn't the first time in the past few weeks that she has considered how this ambition is not so different from the ambition of being a doctor. It is a dangerous thought, and she pushes it away.

Dad and Uncle Ellis used to sit in the evening, drinks in hand, and watch the sprinklers. She used to tease them about that, said they should buy a VCR, but she wouldn't say that now. The light does make the water sparkle and the water does make, eventually, a bright blanket of green grass. She wonders if Tim would think this was beautiful. She wonders at herself thinking about Tim. In the field below, Ray and Susan work in tandem, their voices rising and falling in a duet of muted conversation.

The night before, Susan got off the phone with Ray and danced around the room in her sock feet. Then she made a pot of coffee and stayed up for hours making lists of questions and sources, reading through things she'd printed earlier at the library. Jackie sat awake in bed, listening to her sister. Cold reached her under the covers, worry beating away sleep, remembering those mornings before school in Ray's old Ford.

The Ford was a 1969 and Ray called her Big Blue. He would work for his granddad at sunrise and then swing by their place. Susan always slid into the truck first, so she could sit next to Ray and make him laugh, and on those days Susan always wore her hair down and curled. On those days, Susan shed her need to be cool, and softened into her old self, the one who was goofy and curious and even shy. Jackie had loved it.

Those rides to school had ceased when Camila convinced Ray to join the swim team, which practiced in the mornings. Susan immediately had sex with the quarterback, Ray's best friend, traded him for the point guard, Ray's sister's ex, and finally dumped him for the editor of the newspaper. Jackie never saw any of them make Susan laugh.

In the field below, Ray and Susan finish their set and get the sprinklers started, talking close together in the fading light. Jackie's set almost finished, she tries to pick up the pace but finds her arms and body are heavy. The sun has slid behind the mesa. A coyote calls across the field and Chicken sits back and howls, the early evening sliced through with sound. Ray walks toward them and she pushes away her exhaustion to connect the final pipe, for the satisfaction of finishing alone. She reaches for the opener and cranks.

Freezing water blasts her in the face, in the groin. With a stick, she pokes at the gasket to move and reseat it. Water sprays into her eyes, her ears.

"You all right, Jackie?" Ray shouts behind her, his footsteps clomping through the wet grass.

She keeps poking it, swearing under her breath. Ray looks down at her handiwork, not telling her what to do, not his way, and when she gets it fixed, the water moving back in the direction it was meant, she wipes her face with her shirt and smiles.

"I was thirsty."

"Ha. You look cold."

"I'm fine, really. I finished the set."

"Good girl."

Susan runs up behind them. "Jackie, you've got to get that water off of you. You're sopping. Go, hurry, back to the house."

Jackie looks down at herself and then looks at Ray and finally at Susan.

"This is what I've been saying, Susie. How can you think about writing an article about this? You're irrational about it."

Susan puts her hand on Jackie's arm. "How much is that gas contract influencing your lack of curiosity about all this? Don't be a sucker, Jackie."

Jackie starts to say something and then stops, surprised. "You sound like your old self."

"Jackson, go home." Susan nods toward the house. "And don't be an idiot, get dry. We'll finish."

Jackie marches across the mesa, the dark sliding around her. Ray and Susan's laughter bounces off the poplars, off the clouds, back into her face. She takes hold of her own hand, as if she could fix her own isolation.

At home she heads straight for the telephone, wet hair dripping behind her across the kitchen linoleum. His voice mail clicks on right away.

Hey, it's Tim. Leave a mess; I'll pick it up.

She holds the receiver in her hand, unsure what to say. Tim, of course, is on the Uinta for five days. Her voice is full of poverty. She hangs up mid-sentence.

If she were in Denver, she'd be giving report at changeover. If she were in Denver, she and Jean would go for a run afterward and Jean would make her laugh about something she saw that day and then they'd go have a beer at the dive down the street from their apartment. Jackie goes to the phone again and dials.

"Jackie Dunbar, is it really you? You sound tired. Is it awful?"

"Oh, it's not so bad." Jackie forces herself to laugh and hopes it's been long enough that Jean won't recognize it for a fake. "It's not like the hospital."

"I miss you. It's not the same without you here."

"I miss you too." Jackie smiles at her reflection in the window glass. She pictures Jean's nose ring, her black fingernail polish, her silver bracelets. At the funeral, she had stood behind Jackie, touching her shoulder every now and again. "When can you come visit me out here in my own personal wasteland?"

"I've meant to come a hundred times. I'm just so busy with the path rotation in Dr. Gown's lab. And I'm doing that research project, which is way more work than I thought. When are you coming back?"

"There's so much to do here. I don't know when I can get back."

"Your dad would expect you to finish school."

Jean's confident voice sounds incredibly far away. Jean grew up on Lynx Lane, a cul-de-sac named for the animals it replaced. Her parents, both still alive, are doctors. Their coffee table stacked with medical journals and issues of *The New Yorker*. Jean's embrace of Jackie, her referencing her as a best friend, had at one point been a sign of Jackie's entrance into a world with options, a world of people where no one from Silt had ever gone. Suddenly, the words in Jackie's mouth are slow to form, the effort of making them exhausting.

"The last thing my dad would want would be the ranch to go under." The receiver is cold against her cheek.

"Did he ever say that?"

"He wasn't really making sense by the time I got here. He died really fast. I thought I told you that."

"Don't be like that. I've been thinking about you so much."

"You sound good. I'm really glad for you."

"Listen, I hate to do this, I'm really sorry, but I have to go. I have a date with that guy Robert and I was supposed to be there five minutes ago."

Jackie stares out the window into the empty darkness.

"The mouth breather?"

"I know. But he's so fun to talk to."

"Well go have fun. I have a hot date with my local television station."

Jackie says goodbye and hangs up, shivering in her wet clothes. The clock ticks against the faded wall. It occurs to her that this feeling is something her dad or sister may have shared on any one of the times she herself had called home. Always, she had been the first to get off the phone. Jackie shivers in her wet clothes and watches the clock tick against the faded wall until the minutes have consumed her wasted time.

21

THE SKYLINE SMELLS LIKE cigarettes, stale beer, and men, which is to say it hasn't changed. The Happy Birthday banner still hangs over the door. Behind the bar, a wooden-framed Denver Broncos poster shares the wall with a stuffed coyote. There's a stack of bills on the edge of the pool table and shots of Irish whiskey on the bar. Delores is good at her job; she doesn't ask Susan about where she's been, doesn't say anything about the last time Susan was there and the man she was with then.

"What can I get you, darlin'?"

Susan asks for a club soda—she is there to work—but then she rethinks that and asks for a Bud Light. A reporter should always blend. Her clothes are right, absolutely, positively: jeans, boots, wool cardigan. She fingers her turquoise earrings, a present from Jackie years ago. She'd put them on for good luck but realizes now they were a misstep. A sign of personality. So too, she thinks, is the concealer smeared under her eyes, the lip gloss. She's been afraid to shower, just doing sponge baths with baby wipes. Her long hair, even in a bun, is terrible.

The door is right there. She could just walk out the way she came. She sets her beer on the bar.

"Sue, we're over here." From the back, behind the jukebox, Ray waves.

She picks up the beer. Here goes nothing.

"Stones were flying up off the ground and into my face. It was super fucked up," Jimmy Crowley is saying when she gets to the table. "Sorry, excuse my language, ma'am."

"Oh, I don't care. Thanks for meeting me."

"Well, I owe Ray a few favors. And I remember you, from before. High school cheerleaders ain't easy to forget."

Laugh, Susan. Laugh it off. She's still standing. Should she slide into the booth beside Jimmy? That might be a little too close. Or pull up a chair to sit squarely between them? The notebook in her back pocket needs to be on the table, or it could be on her lap, hidden from view to protect Jimmy. She puts her beer down on the table and shifts her feet.

Ray, thank god for Ray, puts his hand on her arm and smiles. He moves over and motions for her to sit beside him.

"So, um, can we talk about the night of the kick?" she asks, tucking a loose strand of hair behind her ear.

"As long as this is off the record, go ahead. What can I do you for?"

Direct question or second level? Butter him up or not? She smiles at Ray, edges closer to him, and opens her notebook on the table.

"I've heard that you were using a new choke that night, but that you lost control to release some of the pressure that was building up in the well. Did the concussion events happen at each of the openings?"

Jimmy starts to talk about bullshit company lines and cracked casing. There's a St. Christopher dangling from a chain around his neck and as he talks, his fingers drumming the table, the pendant lunges into his beer. She'd bought Kelly a St. Christopher before his first hitch in the Jonah Field. Four different times it broke off; every time she'd bought a new one. As if luck could be so easily acquired.

"You getting that all down?" Jimmy reaches across the table and puts his hand on her notebook.

"I'm sorry, can you say that one more time?"

"I said that the roughneck on the last hitch didn't clean the mud tanks. The drilling fluid was way too fucking light."

"And why's that important again?"

"You sure you're not too pretty to be a reporter?"

You're no Lois Lane. Kelly had laughed when he said that. There is a squeeze in her chest. She drinks her beer. Ray won't meet her eye. He's studying his thumbs.

Laugh.

Now.

Try again.

"You were saying about the nitrogen and foam from the last job?"

"Yep, some idiot on the rig's last hitch didn't clean the mud tanks. And there was no diverter installed."

She should know what a diverter is. Always do your homework. Always know more than they think you do. And she doesn't know. And what was she thinking. And Ray is embarrassed for her. Her throat is tight. Her pen doesn't work. She stands up.

"I'll be right back. Bathroom still in the back?"

The smell of bleach is a salvation. She pulls down her pants and her underwear as if she really did need to go. *You're no Lois Lane.*

There are people in Canada who, according to an article in the *Alberta Sun*, took matters into their own hands when a gas company ruined their land. They slashed tires and cemented-in gas wells. They didn't hide behind a byline. Susan sits on the toilet and bites her nails.

"Sue, you in here?"

Ray knocks on her stall. His boots are so close to her own, they almost touch.

"This is the women's bathroom."

"Jimmy had to get back. His kid is sick. But he says you can call him whenever. I think he likes you."

Susan covers herself with her cardigan. Hiding in the bathroom is a bad sign. She has been trying to ignore the signs, but this is not something easily dismissed. Camila would never hide in a bathroom.

"How did you know all that stuff about the diverter and the foam? That was great. You did good."

"Really?"

"Come on out already, I'll buy you a beer. Oh, and my cousin Carson works on a frack crew. He's having some weird health stuff, says he'll talk to you as long as it's off the record. I told him what you're doing."

As if she were someone that could be counted on. *What you're doing*. As if she were going to actually write and publish something.

"I'll be right out."

When she pulls up to the house, the high beams catch two eyes in the dark. Her sister's lean frame cloaked in Dad's down coat; the dog at her side, tail wagging. Susan steps out of the truck and the night sky is dirty with stars. Jackie's breath leaves her body and stitches her to the outside, one exhale at a time until, by the time Susan has closed the space between them, it is as if her sister were sewn into the air.

"You ever wonder how it might've been if Mama didn't die?" Jackie says, staring up at the sky. "You ever think we might be in better shape?"

The slight catch in Jackie's voice lets her know. Even in the dark. Say goodnight and go inside. Duck and run. But there is Jimmy Crowley's face, how it softened when he saw her listen, saw her believe. Not everyone worries about her.

"I was out interviewing a roughneck for my story."

This doesn't make an impression. Jackie's breath slides in and out of the night.

"Ray says I'm doing a good job," says Susan, trying again.

"It's nice of him to help you."

"I think I'm better. Do I seem better?"

"Maybe."

Before Susan considers the tone of disbelief, before she lets it settle into herself, the lie forms in her mouth. She spits it out.

"My old editor at the *Sentinel* says he'll buy the article when I'm done. He says it'll run above the fold."

Drum beats at her chest. You are lying. Lie down, Susan. Lay down, Susan.

"Really? I mean, congratulations. That's really great, Susie."

"They want three thousand words. And a sidebar."

"Well that's a real start," says Jackie, her voice uneven. "I'm proud of you." Jackie sighs and rests her head on the gate. "I can't sleep. I've been so distracted by the ranch, I can't get this proposal done for my attending. Medical school seems really far away."

Susan stares at her sister with great interest. In the span of several minutes, she, Susan, problem child, has been transformed. No longer is she someone to agonize over; now she is a confidante. The way an older sister should be. She touches Jackie's arm, feeling bones and muscles through the down. Dad wore that coat forever, and still it is the same sky blue. Even in the dark, she knows the color, knows the smell of the fabric.

"You aren't sure about medical school," Susan says neutrally, in the tone of a therapist.

"I know you think it's impossible if we want to keep the ranch."

"I don't think that. I think you can't imagine leaving me to run it without you."

Jackie looks hurt. Not what Susan wanted. This was a conversation about Jackie not having to worry about her anymore. "I mean. Ray and I could get on fine."

"But Ray is going to be deputy again in June. You know that, right?"

Susan pinches her belly through her pocket lining.

"Listen, honey." Susan steadies her voice. "You don't need to worry about me."

Nothing libelous in a little lie if you're lying low.

22

YOU GOT YOURSELF A *Class Four wife there, Ray*. Gramps said that once. As in a Class Four river. As in, you got yourself a complicated home life.

Susan Dunbar, on the other hand, is more like a hanging lake. That girl is hard to get to, deeper than you first think, the kind of pretty that refreshes the soul. Ray watches her from the corner of his cousin Carson's trailer.

Sitting on the edge of a frayed orange couch, Susan crosses and uncrosses her legs. Carson, his leg still in plaster, picks a remote from a red plastic crate covered with pizza boxes and empty beer cans and mutes the game.

"I ain't so sure about this." Carson catches the Pabst Ray throws him. "The squeaky wheel don't get fixed in this business, it gets junked. I got a car payment. I got alimony."

Two sets of crossed fingers tucked behind her notebook, Susan explains that the interview can be off the record. That the last thing she wants is to jeopardize his job. That it's entirely up to him. Ken Singer never said those things. He never looked at Ray with such kindness. Sue has always been good at making a person feel like they're the only person in the room.

"Listen, cuz, Sue is basically family." Ray pulls open a folding camping chair and sinks down into it. "She won't let you down. I swear."

Carson stares at the muted hockey game for a full minute. Wind rattles the trailer walls. Men outside leave for their shifts.

Ray wishes he had got himself a beer, but there isn't one on the table and it seems rude to get up while Carson is considering. Carson used to follow him around at family barbecues, dogging his every move. He'd come to Ray's baseball games and sit near the dugout, shouting out "That's my cousin!" whenever Ray made any sort of contact with the ball. Carson used to talk to Ray about joining the force, about them being partnered up together like in the movies.

"Listen, what happened to me don't matter, not really." Carson sets the beer down on his cast. Decided. Still watching the game. "The big story is all in the MSDSes. Look 'em up for the ingredients in frack fluid. That shit is no joke. Something went wrong on a frack job at Johnson's the other week. We lost hundreds of thousands of gallons. Couldn't pull it back up. Where'd it all go? That's your story."

Susan asks him for some names and he shakes his head, silent. Sue is nice about it, thanks him for the tip. Ray tells Carson to call him if he needs anything. They hustle out to the truck, both of them faster than they need be.

"Damn. I'm sorry, Sue." Ray pulls out of the windblown man camp, the trailers lined up like toasters. "I hate to let you down."

"It's not your fault. He probably took one look at me and knew I hadn't done this in years."

"Nah. If I were still a deputy, it'd be different."

"How's that?"

"Oh, you know how it is. What's that they say? 'The badge makes the man.'"

"You think Carson thinks less of you now? People don't think that."

"I don't blame anyone over it. I mean, come on. I got messy."

There's a half-empty flask of whiskey under his seat. There's an extra bottle in the barn. Another hidden at the bottom of a box of Christmas ornaments in his garage. He's been drinking less since he's been working for the Dunbars, but most days he still doesn't hold off much past four.

"Shit, I'm still messy."

"If it's any consolation," says Sue, "I can't think of anyone I trust more."

"You don't have to say that."

"It's true. There's more light when you're around, Ray Stark. Always has been."

Ray touches her beautiful wrist. But only for a second. His hand takes flight until it finds safety on the steering wheel. He focuses on the road ahead, on driving, and he does a good job of not looking at Sue the whole rest of the way. Outside, the clouds in the north promise a rain headed someplace else. They drive past the muddy Colorado, which moves so slow it might as well be one big eddy, circling back on itself.

That night, Ray bends his head and listens to the highs and lows of his family's four voices mix into one sound. They all say grace in Spanish. Lilly's hand in Ray's right hand is sticky and Monica's hand in his other hand is hot, and after they're done with the prayer he holds onto their small hands for a second longer until they both pull away. They pass peas and chicken and bread around the table. Camila asks Monica what she learned in school, which she asks every night, and Monica talks about the space shuttle and how she needs to find a poem to memorize. The whole time, she looks at her mom.

"Here, Lilly. Eat more peas." Ray spoons some onto her plate.

"Do I have to, Mama?"

"Try a few, baby." When Camila smiles at the girls, she holds nothing back—her lips wide, her front teeth showing, as if everything she has is theirs. She looks at him and even though the smile is still there on her mouth, it's reserved, smaller. "Ray, I called Joanna at the courthouse today. There's a form you fill out to appeal for a shorter probation. I picked it up for you."

"I didn't ask you to do that."

"Well, you're welcome."

"Those forms don't work. Sheriff does whatever he wants."

"It's worth a try. We need your job back."

"It's coming back."

"I miss that overtime pay. Sooner you're back there, the better for everyone."

Monica knocks her milk over, and Camila yells; Ray pats his daughter's hand and tells her it's no big deal, he'll take care of it.

He gets up and stands in front of the open refrigerator for a time, staring and not seeing the half-empty shelves. *Uniforms are sexy*, Mila had told him all those years back, when she was pregnant and he had been running cattle for Gramps and making barely enough for groceries. She was the one who told him he'd make a great deputy. She was the one who wanted to stay in town, near her parents and the church.

He sets the glass of milk down in front of his kid and looks across the table at his wife. Her creamy skin against her black low-cut blouse is beautiful. He wants to tell her how much being outside and working for the Dunbars is helping to make him feel half normal. In four weeks he'll deal with parking lot patrols and meth heads and bar fights and domestic disputes, but not yet. He isn't ready yet.

"You all should come up to Dunbars' this weekend. It's pretty this time of year. You girls want to see some baby cows?"

That seems to get through. Monica and Lilly both say yes, but Mila sets her fork down and stares at him.

"Susan hasn't returned any of my calls. Is she any better?"

"I think so. She did pretty good talking to Carson this afternoon."

"Why do you need to be there for her interviews?"

"I guess she thinks it's useful to have me there. Did you hear about Doc Pitkin's ranch? They found bubbles yesterday in their part of the creek."

"So." She sits back into her chair. "Now that Susan says there's a problem, you believe it?"

"It's not like that."

"Do you want to get involved? I could use help getting the word out about the community meeting next week."

"I'm still not clear what the point is in sitting around hearing people blow sunshine."

"Oh, Ray. You've become so predictable."

"Mama, read me about the zebra."

"I can do it, honey," says Ray. "Bring me your book."

"Lilly, you know the rules. Not at the dinner table. Jackie must be better by now. It's been two months."

"It feels good to help out."

"The dishwasher quit on my brother yesterday. He could use a hand at the restaurant." Camila sets her fork down. Her stare is bulletproof.

"I like being outside, Mila, being up there. It's good for me."

"Good?"

"Can we be excused, Mama?"

With the girls gone, they light into each other, picking over everything and nothing. Camila clears away the plates, still yelling as she walks to the sink. He sits at the round table by himself and stares at his wedding ring.

Gramps stayed married to Grandma for fifty-one years. When there was drought and the hay crop failed, he rodeoed for money. Broke his arm in three places once but didn't lose the bull. Bronco Lou, Grandma called him after that. When the sun hit the water right, Gramps always put his arm around her and pointed to the bits of light. *Betty's diamonds*, he'd call them, and she'd lean into him.

Ray walks into the kitchen and stands behind Camila at the sink.

"Mila." His voice is low, all the fight blown out of him. "Maybe you'd be happier with someone else."

"What are you saying?" She doesn't turn around.

"I want you to be happy. That's all I want."

They look at each other in the reflection of the window above the sink.

"You want to leave? That's not what we do." Her face drops its mask of toughness and for a moment, fear splays her features into the girl who ran across the desert. "That's not who we are."

"I want us to have the best possible version of our life."

"Then make the best of it. Figure out how to be happy and stop looking to me for all the answers."

"OK. Forget it." He touches her shoulder and in a snap, her mask is back on. She yanks her body away from his touch and shakes her head. He stands there for a minute or two, waiting for her to say something, anything. She scrubs the dishes, never looking up.

"I'll get bedtime going," he says at last.

The two girls are watching TV, some stupid sitcom, and he tells them it's time to brush teeth and wash up.

"No. I want Mama to do it," Lilly says from the couch.

"I'm already ready, Daddy." Monica, glassy-eyed in a purple nightgown, doesn't budge from the floor. "I can watch for seven more minutes."

"No, you can't," says Camila behind him. "Come on, girls." She leads them away.

Under the bright bathroom light, the three of them crowd together in front of the mirror. They all have the same dark hair and almond eyes and the same way of talking over each other. The newspaper sits in his lap unread as he watches them from the couch in the living room.

23

THE GLASS DOOR OF the diner swings back and forth, ringing its two-note bell, as a parade of muddy boots, sneakers, sandals, corrective shoes, a muted landscape of practical footwear, enters and exits. Tim and Jackie sit across the table from one another in a booth near the front.

Cheryl, the waitress who has worked the lunch shift longer than Jackie has been alive, is a powerhouse of efficiency; she glides her solid frame between the crowded wooden tables in her white high-tops. The room is filled with people who knew Jackie's dad, old ranchers eating pie and hash, their hats on the chair beside them, their confidence about how the world works intact.

"I'll take a Coke and your banana cream pie," says Tim.

"You got yourself a sweet tooth, honey," says Cheryl, her voice the sound of cigarettes before breakfast.

He looks at Jackie across the table and winks. "Yes ma'am."

Jackie rolls her eyes at Cheryl and orders the salad bar and french fries.

Tim smiles at Jackie and then nods hello to Alan Gibson, who is looking at them from the next table over. She'd heard Gibson used the money he got from the gas royalties to buy a Zamboni and turn his backyard pond into a hockey rink for his kids.

"Nice to see your shining face, Dunbar. Now, what can I do you for? You sounded strange on the phone."

She frowns. "Something weird is happening to our water and it's got us all a little spooked. I can't get you that gas lease by the end of the week when it's due."

"What kind of weird?"

She leans across the table and lowers her voice. "Divide Creek is bubbling and my sister is real worried that it has to do somehow with the fracking up-valley. We've had the state out to test the water but no word back yet on the results. Susan's convinced we're being poisoned."

"Poisoned sounds like a stretch."

"Maybe. But I'm not naive. You can't tell me that kickdown was normal operating procedure."

"Definitely not. But you have to think about it like a doctor would. How often do patients come in worried they've got some rare parasite and it turns out to be the flu?"

Jackie nods. *Don't hunt for a zebra*, that's what her attending had said just last November. "But that doesn't mean you don't take it seriously."

"Of course. You know I love your creek. I love all the creeks around here. I'm not in this business to watch things get wrecked."

Jackie fiddles with her fork. "Susan's not budging on the contract."

"Listen, I don't have a dog in this fight. Sign the contract. Don't sign it. I get paid either way."

"She doesn't think we can trust the people you work for."

"Here's what I'll do and hopefully it can bring your sister around. I'll see if my company can get you all drinking water delivered. That's just being a good neighbor; it's good for their PR, they'll like that." Tim bounces his knee under the table, so fast the water sloshes in their glasses. "And I'll personally call the folks at the state and see about coordinating with their results, make sure everyone's talking to each other. And let's say there is something weird going on, there's things we can do. There's charcoal filtration systems and aerating devices, whole bunch of things." He takes a long sip of water. "If I were you, I'd want an extension on that contract until this hoopla settles down, yes?"

Jackie nods and exhales the crimp in her chest. She settles back into the booth, lets it hold her.

"Consider it done."

Jackie squints at him as if he were a puzzle she was trying to solve. "Don't tell me you're actually a nice guy."

"Watch out, Dunbar, you might have yourself a friend, despite your terrible personality."

Jackie smiles and heads to the salad bar, scooping bean salad, macaroni salad, and potato salad onto her plate. Across the room, Cheryl delivers Tim his pie and he takes a huge bite, his top lip becoming covered in cream.

What she has wanted, when it comes to relationships, is not something she has ever understood. There was the snowboarder who had dropped out of college, with the great arms and nothing to say. There was the aspiring novelist with the job selling vitamins, who was moving, and then did move to Buenos Aires as soon as he saved enough money. There was the medical student with Aspergers who would only see her on Friday nights from seven to nine.

She has always picked people she is certain to avoid falling in love with. A defense mechanism that always fails: she has never managed to completely sidestep hurt.

She slides back into the booth.

"I want to thank you. I mean it, it means a lot to me to have your help."

Tim waves his hand as if it were nothing. He points his fork at her plate.

"How is that a salad? There's no lettuce."

"How is that lunch?" She nods at the last bite of congealed syrup and store-bought crust on his plate.

"This is fruit, dairy, grain; it's practically a model of the USDA food chart." He cocks his head to one side, laughter in his eyes, searching her face. "Explain to me how you don't have a cell phone. You're impossible to reach."

"There's no point. They don't work up at the ranch. I put my plan on hold."

"You put your plan on hold. That sounds like a metaphor."

She laughs at the surprise of again misjudging him.

"Want to go to Farm and Home after this? I need a new post hole digger."

"That sounds romantic."

"Yeah well, romance has always been slightly lost on me."

"Another thing I like about you."

They grin at each other through the din of the doorbell, of silverware clanking against earthenware plates, through the talk around them of weather and feed, through the smell of coffee, bleach, and bacon. Neither of them moves to pay the bill; they let the minutes pass unused, squandered on the pleasure of being together.

24

THE UNEASY FEELING STARTS early in the day for Tim, as he is riding single-track cut into the side of a river canyon. His full suspension bike is already splattered with mud, a sign of a good ride. Juniper blur at the edge of his sunglasses. On his iPod is Killer Whale, the most awesome band he's heard in a long time, a band that should, under normal circumstances, especially on such a technical ride, clear his head. Killer Whale, or the Orcas, as their true fans call them, were originally out of a small logging town in Washington, three guys, heavy loops, and Tim knew when he first saw them a few years back in a tiny smoky bar in Casper that they'd make it big. Now, just like he'd predicted, they're playing Radio City, living in LA, dating models. Tim focuses on this and sees how he has always been good at making a good bet, especially on people like himself, people who come from not much.

At the bridge, he opts to ride through the shallow stream, mud from his tires splattering his face and calves, a sign of hard work, of someone who keeps after it. He had considered inviting Jackie to join him for the weekend but is relieved he hadn't. He needed the time to think, to consider what to do.

As he hits the steep section, he grinds up the trail, pulling his body forward off the bike; he listens to the same track, "Day Fight," over and over. There is a part in the song, where the verse slows, where the music becomes predictable, almost boring, but then, there's a pause and the chord changes and the rhythm picks up, and suddenly the song is saved. Tim marvels at the upbeat, at the guts it took to write a chord progression where its near miss with failure is its setup to success.

Without wanting to, his mind wanders back to Jackie. She hadn't gotten around to listening to the CDs he gave her and he didn't like that. In fact, he can't remember her ever knowing that much about music. To move away from the country and classic rock stations of rural America was as much the central motivating idea of his adolescence as his longing to squeeze the juice out of life. Would Jackie embrace the moment before the pickup? Would she know what that means? She rarely talks about medical school. It's no longer obvious to Tim that she is the same person, the one who would do what needs doing, see things from a no-nonsense distance, in order to achieve her personal goals. Like most people, she probably only tracks the lead singer. Doesn't notice the bassist, the one communicating between the drums and guitar, the one holding it all together. Although at some point, she had noticed him.

She had come by herself one time to watch Chewbacca's Foot, his high school band that everyone had said was certain to make it big. He'd been impressed by how unafraid she was of being different, of not traveling in a pack like all the other girls he knew. After his set, she'd been shy and awkward, not someone he would normally go for but then he'd made her laugh and he'd been surprised at how satisfying it was, how special it made him feel. So when Don got into meth and Bunny got pregnant and the sixteen labels they'd sent their demo to never responded, it didn't matter as much because he was dating Jackie. She wanted things from life, things that no one had ever told him it was all right to ask for. Without her influence, he never would've taken the SATs and surprised everyone including himself with his high scores. If they hadn't dated, he might never have gone to college, gotten such a good job, been able to help his family and certainly to help himself.

Her message on his voice mail the day before had been sweet, but he had blown it off. And while she certainly took her time returning his calls, that didn't mean he had to be a tit-for-tat sort of person, he didn't want to be that guy. He had woken up this morning, sunlight streaming through the tent, warming his bag, with nothing but the sound of the creek, which should've been the start to a perfect day, but he found himself worrying about Jackie, about what he'd seen at work the day before, about his confidentiality agreement. And he doesn't like to worry. That's not his jam. He turns the music up and hammers out the last pitch, his lungs burning, his legs heavy, until he clears the crest and his thoughts narrow to the gravel under his tires.

Driving back toward town the next day, he idles on the frontage road to call his folks, just to give himself a boost, because today, they should be happy with their baby boy. If they were anyone else they definitely would be.

It takes a minute for his dad to pick up the landline.

"How's it look? Is it amazing?"

"We missed you this weekend. Your mother thought you'd be in town. We were expecting you back for church."

"I see you all the time, Dad. Did the dishwasher come?"

"Hold on a minute, son. I'm just finishing gluing this mast; let me pass you to your mother."

Tim winces. Ever since his dad had to close the mill, he's built model navy ships, the kind used during his Vietnam tour. A completely dull, useless, old-fashioned hobby. His mom dusts those damn toothpick boats every week and never says a word.

"Hi, honey," his mom picks up. "Tell me everything."

"Mom, how's the dishwasher? I thought they were delivering it yesterday."

"Oh yes, it's the most beautiful thing I've ever seen. Thank you. It's just wonderful, honey."

Tim frowns. *It's just a dishwasher*, he wants to say. Everything with his mom is always the most wonderful, the most beautiful, so much so that it can't possibly be true. But then, wasn't he hoping for this kind of reaction? Wasn't the point to please them, to hear them go on and on about his generosity? The money Tim gives his parents every month has been the only reason they're still in their house. And he doesn't want them to feel like they owe him anything, except maybe he likes it that they owe him, that they depend on him, and what does that say about his character? He yanks the parking break, annoyed with himself for going down what he has taken to calling The Doubt Spiral.

"How did the install go? Did they get out of your way pretty fast?"

"Well, um. It's still in the box. Your father will set it up when he has the time. We just love it so much."

Tim slumps against his seat. On the road, he never gets this squirrelly feeling like the one he has now. He sighs.

"Mom, I paid extra for them to set it up for you."

"You know your father. He didn't want to waste money on something like that. But he just loves it, Tim. We both do."

He should let it drop, right there, but pathetically, he can't. He tries one more time.

"The color was good, right? I thought you'd like the silver."

"Oh yes, honey. It's just perfect."

Then his mom wants to talk about the weather and about her neighbor's new peonies, about how the dog has learned to roll over. Tim stares vacantly out the window until he can interrupt her to tell her he loves her, to say goodbye. *They're not bad people, they're just not like us. Their dreams for their lives are pocket-sized.* Jackie said that once, before they left for college, and it was something he'd remembered and retold himself again and again over the years.

The thing he has always liked about Jackie is how she tells it straight. This point is troubling and he throws that in the pro column. Then he considers the cons: his lack of real choice, all the people counting on him. Clearly, Jackie can relate to the constraints of obligation. He banks on that and the more he thinks about it, the surer he becomes. He drives to the office. There is no need to think about it again.

25

On a cloudy May afternoon, Jackie walks through the Kum and Go gas station on the edge of town by the highway, berating herself for being there, but sometimes procrastinating to the point of self-loathing is the only way to truly buckle down. She stares for a long time at the four shelves of gum, which for a town of two thousand people seems like way too many choices.

She had woken up that morning, resolved to complete her research proposal, resolved to ignore the specific anniversary of the day. But Susan bowed out of work, something about her deadline. And then the ditch needed burning, and there was a cow with an impacted and infected udder that needed to be put in the squeeze chute and nursed out, too much for Ray to handle alone, and there was three hours gone. They had needed more wire and she'd offered to run to town, thinking she could sneak in an hour of uninterrupted research time at the library before heading back. But on the drive, her head kept nodding off to one side, which has been happening lately, every time she stops working the fields.

She picks up a pack of Trident, sets it back, reaches for Juicy Fruit.

"Don't overthink it, Dunbar." Tim appears at the end of the aisle, by the cold case. He couldn't look more relaxed, a sort of Teflon-human, his smile is slack, his skin tan. A twitchy, high-pitched thrum fills her blood. Her breath is stale. Her breasts are too small. She waves hello and drops the gum on the floor. Then kicks it, awkwardly, weirdly. She doesn't know how to be and she doesn't have time for another thing she doesn't understand.

"How was your weekend?" She crosses her arms over her ribs. She should've said something else, something that took the conversation far away from the fact that she'd noticed he'd been away, that she'd left him a message that he had never returned.

"Fine enough." He speaks really fast, smiling his big broad easy smile, going on and on about the sick single-track in Durango. "I got your message. Something about good news?"

"Fisk called," Jackie tells him. "The water samples came back in normal range, maybe on the high end of normal but still, nothing to worry about. He says it's probably biogenic methane, just extra peat in the river. You're nodding. Did you hear?"

"I'm glad you're feeling good about it." His smile is strange. "I've been thinking about you."

If this were true, if he really liked her, he would've called her back. He would've called when he first got to town. Jackie grimaces at this needy line of thought. For the twentieth time, Jackie reminds herself that she doesn't want anything complicated from Tim. That she is in this for friendship, and friends don't always return calls in a timely manner.

"Sounds like you had a great trip." She tries for breezy, talking over her shoulder as she grabs a Coke from the cold case. "I've got to get going but welcome back."

"Hey, what's the rush?" He grabs a Coke and then grabs hers and takes them to the counter to pay. "Can you take five minutes?"

To say no would be to admit something.

They walk to his truck, parked at the far end of the concrete pad behind the gas station, near the dumpster and the highway. They climb on the hood and watch the semis and cars, new and old, heading east toward Denver. Their knees touch.

"You as sick of this place as I am?" He looks better in his jeans than she wants him to. "Hometowns are kind of the worst."

Although she has had this same thought multiple times in the past months, it isn't something she would say to someone, a potential something or other, if she liked spending time with them.

"It's beautiful here."

"Come on. You must be gunning to get back to Denver. I know you."

"Do you get lonely being on the road all the time, Tim?"

"Sometimes." He nods, unaware of the dark alley he's about to walk into.

"If I were you, I'd have a special lady friend in every state. Seems normal."

"What are you talking about, Jackie?" Tim rubs his forehead, his smile drained of effort. "Obviously, you're special to me."

Jackie is aware that what she is doing is what her friends with better home lives might call "self-sabotage." These same friends have missed out on the comfort that comes from clearing a radius around yourself by setting a brush fire. She narrows her eyes at him. "You sound like a used car salesman." Her feet hit the cracked concrete. She wants to run all the way to her truck but she makes herself walk. He swears quietly, "what the fuck," his words bouncing off her back.

In the safety of her own truck, she drives quickly to Farm and Home for the wire she promised Ray. There, in the back, near the tools that smell like her dad, she is sure to be able to get a grasp on the things that matter.

But no. Later in the day, as she is lying on her back in the grass to change the oil in the 8N, a job that's needed doing for weeks, she is still thinking about Tim and wishing she wasn't, wishing for things to be different. It has been sixteen years to the day since her mom died. For the first time in her life, her dad's voice, her sense of him, has gone radio silent. Lying on her back in the grass, in the muck under the tractor, only a thin slip of sky is visible. She leans all her weight into the crescent wrench and pushes against the bolt. It won't give. She tries again, harder.

The bolt still won't give and she is just about to get the correct open-end wrench, the one she should have grabbed in the first place, when she gives it one last push and it gives, oil dumping into an old glass spaghetti sauce bottle. But she'd forgotten how big the plug is, and oil spills over the sides onto the ground. Worse, the oil isn't black. It's clear. Ray must've just changed it.

"Dammit." She gets out from under the tractor and throws her wrench at the ground. Inefficiency is akin to sin. She kicks the Ford tire with her sneaker. The day hasn't been worth its weight in air. She kicks the dirt. A cloud of dust spits in her face. Her body is sore, still not as strong as it was before the cow trampling. She yells at the flat gray disinterested sky.

To have Ray up here working for them, to care if Tim has called or not called, to rely on any man, this is not the person her dad raised, this is not who she wants to be. Her jean shorts streaked with oil, she marches across the wet field. There is only the sound of wind through the poplars and the screech of a far-off pump jack. She finds Ray oiling the head gate, brown water running quick through the ditch.

"Almost done here." He doesn't pause, set to the task.

"Ray." Out of breath, she puts her hands on her hips to open her diaphragm. "You have your own life, Camila, your kids. I can't let you keep working up here for free."

"I like working here." Ray stops working and straightens, pushes the brim of his hat up to look Jackie straight on.

"But we're not your family. You don't owe us anything."

"Well shit, Jackie. I ain't here because I owe you."

"We're taking advantage of you. My dad would hate it that you're still up here when I'm well enough."

He stares out over the mesa, up at the sky. Finally, he asks, "Sue want it this way too?" He cradles the sound of her name.

Jackie pauses. An eddy swirls in the ditch below the head gate, so much water running counter to the main. Susan would see a metaphor.

"Susan's not looking for another problem."

"All right then." Ray spits at the dirt. He pulls a small notebook from his T-shirt pocket and hands it to her. Inside are pages of lists. Who he's vaccinated and who's been snipped. When he tagged. He won't make eye contact. His brow a plank. "There's a stretch of fence up top that needs mending. And a few calves don't have their tags yet."

She is a complete shithead. She feels like crying. She would give anything to go back to the Kum and Go and erase the entire afternoon.

"You've been so good to us, Ray. I don't know how to thank you."

"Right." He squints, his face hard. He puts the dirty rag in her hand. "I guess I'll go then."

If she were a better person, she would call out to him, tell him to stop. Then she would call Tim and apologize. She is far too much like the stubborn rancher who raised her. If she had known her mom for longer, maybe she would know how to find a soft place inside herself and live there. Instead, she keeps her mouth shut and oils the metallic corkscrew on the head gate until it shines, until the scattered, awful feeling in her mind gets in line.

26

THE GREEN LIGHT ON the old Dell blinks at Susan. The cursor is impatient. It asks: What else? Why?

"Let me think a minute," she whispers to herself, to the screen, to the empty house.

Over the past few days, again and again, she has reread her notes. Again, she called Benny Fisk about the samples he took from the creek; again she was told he is away on vacation. If the data is right then she has it wrong, and she can't get anyone to parse the data. She paces the hall, the kitchen, the living room. Her ship has had too many hits. It's sinking. This isn't even a good metaphor, not like a real writer could think up.

She had stayed up all night rereading articles about activists in Alberta, in Alaska, in Peru, about people who do something. At breakfast, she'd told Jackie that with her deadline only a few days away, she needed the day to work. This is not technically a lie. People set their own deadlines all the time.

In the mirror above her desk, she sees the bags under her eyes. Her hair is limp from bottled-water showers in the sink. She smells like baby wipes. She tries lying. You look pretty, she tells herself. She smiles. She read about it in a magazine. Even if you don't believe it, it creates an air of confidence.

Ha.

She writes something. She deletes it. All she has are fragments.

Deep underground, beneath town and the interstate highway and the Colorado River, beneath the new Holiday Inn and the cattle guards and the hundreds of new roads, the ground gives way to hundreds of vertical faults. Ancient rock formations, like pancakes stacked sideways, extend into water and sand and a kind of gas called methane.

She was always good at finding a story. Whether she can pull off the writing, the reporting, the thinking is not a given. Her keyboard is sticky from the orange she ate two days ago; an ant crawls from the f to the r. Her notebook, receipts scrawled with ideas, crumbs from corn bread, and three coffee mugs clutter her desk. The AP Stylebook, outdated, sits in her lap. She tries again.

No one can comment on the connection between the fireballs over Amick's place—the kick, they have settled into calling it—and the fracking and the bubbles in the creek. Carson said the frack fluid escaped from Johnson's, but he couldn't say where it went. She needs an expert. She needs an editor. She needs a goddamn guidance counselor. Her outline has so many points it looks like a Christmas tree. She should be better than this. She's wasted everyone's time. *Do yourself a favor, kid. Don't write about anything you care about.* No one is going to publish this. That asshole in Wyoming could've told her that.

The toe of her rubber boot tap tap taps the concrete step. Hurry, Ray. The cup of coffee in her hands is getting cold. Black, just the way he likes it. She needs him to get here, to get back from the fields and give her that half-smile. The irrigation spigots spray long spinning arms of water. *Getgoinggetgoinggetgoinggetgoing*, they whisper.

Again she checks her watch. He always comes in for the day around twilight. It's almost dark.

When you start to feel anxious, whistle. That's what the meditation lady on one of those tapes says. The air leaves her teeth. The roadrunner drops down the canyon. *You'll get her figured. You've got time.* Ray's going to tell her that.

Tap tap tap.

But it is Jackie who comes down the dirt road.

"You seen Ray around?" Susan asks.

"He went home a while ago." Jackie scratches the skin below her right ear. It's always been her tell. She's never been a good liar.

"Why?"

"I told him to stop bothering with us." Jackie's words fall like gunshot around her. "We're fine. It's enough already."

Susan holds the coffee cup in front of her chest, the tiniest armor ever made.

"Why would you do that? We need him."

"We don't. I'm not sure I'm going back to medical school. So there's that."

It has been a thing she has longed to hear for so long but now that it's there, she feels the heaviness of Jackie's words settle across her shoulders. She stands up as if to let her sister's baggage slide off her back.

"Jackie. He likes to be here."

"He's married."

"I know that." She is walking to the truck. "I've always known that."

When Susan finds Ray slumped on a barstool at the Skyline, he doesn't smile. He doesn't stand. Jonny St. Clair is playing blues and the bar is thick with bodies, men in tight jeans, women in dresses that leave little to the imagination and a lot to be desired. Delores nods hello from behind the bar, where she's filling a tray of tequila shots.

His sad eyes say, come sit with me. Come make it better. You aren't the only one who needs saving in this disappointing world. She takes a seat beside him, her arm touching his arm.

He might say, this is perfect. He might say, only people like us who have truly suffered can appreciate a quiet moment shared. He might say, how did you know what I've always wanted?

Except Ray doesn't talk like that.

"Don't stop working our cows." She touches his empty glass.

"Your sis is right. You all don't need me in the way up there. I mean, shit. I'm not good for shit these days." His voice is a little loud, forced. "Delores, will you get me another? And something for my partner here?"

"Ray, honey, I'm cutting you off." Delores pats his hand, her wide red face a landing pad of sympathy. "I promised Camila not to serve you more than four."

"I thought you were on my side, D." He slurs, his words loose and heavy.

"Come on, Ray. Let's go." Susan stands up. She tells Delores she'll get him home. A hundred eyes—their neighbors, their ex-classmates, old friends of her dad's—watch them leave the bar together.

They take her truck to the liquor store, his idea, and buy a bottle of whiskey, her idea, and drive out to the shoulder near the new hotel beside the Colorado River, also his idea. It's a cloudy night, the moon tucked away, and the river running dark before them.

They trade the bottle back and forth for a while. There's an old Mexican blanket covering the cracked seats of the truck, her dad's old truck, and it's not so different than the old thing Ray used to drive in high school. Their arms are inches apart.

"Sky's threatening," Ray says at last. His voice has a quiet to match his whole self. He stares out the window toward Grass Mesa. She follows his chin toward the fishing holes he likes, that Dad used to like. The wind bothers the sagebrush and the river, and if she can notice every single thing just how Ray might see it, she'll know the right thing to say that will fill the space between them.

A car passes on the road. A train hollers from the other side of the valley.

"It'll be awful up there without you," she says finally.

"You're sweet. So pretty." The rough of his hand brushes her cheek. "Always have been."

Her eyes drag his face like a net, collecting every feature, old acne scars, stubble. His eyes are deep pools in a windswept face. The liquor makes her bones soft, her will strong. She leans over and gives him a wet kiss, and it feels like falling. He kisses the skin under her temples, at her collarbone. He smells like wood smoke and whiskey. He tastes like a different life.

She is straddling his lap, both of them half naked, when another car passes, this one seeming to slow, letting the fullness of its high beams settle on their bodies. Spinning red lights follow, the wail of a siren, chasing. Ray pulls back. Terror in his face.

"Ray, it's OK. They're gone."

"What are we doing."

It isn't a question. Cold air fills the gap between their bodies.

"I've always wanted this." She cups his face with her hands. "You're the best person I know."

"I'm not this guy." He lifts her off his lap. Sets her aside. "Shit. We can't do this. I fucked up."

Susan pulls her shirt from the floor and holds it to her chest. Ray thrashes around, yanking on clothes. Twice he says sorry. He puts his shirt on backward. She stays very still.

"I'll see you around." Ray squeezes her leg and opens the door.

Susan concentrates on the AM/FM dial, the one that hasn't worked for years. Mama was tuning a dial in their old Honda at the moment of impact. This moment, Ray stumbling away on the other side of the window toward town, her bra in a ball beside an ancient pack of cigarettes and an empty Coke bottle, this isn't as bad as life can get. She picks up the pack and lights one, letting the stale tobacco burn her lungs. Through the smoke, she watches Ray start to run. In no time, he recedes into the darkness. She is alone. She will not cry. She smokes the stale cigarettes. She pukes by the riverbank. She drives home to her cold bed.

27

The next morning, a Saturday, Ray tells Camila to sleep in. He watches his kids eat corn flakes in their pajamas. He shuts off the radio and opens the curtains onto a sunny day. Life can be simplicity, boiled down. If he works hard enough, it will be that way again.

In the basement he finds a box and he moves through the house, filling it with bottles and cans.

"What are you doing, Daddy?" Monica asks from the kitchen table.

"Cleaning up."

The girls watch cartoons on the little TV in the kitchen, and Ray takes the box outside into the too-bright morning. Dandelions pop all over the yard. The chain link is thick with wild peas. There hasn't been anything in the beds since he hitched out. Three green plastic chairs, left outside all winter and spring, lie facedown in the long grass.

In the back corner of the yard, away from the swing set, near a pile of broken chairs, old paint cans, and rotting leaves, he sets the box down. First bottle to go is the JD. He tips it sideways and it waters the ground. Then the full cans of beer, the box of wine, all of it.

He smells like rot gut, like a dead rat. He slept on the couch, and his neck has got too small for his head. The headache feels right, feels like penance.

In his pocket is Bill Dunbar's knife. He pulls it out and taps it against his wedding band. *I've always wanted this*. For a while when they had been kissing, he had felt like she was a part of him, like they were both part of the river, the moon, and the dirt, and it was OK what they were doing, even beautiful, to be so connected to another person. Her body had fit against his like they were parts of a motor. It had been a wonder.

All these years she'd never been more than a friend. But sometime in the past weeks, somewhere in the fields, the sweat and ease they shared, something had broken open. He felt alive around Sue, like life was still full of possibility. It wasn't anything he'd wanted or looked for. He throws a full bottle of Bud at the ground. It doesn't give him the satisfaction of breaking. It bounces.

He stares at the pink curtains inside the girls' bedroom window. Camila made those. They had hung Monica's baby picture in the hall and found a couch at the thrift store that looked to them like it belonged in a Denver apartment. The first night they moved in, they sat on the floor, eating enchiladas and drinking beer, Monica chattering between them. Camila had held his hand. She had said she was happy.

He can shut down this feeling for Sue. Work will help. It's the only thing that ever does.

A while later, after he's mowed and swept and worked up a sweat, the back door opens and Camila steps through it, wearing the purple bathrobe he bought her for Christmas. In her hands is a plate of pancakes, an orange slice on the side. His thinking and movements get wooden.

"I invited my parents for dinner," she says, offering the plate.

"Sounds great, honey. Whatever you want."

His back is too straight. His eyes give him away. He tries to smile.

"What're you doing back here?" She leans around his body and sees the stack of bottles in the grass. "Ray." She inhales sharply. "I've prayed to God a thousand times that this will happen."

"I thought I'd try to cut down. It's been too much."

"Oh, Ray." Tears fill her eyes. She looks at him like she looks at the kids when she watches them sleeping. She touches his cheek. He touched Susan's cheek in this same way. He looks away.

"It's not that big a deal, Mila."

"It's a good start." Her face serious. "The neighbors will be happy about the yard."

"I called your brother this morning, told him I'd be in Monday to wash dishes."

"What about Susan and Jackie?" She folds her arms across her chest.

"They've got things under control."

Camila pauses, searches his face. Grenades hit his heart.

"Do you want some help? I'll just go change."

"No. I got this." He swallows sand. "It's all right."

"Eat, before it gets cold." She kisses his cheek.

After that, there isn't much more to say. Camila goes inside to see about the girls. Ray stays outside for the rest of the morning. He throws Roundup on the weeds and tills up the old bed and sets things in order.

28

At dinnertime, Jackie tries again. "You need to eat something," she says to Susan's locked bedroom door. The hallway is cold and dark, full of dusty pictures of dead people. Her sister hasn't left her room since she got home late the night before. "We should've branded today. I fed out and moved handline." Jackie leans her forehead against the cheap wood paneling. Susan knows from a lifetime of practice that the worst thing to do to Jackie is ignore her. Jackie tries again. "Fine. I'll call Ray. I'll tell him to come back."

At that, the door opens. A hard edge of light bisects Susan's face.

"Don't call Ray," she whispers. She leans against the door in her sock feet, her hair in braids, wearing only underpants and a T-shirt.

"Are you all right?" Jackie asks, staring at the floor behind Susan, a mass graveyard of books, newspapers, dirty underwear, and coffee cups. White papers and old newspapers are scattered across the desk, the bed, the chair. "Where'd you go last night?"

"I went to the Skyline." Susan bites her lip. "St. Clair was playing."

"You went to see Ray?" Jackie keeps her tone casual, her face neutral.

"He was there." Susan shrugs.

"You got home awfully late."

Susan picks at the watch on her wrist, turning the dial backward and forward. Quiet fills the room, sucking all the air between them. Finally, she meets Jackie's eye. The look that passes between them spans a decade. That Jackie couldn't prevent this from happening is one more failure. She walks into the room and throws herself on the unmade bed.

"Of all the husbands in this town, you pick Camila Stark's?"

"Nothing happened. Not really."

"Is he going to tell her?"

"There's nothing to tell. Honestly." She spins away from the door and folds herself into her wooden desk chair.

There is a bald spot in the rug near the desk leg. Jackie stares at that for a long time. What makes the Starks' marriage work has never been obvious. They have no shared interests. They don't laugh together. It's never been a relationship Jackie wanted, but she has respected its durability. It has been something she could look to, to believe that relationships worked if you just worked hard enough.

"Stop judging me." Susan talks to her computer screen.

"I'm not. I just—" She is unsure what to say to her sister's back. There are sisters who share clothes, who share secrets. There are sisters who call each other every day. Jackie shivers. "Do you really think it can go anywhere?"

"Remind me how many relationships you've had that've lasted longer than six months?" Susan's anger sets her face at an angle, all her features bent.

"Things don't stay quiet in this town. People are going to judge the shit out of you."

"Well, that'll be a change." Susan shrugs and knocks on a stack of papers. "I need to work on this."

"We have to brand tomorrow. First thing."

"Fine."

Jackie gets up and gets out, slams the door, then stands there, listening. There is no typing. There is no shuffling of papers. Whatever Susan is doing in there, it's not productive.

Dad and Uncle Ellis understood one another in a way that never required much talk. The two of them worked the ranch together for thirty years, not one of them the boss. Uncle Ellis, the better cook, used to make dinner for them both, before heading out to the cabin he built by the creek. They shared the same shyness in groups of people, the same brown eyes, the same gap-toothed smile. They both loved fishing and chess, things they did together every single week. At Uncle Ellis's funeral, Dad said he felt like he lost his left hand. Then he drank too much and threw up all over the bathroom floor.

There is no one in the world Jackie knows better than Susan. She can read her moods better than weather coming over Mount Baldy. She knows, for example, that anger in Susan breathes with gills underwater, but that given a few hours, the anger floats away. She knows that Ray can act in many terrible, thoughtless ways before Susan will stop loving him. She knows that Susan will spend no time considering that Jackie will worry.

But knowing and understanding aren't the same. Why they aren't closer, why Susan makes her own life so hard, why she would fool around with the husband of a friend, even an ex-friend, all of this escapes Jackie.

She tries to back up from the situation, to see them both from a scientific distance, her sister inside the bedroom smelling of stale cigarettes, herself in the dark hall. From that place, it's easy to see the journal articles she's ignoring in the living room, the old clothes she has on, the empty place on her ring finger, the bruises and cuts from falling on the ranch. She doesn't linger for long at this bird's-eye view. To stay up there, to make connections between herself and Susan, to see the sadness left behind by their missing parents, puts her dangerously close to the pool of grief she wants to avoid.

Jackie jumps away from the bedroom door and walks to the kitchen telephone to call Tim. She tells herself that inviting someone, him, on an outing is a demonstration of her innate strength and independence, of how she and Susan are different at the cellular level.

Half the county are on their feet, yelling. Jackie joins in, letting the crowd drown her out. White smoke pours from the hood of Randy Pyle's tiger-striped Escalade. Ricky Colton slams his silver Cadillac into the back fender, backs up and hits it again; the smoke turns black and rises above the families in the stands. The evening light of early summer is soft. The smell of exhaust mingles with the freshly-cut grass of the ball field across the road. Joey Arnet's black station wagon, advertising his portable welding service, slams backward into Colton's driver's side, crushing the door, his wheels spinning in the fairground's mud. A boy and girl, teenagers, stand beside Jackie, their hands in each other's back pockets.

She had left Tim a message, inviting him to come to the demolition derby, telling him she'd be there. Her voice had been upbeat, almost perky, a voice that didn't belong to her but to the person she was trying to be. Again, Jackie scans the crowd, the beer tent, the trailer selling hot dogs, looking for Tim's familiar wide back.

A pack of kids jump off hay bales that someone brought in for extra seating. The women lean over smaller children, helping them eat their popcorn. All around her are men dressed like her dad, with their pearl button shirts and felt hats, who hold their mouths in the same sort of frozen way when they listen, their arms resting lazily against their wives' lower backs. The crowd takes a collective seat, waiting for the next round. The sound dies down for a minute. The talk, spoken over cups of burnt coffee and cans of beer, is not much different than it has always been: the expected price for calves, predictions for a dry summer, high school baseball. They look to Jackie as perfect as the summer night, an extension of the life she knew when she was very young, before her mom died, when life was predictable.

Jackie turns around, looking up behind her. Looking to see if maybe, possibly, Tim had gotten there early, found a seat but not found her. Instead, she sees Ray. Camila sits beside him, leaning in to say something. Lilly sits on his lap. Monica hops up and down, pointing to one of the smoking cars. They look contained and happy and immune to any outside threat. Susan was right. She, Jackie, doesn't know anything about relationships.

A beer will help. One beer and she will go.

After she has collected her drink, and the sun has set, leaving behind a blank sky, she stands near the kids by the hay bales watching Randy ride up over the back of the station wagon, pushing it back. The two cars reverse and square off, then Randy pummels forward and clips the station wagon. She isn't clear on why this is fun. Why this is looked forward to all year. She doesn't understand anything.

"Enjoying the best this place has to offer?" Tim's voice from behind makes her jump. She spins around and seeing him there in the fresh grass, something small compresses in her diaphragm. Dressed like a hipster, in sneakers and a T-shirt for some obscure band, he looks out of place.

"You came. I wasn't sure you were coming." She bites her thumbnail.

Behind her, two cars sideswipe each other; metal slides and screeches against metal. The crowd is on its feet, cheering.

"I'm here."

"I was a dick earlier. I'm sorry. I don't know why I was like that."

"I like you. You know that, right?" He has to shout to be heard over the crowd.

"What?"

"Don't make me say that again."

Something lightens inside of her and she laughs. "No one has a relationship talk at a smash-up derby."

"Fine, Jackie. Forget it."

"No, I didn't mean it that way." She grabs his arm and leans in. "Could we go someplace together? Someplace not here?"

"Where?" The floodlights shine in his eyes.

"It doesn't matter." She presses her arms to her sides to hold herself very tight, to wait to see what he says. "Anywhere."

"Hell yes. Let's go."

They head north in his truck. Some terrible band she doesn't know sings about logging camps and depression. The lights of town disappear in the rearview. Outside, the odd hills rise up and down, interrupted only by sagebrush, an endless, unchanging landscape.

"There's nothing subtle about this place, is there?" She talks to the closed window. "All my life I never saw that, never noticed how the land here goes to extremes."

"How you doing, Jack?"

"Fine." She pauses. "I don't know."

He shakes his head silently in the dark.

"You wouldn't like it if I laid it all on you." She waits for him to turn up the music, to make a joke, to turn the car around, for any sign that he feels suffocated, that he feels like she does around Susan.

"I'd like to know."

"It's boring."

"I doubt that. I know you want to be all tough and self-sufficient. I'm not a threat to that, you know."

It's quiet for a long time. She rolls down the window, letting the darkness come inside to swallow her. It had been hot for April and now is hot for May, the extreme of it another thing to worry over but in the safety of that darkness, the warm wind on her neck, she loosens her hold on herself.

"I haven't been sleeping." Her arms tremble against the windowsill. "I wake up at night convinced a cow's running over my ribs, its hooves crunching my bones. And in the dream there's coyotes trying to rip apart my intestines. It takes hours for the adrenaline to leave my bloodstream. I just have this nagging uncertainty about all of my choices." Her heart is beating fast. "I don't know if I care enough anymore about becoming a doctor." She takes a deep breath. "I'm mad at my dad." She stares at the rubber strip on the windowsill. "I haven't told anyone that."

A large steel hasp inside Jackie's gut unlocks. Tears fall down her cheeks.

"This is just a hard time," says Tim. He pauses and stares at the road ahead. "I think you're fearless."

"Not anymore."

"You don't give up. We have that in common."

"That doesn't make us fearless; that makes us stupid."

"Nah. We're pragmatic. We see the choices presented to us and pick the best one."

She squeezes his hand and listens to the tires as they turn onto a narrow dirt road that snakes through the canyon walls, dropping down, away from the highway. She doesn't know what to say so she keeps her mouth shut, a thing she learned from her dad.

At the Dominguez River they get out and hike across the boulders back into the red rock canyon, the moon casting a blue light across their bodies. After a half-mile on the well-worn path, they come to the lake, a dammed man-made thing that shines in the moonlight. Without saying anything, they both strip, tossing their clothes at their feet. Neither of them is the kind to wade. They climb to the cliff edge and jump, the cold a shock. Jackie comes up laughing at the first stars.

Afterward, they lie out naked on the big flat rocks, still warm from the day. They've done this before, a million years ago. It's a moment she would pick again and again.

"How's your mom?" she asks, facing him, their feet touching.

"You want to talk about my mom right now?"

"She was always nice to me."

"I don't know." He shrugs. "She still works at the Village Thrift. Her idea of a big night out is eating someone else's chili. My parents' life basically revolves around my cousin's kids and the Broncos."

"They're good people."

"It's just too easy. I want way more than they can possibly imagine for themselves."

She squints at Tim as if to see him better. The moonlight glints off the water caught in his stubble. She climbs from her rock onto his and lies down beside him. He puts his arm around her and her head fits nicely into his chest. They lie on their backs, breathing each other's air.

He speaks quietly, seriously. "You know, you're the only person who I ever told about that stuff with my dad. About my brother."

It comes back to her then, the secret she'd kept. Tim's dad had fathered a son while he was in Vietnam during the war, a son he sent money to, but he'd never told Tim or his mom. When Tim had found out accidentally that summer they were eighteen, he'd been a mess, making her promise not to tell anyone, sleeping in his car. He was the first boy she had ever seen cry.

"Thanks for taking me here," she says.

"I'm not such a bad guy."

"It's possible you're actually a good guy."

She kisses him, her tongue losing itself in a rhythm of its own making. When they break away, the need and want and dirty mess of her dark insides is on her face, exposed.

"Even with everything you know about me, you like me, right?" asks Tim, threading his hand through her hair. He takes a long look at her.

"Remind me. What is there to like about you?"

"My winning personality. My moves."

"I don't think I'm familiar with your moves," she says, rolling over to straddle him. "You better acquaint me."

His touch is light, like he is mapping her body with his hands. The river moves westward and the wind doesn't blow and the moon tracks higher through the night sky, the light of it seeping across their bodies.

29

THE CALVES' HOLLERING IS a symphony of dismay. On the other side of the fence, out in the lower field, the mother cows bellow back at their young, desperate to be reuinted. The calves, black and white and red, pile against each other in the narrow corral behind the squeeze chute. Their snouts tip skyward. The irrigation in the lower field whispers at them: *gogogogogogo*. Inside the corral, piss hits the dust.

Jackie is busy. She's in charge. She sets out the vaccinations, the needle, the bander on the small table she brought from the mudroom. She plugs the branding iron into the outlet in the base of a post. Susan sets one foot on the lowest rung of the corral and rests her elbows on the third.

The water in the stock pond has a reddish tint, and Susan can't remember if that's normal. Tina Krest's goats had another stillbirth, and that is definitely not normal. Driving home the other night, the gas wells along the highway flared into the sky and it looked like something out of Dante's Inferno.

"What do you want to do about bulls this year?" she asks Jackie, which isn't a direct question, at least not enough of one.

"I set it up with Pete to bring one over two weeks from Wednesday."

"But what does that mean about next year? What will we do next year?"

"I guess I figure one of us will stay on."

"I guess."

There was the time when she was sixteen and she had a note from Ray Stark in her back pocket, asking her to hang out after school, and when Camila had asked if she could come with, Susan had said sure. There was the time when Kelly had told her that if she ever cheated on him he wouldn't want to know, raising a question Susan hadn't dared ask. There was the time when Dad had told her not to tell Jackie that he didn't want to have the surgery, when she'd agreed not to try to convince him otherwise. Even the other night, she hadn't tried to stop Ray from leaving. She'd just sat there and watched him run.

Her entire life has been a study in conflict avoidance.

"You about ready?" Jackie asks.

The answer is no, but that isn't something Susan is going to say. Not today, when they have to brand one hundred calves in the heat of the afternoon without any help, because Jackie was too stubborn and Susan was too the way she is to call any of the neighbors.

Susan tightens her grip on the fencing. She needs to get calm, to be gentle; the calves, they smell fear. *Gogogogogogo*, the handline sprays from its cheerleader arm. She climbs up and over the fence and down into the corral among the calves, their legs and tails knocking against her knees.

Both Dunbars wear jeans and boots with thick soles, and tank tops with long-sleeved shirts over them, and ball caps they found in the shed. Jackie has on their dad's old leather gloves and they're too big, they're certain to slip, but Susan doesn't say a word. She pulls the bandana from around her neck up over her mouth.

"OK, little calves," Jackie calls from the calf table, her hand already at the ready. "Who wants to be brave?"

Susan gets behind a small chocolate one, number 27, her body close against its butt. It's best if they know it's inevitable. Life isn't about to hand anyone options. "That's right, honey. Go on."

The calf hangs back, unsure, uninterested in leaving the herd.

"Push a little harder, Susie."

Susan pushes her knees against the calf's butt; it doesn't budge. She places the flat sole of her boot against the hindquarters and pushes. "That's the way. That's it." The mama cows keep bawling. The calf's tail swishes frantically.

"Don't give them room to kick you," Jackie calls, from five feet down the long, never-ending squeeze chute. As if Susan hasn't done this before.

Susan grabs the prod and whacks the calf, and finally the animal snorts and trips forward into the head gate, where Jackie gets it shut around her neck. They spin the calf table sideways, the calf pressed between the metal bars, and she kicks and rattles the cage, which is what a calf table should really be called.

There is power in what a thing is called. Natural gas and clean coal sound like something benign, something safe. Call an activist a defender or a terrorist and the headline reads different. Free-range cattle evokes the life of a beat poet, the living easy.

Jackie lowers the orange-hot brand to the flank, and *sssss*. Pale yellow smoke billows into her face. The sharp smell of burnt hair. The calf kicks and squirms against the metal wall and bellows, and Jackie picks up the brand only to lower it down a second time. Green shit leaks from under the tail, against the blue metal. It's illegal to buy a cow that isn't branded. There's no choice here. This is the only way to be a rancher.

"Dammit." Jackie steps back, both hands on the branding iron. "I didn't get the second brand in the same spot."

Jackie nominated herself to be in charge, to be the one to know. And she doesn't know. She isn't Dad and she isn't Uncle Ellis and she isn't Ray and they, the Dunbar girls, do not have one small clue what the hell they're doing with these thousands of pounds of animals.

Jackie spits and steps back to the cow and again lowers the brand, and again the calf yowls and kicks. There is more shit and flies and dust. The brand makes black tar of the skin. The DCR for Divide Creek Ranch a brownish-red line into the hide.

It takes six hours for them to run through the rest of the calves. A few more times, Jackie doesn't push the iron in hard enough and has to redo. And once she lets a calf run through the squeeze chute, out into the corral, they have to herd it back and do the whole thing again. Susan gets kicked twice in the shin. It could've been worse, probably should've been.

Afterward, they let the calves join their mothers in the lower field to nurse and graze. Reunited, they all quiet down. There is only the sound of flies buzzing, of water trucks headed to or from gas wells down below on Dry Hollow, and the irrigation, *gogogogogogo*. Sitting in the dirt and shade, their backs against the posts, the Dunbars drink bottled water. A thin line of black ash edges Jackie's lips. Susan doesn't mention it. It's too hot for May. There's no wind, and even in the shade the heat is suffocating.

Jackie tells Susan that her landman friend has given them an extension on signing the gas contract. She tells her this as if she has won a blue ribbon. She is eager for praise.

Susan turns her head away from her sister and stares at the empty corral.

"Why do you trust that guy? He works for a multinational corporation. We are like ants on the bottom of their shoe for how much they care about us."

"Tim's a good guy. I've known him a long time."

Jackie blushes and smiles awkwardly, which isn't a thing she does easily or often.

"I don't believe it. You never fall for anyone."

"I wouldn't say I'm falling for him. I mean I like him but I'm thinking straight about it."

Implicit in Jackie's comment is a critique of Susan: that she has always leapt for love, every time, into the chute.

"You know, Jackson, you can't control everything." Her nostrils flare.

"I know."

"Dad would be proud of you; I'm proud of you."

"I haven't done anything, Susie."

"You realize how stupid your plan was, right?"

"What?"

"No one goes to medical school to save the family ranch. It was totally inappropriate of Dad to encourage that idea."

"It was?" Jackie's voice is scarcely audible. "Why didn't you ever say something to Dad?"

"I want to sell the ranch," says Susan quietly, staring at the cows suckling at their mother's tits.

"You're joking."

"They're going to deliver bottled water for what, a few weeks? It won't be forever. They put diesel fuel down those wells to frack. That shit causes cancer, Jackie. There's probably all sorts of chemicals in our water, things that hurt the brain and nervous system."

"Come off it, Susan. You know the levels are normal in our creek."

"I've been reading. I have a stack of things for you to read. The gas company should buy us out, and we should leave."

"How can you even consider that? Dad would disown us."

"Dad is gone. And we can't afford this place. And we can't do this by ourselves." Susan folds her bandana in half; she folds it into thirds. She pushes each of her fingertips into the dirt until the skin below the nail turns white. "I don't want to. You won't admit it, but neither do you."

"You want to give away the only thing Dad gave us." Jackie keeps herself contained, unemotional. "Because it's hard?" She has always dressed up fear to look like righteousness.

Susan sits very still. She bites the tip of her tongue between her teeth. Jackie has never been told off. She has never taken a real risk, with men or otherwise. Sure, she has worked hard, but only within a structure of benchmarks—get good grades, get into medical school, pass a certain test, feed the cows, irrigate—none of it an idea she had to create.

Susan's fist hits the bottle of water and it skitters away. She sits up, and then she stands up.

"Hard? You want to talk about hard?" Susan's words bounce off the posts. "Ask me one goddamn time how all of this is for me. Ask me one goddamn question, Jackie."

"Susie, you matter more to me than anyone. If you don't get better, my life doesn't get better either."

Tears slide off Susan's cheeks. Her heart pounds. She can't swallow. "You don't really care about this place. You just need to be Dad's favorite."

"This land is all we have. I've given up everything to be here."

"But I haven't?"

"You didn't have anything to give up. You came here to get away from your life."

"How dare you. You have no idea about my life. You never ask."

Jackie blinks. Her look of superiority falls to dirt. She leans her head back to look at the sky, her shoulders slumped. Susan presses a smile between her lips, considering the headline: *Spineless Sister Takes a Stand.*

"Where would you go?" Jackie asks. "If we sold the ranch, where would you want to go?"

It's so obvious a thing to ask, but it takes Susan by surprise. She stares blankly at Jackie.

There is Pinedale, where Heidi Hooten is probably naked in Susan's old bed. There is Grand Junction, where she had her first and only studio apartment. A place with a red kitchen, her dad's old record player, a futon on the floor. It had been a half-mile from the newspaper, which was where she really lived. It had been perfect. But Grand Junction is full of ghosts, old newsroom pals who she'd be embarrassed to see. There are cities she's wanted to visit,

Oahu, Juneau, New York, but it's impossible to imagine them as anything more than a two-page magazine spread.

A forced, harsh laugh leaves her chest. "That's a good question."

Jackie stands up and offers her bottle of water to Susan. It's not a hug, it's not a kindred-spirit, *Anne Of Green Gables* moment, but Susan does take the water, and Jackie does sit down beside her, their sleeves almost touching. The pounding of Susan's heart slows. The sun falls out of the sky and rolls across her body. They stay like that for a long time, not talking and it reminds her just a little of the way she often came upon her Dad and Uncle Ellis. On the other side of the corral, the mothers and their calves stay close together now, light breaking around the pairs.

30

JACKIE IS ALREADY HALFWAY toward town, toward Tim and a beer, before she realizes that she still smells of soot and burnt hair. Her dad would say she smells like hard work; Susan would probably say she smells like trying too hard. She turns the radio up. She turns the radio off. Her heart is pounding. Susan would sell the ranch. What heresy.

When Jackie was thirteen years old, she found a faded picture in the attic, a woman with a tiny waist, smoking a cigarette, a big sombrero on her head. Fay Henry, her dad had explained, her great-grandmother, the first white child born on this land. A midwife, and good with numbers, and what Dad described as *fun, not in the usual way*. But why, Jackie had wanted to know, why did the imprint on the picture say California?

Fay left the ranch one fall, after, Dad made sure to point out, the cows had gone to market. She drove to California with her three young daughters, to visit her sister. He didn't say why Fay went all that way without her husband. Jackie knew even as a teenager, especially as a teenager, that the ranch could not be left alone. After two months, Fay came back. With her were a lace cape and a Chinese marble figurine, not the sorts of things one needs to work with cows. Fay never left again, not even for Wyoming. Jackie, even then, had understood the moral of the story. She had understood the bottom line: Dunbars always choose the land.

That Susan doesn't know this, or that she knows this and doesn't care, makes her a stranger, someone with no shared DNA. Jackie rolls down the window and screams at the wind and empty road. By the time she rolls into the Skyline parking lot, she is hollowed out.

Of all the people who might possibly have something helpful to say in this moment, Shorty Lee isn't one of them. But it is Shorty, wearing a pink leather jacket so new it squeaks when she walks, who makes a beeline across the cracked concrete to Jackie.

The first Christmas Jackie came home from college, Shorty, a middle-aged widow with a push-up bra and purple lipstick, had draped herself all over their dad as if she were tinsel. But by summer, Shorty was living with Mike Miller, the banker, the owner of a hot tub. Her dad hadn't wanted to talk about it.

"I've been wanting to talk to you, honey," says Shorty, standing far too close. Her chest is wrinkled, too tan.

Jackie stares at Shorty's cleavage, breasts her dad must have touched, and freezes.

"We have a phone." Jackie backs up until she is wedged against the side mirror of her truck.

Shorty pauses, smiles.

"I hear your sister is writing some big story." Shorty fingers a diamond cuff on her left earlobe. "I hear she been talking to lots of guys."

Jackie spots the new blue Cadillac with the SHORTE plates a few feet away. Natural gas royalties seem to have thrown up all over her dad's ex-girlfriend.

"You know, your dad always had both feet on the ground." Shorty touches her tongue to her purple-stained upper lip. "He was sensible, if nothing else. Commonsensical. You girls ought to keep that in mind."

The air is corn syrup. Sweat drips down the backs of Jackie's legs.

"We're doing great."

Shorty puts her pale, clean hand on Jackie's arm. She leans in. She smells like bubblegum and Febreze, like something manufactured to pass as sweet. "Your dad ever tell you he was hoping to retire someday? Wanted to get an RV and drive to Florida. Can't you just imagine him on a surfboard?"

Jackie can't remember once seeing her dad in a swimsuit.

"Aren't you hot with that jacket on?"

"You know, if you don't sign, all that gas will just flow to your neighbors. You'll just be lining their pockets with your money."

The back of Jackie's throat is dust.

"I've got to go, Shorty. I'm meeting someone."

"Would that be Tim Layton by chance? Now that boy is someone with his head on straight." Shorty reaches over and tucks Jackie's hair behind her ear. "You sure look like your dad." She pats her arm. "See you inside."

Jackie blinks dumbly. She is fairly certain her dad wouldn't follow that woman into a dark place on a sunny day, but then, what the hell does she know. Slowly, she walks into the bar; the air conditioning disconnects the room from all outside realities. A few old guys sit at the bar, watching baseball on television. The place has an appeal.

Tim is in the back, in a booth, staring at an empty pint glass. Repeatedly, he picks up a crumpled cocktail napkin and sets it down.

"You look about as crap as I feel." She sets two beers on the table and sits down across from him. He looks up, surprised, and in a flash, his face is bright, smiling, his pathological good cheer returned.

"Hey you." He reaches across the table and grabs her hand. "I'm glad you called."

Across the room Shorty is tucked into some new man, giggling into the booth's imitation leather. Shorty would've giggled like that with Dad. They might've gone and picked out bathing suits together. Jackie pulls her hand away and downs half her beer. At some point on the drive into town she had imagined telling Tim what Susan had said, but she glances at Shorty and realizes that's a bad idea.

"Have I asked you any questions?" Jackie looks at Tim. "Do you feel like I ask how you are?"

"You want to know about my life?" Tim looks at her uncertainly. Then he does a startling thing and answers her. "Well, I didn't go to church this morning because I don't see the point, but I went to my folks' for lunch, to be with the family. And anyways, I told my dad I couldn't go hunting next weekend, that I had to work, and really, why go hunting anymore? There's a grocery store across the street. But he got really upset. He thinks I don't spend enough time with them. And then he told me that it's my fault the mill went under."

"That's not fair." She looks across at Tim, at the beer foam on his upper lip. "I'm so sorry. After lying to you for your entire childhood, you'd think he'd feel grateful that you still talk to him."

"Well, I don't know that he lied. He didn't tell us something, that's different."

"Omission of truth is a lie."

"You think so?" He shifts uncomfortably in his seat.

"You're not like your dad." She says.

"Thanks." Tim chews on the side of his lip. He stares at his empty beer.

"Families are brutal," Jackie says. "I'm sure my sister would tell you the same thing."

"She loves you."

"You barely know her. We just had a terrible fight."

"My job depends on my ability to read people quickly and that gal of yours is fierce and loyal. Trust me. She's in your corner."

Jackie stares across the table at Tim for a long minute, startled. Susan had in fact acted with spirit. She had in fact been fierce. Jackie touches the thought gently as if with a stick, afraid and hopeful both.

"Did I say the wrong thing?" he asks, his eye twitching.

She shakes her head at him, smiling.

"I guess with families you have to grade on a curve." She walks around the table, careful not to look over at Shorty and sits down beside Tim. He winds his fingers into hers and kisses her. A light buzz settles on her skin and it could be the beer but Jackie hopes it's something else. She holds onto him, glad for him, trusting in it. Unlike whatever it is that Shorty is doing on the other side of the bar, this is something real.

Late that night, the two sisters sit at the kitchen table, eating quesadillas. The clock ticks. Chicken snores under the table. A fan pushes hot air around the room.

Susan sucks on a piece of ice, reading that same endless novel. Jackie considers what it would be like to be alone at the table, if there had never been a Susan.

When they were young, after their mom died, Susan used to soak Jackie's feet in Epsom salts in an old turkey pan. She used to read Jackie stories about brave pioneers. When Jackie got her period, it was Susan, not Dad, who explained how to use a tampon. It was Susan who had made it OK for Jackie to leave. Where their dad was concerned, in life and in dying, it was Susan who had done most of the heavy lifting.

"How about I wash your hair in the sink?" Jackie says. "I'll use the bottled water."

Susan doesn't bother looking up from her book. "There's no one I'm looking to impress." She glances down at her faded green swimsuit, at the rip in its side. "Clearly."

"I'll massage your head. You know I'm good at that."

Susan raises an eyebrow. "You gotta stop trying to fix me."

"I just want to do something nice. I thought it would be nice if we could be nice to each other."

"Why?"

The kitchen light above the sink is behind Susan, and with her back lit like that, it's hard to make out the expression on her sister's face.

"I have no idea what Dad would want us to do about the ranch. I don't know anything. Really. I'm sorry about earlier."

She gets up and busies herself, scrapes the dishes into the garbage, fills a plastic tub with bottled water and dish soap. Fills another tub for rinsing. Susan comes and stands on the other side of the sink with a dry towel. They wash and pass and dry, a familiar rhythm and pace to a chore they have done together forever.

"Did Dad ever tell you he wanted to move to Florida?" Jackie asks.

"What, like to drink piña coladas on the beach?"

"Shorty seems to think Dad wanted to move."

"Shorty's got her angle."

"Shorty's a bitch."

Susan laughs. "Dad did surprise me there. He must've been lonely."

"It freaks me out. It makes me feel like I didn't really know him at all."

"You did. But who the hell knows what anyone else really thinks?"

"I'm not as controlling as you think I am." Jackie's voice was not meant to tremble. She scrubs the counter with a clean sponge.

"Oh, girl. You're the strongest person I know." Susan stands behind her sister and rests her head against Jackie's back.

Jackie's eyes soften. Feeling unspools inside her body. Her shoulders slump.

"How about I wash your hair?" Susan sets her hand on Jackie's shoulder. Her hands are cool. "You don't look so fancy yourself."

"You'd want to do that for me? After everything?" Jackie turns around to look at Susan. The familiar shape of her body stands in relief against the fresh darkness pooling outside the window.

"I've been trying to tell you for months," says Susan. "I'd do so much more."

31

"HONEY, PASS JOYCE THE petition," says Camila, speaking to Ray over her shoulder, a crowd growing around her. "It's there on the chair."

He does as he's told. They've come to the Elks Lodge early so that Camila can collect signatures for her moratorium on gas drilling. He stands at her side while she does all the talking. Out the wide window, the sky is streaked orange and pink. A sunset that looks like a painting of a sunset.

When Ray had said he'd like to go with her to the community meeting, Camila had laughed and said, "Since when do you care?"

For nine days, Ray has worked hard to not think about Susan Dunbar. He's scrubbed forty-seven pots at his brother-in-law's restaurant. He's made three spaghetti dinners and nine batches of scrambled eggs with cheese. Twice he's called Sheriff to try and schedule a meeting about getting probation lifted. He hasn't had one drink, except for a few beers. He's tuned his guitar and tuned it again and tried to remember how to play the songs he used to know, the ones Camila liked and asked for. He's taken the kids fishing up on the mesa and taken them to the park and taken them to see their grandparents. The tools in the garage are all put away.

The oil is now clean in both of his vehicles, his brother-in-law's Ford, and his mother-in-law's Civic. He hopes that enough good deeds will make up for the bad.

It isn't clear that Camila has noticed. She is always running off to another meeting or to work, leaving him with a list of things to do and a quick kiss on the cheek. She rolls her eyes at things he says. She rolls over in bed and shuts off the light without touching him. At night, he dreams of a woman with dirty red hair.

A bunch of men with collared shirts and gas company logos printed on their hats lean against the wall. Camila says they've bussed in roughnecks from all over the western slope. But the hall is filling up with all sorts of people he didn't figure to be interested in gas drilling. There's guys he knows from playing ball, from swapping bulls for his gramps, from the bar, from law enforcement, from his kids' school. Up in front on stage are the bureaucrats and corporate drones, shifting paper around the table and looking at their watches. And far in the back, standing under a stuffed pronghorn, are the Dunbars, their heads yoked.

While Joyce Marbel signs the petition, he leans in to his wife. "I'm going for coffee."

She doesn't look up, keeps on about eighty-acre spacing and the need for a scientific baseline.

Ray passes the table with the donuts and the Styrofoam cups. As he closes the space between himself and the Dunbars, he tries to set a smile on his face that is casual. There's a flapping in his chest. His thinking is squirrelly. Jackie leans down to her sister and whispers in her ear. Neither of them smiles his way.

"This whole thing is icing on a shit cake, ain't it?" He looks at Susan, his legs loose. She stares at him with doe eyes. She doesn't blink. "How's things up top? Is that one cow still lame in the back leg?"

"She's doing fine," says Jackie. She slips her arm through her sister's arm. "We're all fine, Ray."

"Well, good. I've wondered about that. About how you all are."

There is a long pause where no one says a thing. Ray's insides race. Sue's hair is prettier than in his dreams. Cleaner. All combed back and tended to.

"How's your story coming along?" He nods at Sue. She smells like hard soap and sage. "I bet you got some good questions to ask, don't you?" His hand, acting without his say-so, reaches out and touches her arm.

Sue jumps away, stumbles into her sister. "You can't do that."

"I'm sorry, Sue."

Sue's eyes go soft and then they go scared, looking at something behind him.

"What are you sorry about, honey?" Camila says behind him. He feels his wife's body against his side, watches her look at the Dunbars, watches Susan duck her glance to look to him, watches Jackie hold her breath, all of it in slow motion. All three of them look at him.

"Just saying I wish we weren't here. I wish the gas men didn't ever come."

Camila smiles and pats his hand. "Don't let him fool you. He doesn't really care about any of this. He just didn't want to be the only husband of all the ladies on the committee to not show."

Ray looks blankly at the stuffed pronghorn on the wall.

"How's your article coming, Susan?" Camila looks Susan over with eagle eyes. "You must be real busy with that."

"I am. In fact, I see someone I have to talk to." She nods and starts to move away. "Nice to see you."

"You know, we don't have to be friends." Camila looks Susan up and down. Her laughter is a string of jagged tin cans. Ray puts his hand on her arm to move her away, but when has she ever paid him any mind. "But stay away from my husband."

Susan's face turns red. Jackie stiffens.

Ray steers his wife away.

"I thought you were getting coffee." Camila hisses in his ear. "Where's your coffee?"

Ray wishes his body were made differently, in a shape where it would be easy to punch his own face.

They sit down without speaking. Camila crosses her arms and sighs. Ray stares at his hands; they rest on his thighs. They're weak, limp. In another week, the calluses on his palms will be gone, all sign of his time at Dunbars' will disappear.

The men on stage start the meeting. The gas men, the government men, they talk plans and sunshine. Ray listens without listening. He has heard such talk before. He tucks his hands under his legs.

There had been a day when he was seventeen, when Gramps had seen him and Susan talking before school. *You seem yourself with that girl*, he'd said later. Ray had shook his head no, Camila already pregnant, the rest of his life already in motion.

For too long he has chosen to wait life out. He has believed that nothing is his to change, none of it his to hold. Iraq has been to blame. Camila has been to blame. Being a soldier, being a deputy have been costumes to hide his cowardice. Only up at Dunbars', only working the land, working with Sue, has he felt like he held the reins to his life.

He looks over his shoulder, through the crowd to where she, brave and serious, writes something in a notebook. He waits for her to look up. He has to make her see.

32

DANNY JAY, THE GAS company's PR flack, stands up and asks people to take their seats. His manicured goatee sits on his face like a neon sign: *I am uptight. It doesn't matter that I never got a date in high school. Look at my suede boots: I make more money in PR than an entire news desk.* He says they plan to reintroduce native plants after they're done drilling. He holds up bags of seeds. He shows slides of elk and deer grazing near a pump jack.

When the county commissioners speak, they use the term *win-win*. They're so obviously in bed with the gas people, they could share a pillow. Susan's neighbors ask simple questions and are easily satisfied by the argument the gas men have crafted and that the politicians parrot: that this is about jobs and energy versus the environment, that it's not possible to have all three. They've managed to make the truth, that natural gas development has the potential to pollute, controversial.

If she weren't a reporter, she would say that this controversy is a fiction. That anything is possible; it's a matter of scale and priorities. But journalists don't get involved. They have no comment.

In her pocket is a piece of paper with three good questions concerning geology, hydrology, and transmission. They are not, however, the questions she most needs answered.

Ray's head is bent toward his wife and he nods at whatever she is saying to him. Camila, with her perfect skin, with her tenacity. Susan will always come in second. She will never be the one that matters. This is as it should be. Camila would never consider stealing a husband, especially one with two kids.

Halfway through the meeting, when Camila scoots her chair backward as if she is about to stand, to ask the questions written on her yellow notepad, Susan throws her hand in the air. Danny Jay nods for her to go ahead, to be first for once, and she can only look at Jackie, stunned, and feel for the thin paper in her pocket.

"You got this," Jackie whispers. She is the most reluctant of wingmen.

Susan takes a deep breath.

"A few weeks after that well on Amick's place kicked, Divide Creek started bubbling." Best to play dumb. Let them underestimate you. "Can you explain that to me?"

"Well," Danny Jay leans forward in his chair. "You heard of Dimethoate? Write it down."

Always stall by asking a question you already know the answer to.

"Can you spell that?"

"I don't know how it's spelled, Susan; you can look it up. It's a pesticide."

"What's a pesticide got to do with gas development?" Sweat pools in her armpits.

"Exactly. From what I understand, pesticides from the fields beside yours ran back into the creek due to some faulty hydro equipment. That's where you got those bubbles."

Danny Jay doesn't have to tell her: a story about pesticides in the water isn't a story. People lean over the backs of their chairs to stare at her. At last they have found their skepticism and concern.

She hasn't seen many of them since her dad's funeral, since graduation, since she was someone they thought they knew.

"So you're saying there's no connection between the blowout at Amick's place and the bubbles in our creek?" She shifts in her ballet flats. She tugs at her hair. She can't think of her next question. She needs to ask the right question.

"Ms. Dunbar, you see too many movies." Danny Jay shows the crowd of sheep his very white teeth. "Come on, now. This is a multi-billion-dollar business; we only get access if the state gives us a permit." He slaps his pinky ring against the podium. "This company will not risk its reputation with shoddy work. We're running a top-of-the-line operation here, folks."

Not everyone in the crowd smiles and nods at Danny Jay. Some people watch with curious eyes, with affection, as if they want to know what she, Susan Dunbar, one of them, will say next. If she looks at Ray and Camila she will sit down, so she doesn't. She does her very best to look like someone who is good at something. *Fake it 'til you make it.*

"Then how do you explain why we could light the water on fire? Pesticides don't account for that. And how do you explain why your company is willing to deliver us drinking water, if you have no culpability?"

There is a murmur in the crowd. Jackie stands very close to Susan, puts her arm on her back.

"There are more than thirty-two hundred wells in this county, most drilled in the last five years. I understand that there are plans to drill ten thousand more." Susan's voice cracks. "Industry documents say as much as 30 percent of frack fluid remains underground after a well has been fracked. Can you tell me where you think all of those chemicals go? Isn't it possible, based on recharge, that it might be frack fluid in our creek?"

A few of the guys standing against the wall start booing. "Sit your sweet ass down, Dunbar," someone yells from the back. Someone else yells, "That's enough with the language." Camila looks at Susan like she's doing something funny, not in a ha-ha way, but a weird way. Susan tucks her hands under her armpits. Jackie raises her hand, she tries to say something, but Danny Jay won't look at them. He opens his PowerPoint to answer not one of her questions, but to talk about their commitment to environmental stewardship.

All Susan's thoughts run off. There goes one, and another, flung beyond her grasp. She wipes the sweat off her face with a napkin, but it pills and she picks at the balled-up wads of paper on her cheeks.

Ray stands up, his chair scraping behind him. He is leaving. He doesn't care and he is leaving. There's no point to Susan's article. There never was a point, an important point anyways.

"I don't hear you answering her, Danny." Ray, his voice soft, interrupts Danny as he's talking about elk migration. Ray's jaw clenches. His face looks boiled.

Susan forgets to breathe. She flattens her back against the wall.

"Give me a minute, Stark." Danny Jay holds up his hands like Ray is trying to shoot. "I'm getting to that."

"Nope. Answer her now." Ray pounds his fist on the back of the empty metal chair in front of him. "The truth would be nice."

No one boos at Ray. No one tells him to shut up. A deputy sheriff is not the same as an unmarried, fake reporter. The crowd looks at Danny Jay and Danny Jay scratches his shoulder, his elbow. Ray doesn't sit down. The only sound in the room is Susan's heartbeat.

Danny Jay sighs. "Listen, folks. We're providing water to the Dunbars because we want to be good neighbors, and when we hear about people in trouble, we do what we can."

"That's a line," Ray says quietly. He looks at his hands and pauses, then lifts his head. "Far as I can make out, you got yourself a golden goose, and it just laid a bunch of goose shit."

"Mr. Stark, please sit down." County Commissioner Lomax adjusts his bolo tie. "You're disrupting things, son."

Ray looks around the room, his back straightening. "The Dunbars have had it rough. You all know that. They deserve an answer."

Ray has never been so beautiful. Susan wants to touch the wrinkled skin at the corner of his eye, his hip, his red ear that looks so very hot, the cuff of his maroon pocket T-shirt. Jackie squeezes Susan's arm. There's a murmur in the crowd—not the whole group, but maybe half, nod.

"I'd remind you that you're a public employee." Lomax frowns. "You're out of turn."

Ray pauses. Camila tugs at the hem of his shirt. He nods and takes his seat. Camila leans over and kisses him on the mouth. And Ray rests his arm on the back of his wife's chair, and they hold hands for the rest of the meeting, and he never once turns around. When Camila stands up and presents her moratorium idea, she doesn't sweat. She is eloquent, her accent unnoticeable.

"Let's get out of here," Jackie whispers in Susan's ear. "You don't need to watch this."

"No. It's good for me." She pinches the inside of her left arm until she can't feel anything.

Number of people in the room: 104. Average length of public comment: six minutes. How many times Danny Jay touches his goatee: nineteen. The ways that Ray shows how much he loves his wife: too many to count. The point of trying to make anything different than how it has always been: zero.

33

Again, Jackie touches the unsigned lease agreement stuffed into her back jeans pocket. It's too long and it juts under her shirt, scratching her bare skin.

When Susan said they were going to the Elks Lodge, she'd handed her a phone message from Tim—he needed to speak with Jackie, he'd be at the Skyline after seven—and rolled her eyes. As if to say, we're in this together. Jackie hadn't said anything about the contract, due in four days.

If it weren't for the contract, it would've been Jackie, not Ray, who had yelled at the jerks who yelled at Susan. If it weren't for the contract, Jackie might have asked her own questions. She reminds herself what she has told herself before: signing the contract is pragmatic. Signing the contract offers them a seat at the table, a bargaining chip. Such phrases, she knows, are what her sister would call clichés. Such phrases, she sees now, expose a lack of intellectual curiosity.

The room is stuffy and hot. An industry geologist talks about projections without citing any data. He doesn't offer a single scientific explanation. Susan asked a series of good questions and they, those men up there, Tim's colleagues, they shut her down.

She scans the crowded room, looking for one person that she can relate to. The people who used to be her age, the ones she knew in high school listen quietly, kids on their laps, to what the men on stage have to say. Beside them are their parents and grandparents, whose faces are weather-beaten, tight at the eyes. Whiskey and dust and sun have pickled the worst in all of them. The stuffed pronghorn and elk and lynx and coyote and hawk mounted on the wall stare at Jackie with their glass eyes. You're not better than any of them, the eyes say. You're just the same.

She had brought the contract to the meeting hopeful that after hearing what the gas people had to say, the drive home would be the right moment to remind Susan that leasing their minerals would allow Susan to have whatever life she might like. It would, Jackie had thought, be the right moment to present the gas lease as an alternative to selling the ranch. The faulty thinking of such an argument is now obvious. The wood-paneled walls and pea-green floor fold up around her.

Her sister, the only person she has left, stands to her side, smelling like onions, which is to say she smells like fear. And Jackie has done nothing, she has said nothing. Throughout all the weeks she has stolen away from her sister, from the ranch, to review research on purkinje cells, she has not spent one minute researching the possible public health or environmental impacts of oil and gas development.

She pulls the contract from her pocket and hands it to Susan. "Here. Take this," she whispers, the men in the front still droning on. "I don't want this anymore. I feel gross that I ever did."

Susie doesn't smile. She doesn't say anything.

"I'm sorry," Jackie says. "I thought it would help."

Susan nods and takes the contract. She folds it behind her notebook. People in the back row turn and stare at the two of them whispering against the wall.

"Your landman know about this yet?" Susan keeps her eyes on the presenter; she talks out of the side of her mouth.

"I'll tell him tonight."

"He's waiting for you, isn't he? Just leave me the truck."

Jackie nods to herself and exhales. "I don't want to leave you here alone."

"If you mean it about the contract, you should tell Tim. Go on, get out of here." Jackie isn't sure what is more unsettling, to see Susan act so much like her old self, or the fact that she is relieved to be told what to do. She kisses her sister on the cheek and walks through the crowd until she finds the exit sign and leaves.

She finds Tim at the back of the Skyline, his knee bouncing up and down under the table. In his right hand is a white business-sized envelope and he's tapping its edge against his beer.

"Why weren't you at the meeting," asks Jackie, sitting down across the table.

"I couldn't go. I couldn't do it, not today."

"I want to tell you something and I don't want you to interrupt me. I've been thinking about it on the walk over here from the Elks'."

"You've got my attention." He continues to bounce his knees under the table like crazy, shaking the glass and the last inch of beer inside of it.

"First of all, I want to thank you for everything. The water deliveries and the contract itself have been a very big deal for me and I appreciate it. More than you could know. But the thing is I only have one blood relative left who means anything to me and the people in that meeting, the people you work with, they were dicks to her."

Tim nods, his entire body agitated.

"I don't think my dad would sign something his brother was against. I just can't sign it."

"I can see that." He shrugs and smiles his thin strange smile.

"You're not disappointed? Don't you get a bonus or something if the whole section signs on with them?"

"Oh man. It's so much more complicated than you know."

"Why didn't you go to the meeting?"

Tim puts his palms flat against the table and stares at his beer. "I can't stop thinking about what you said the other night. About omission of truth being kin to a lie." He looks up at her. "I can't stomach the idea that I'm like my dad. I can't be like him. I'm not him."

"What are you saying?"

"The DNR gave you an average of the levels of contaminate in the creek. They never showed you the individual data points from each water sample." He pulls a sheet of paper from the envelope. "Look at this."

A graph describes twelve water samples; in two of them the levels of benzene and hydrogen sulfide reach far above the safe drinking water standard, which is marked by a broken red line. In the corner is their address and the longitude and latitude of the creek.

Tim speaks quickly. "Those levels truly are outliers. Fisk could've just collected them incorrectly. That happens."

Jackie stares at the graph and starts to feel anxious.

"They should've retested to be sure. How could you not tell me?"

"There's a nondisclosure clause in my contract. I can lose my job for showing you this."

"I feel so stupid. All this time I thought Susan was crazy, I told her she was crazy."

"My parents rely on my paychecks, Jack. You of all people can understand that."

"If something is a fact, you can't pretend it out of existence. My god, you really are like your dad."

"That's low. Shit, that's low. My dad never told us, he never fessed up. I had to figure it out by accident. I'm coming to you with this. It's totally different."

"You're a real hero."

"Come on, Jack, don't be like that. You have a ton of choices. You're smart. You can be a doctor if you just get it together and leave this town. Stop acting like you're a victim to circumstance."

"I liked you. Oh my god. I let myself like you."

"What would you have done if you were me? Really think about it. I'm not sure you would've made a different choice."

34

RAY STANDS AT THE window of his kids' bedroom and stares past his dirt yard, past the garbage clogging the street's storm drain, past the short spindly trees, up at the stars. *You only see them when it's dark outside*. Marcus Wilson had told him that, the day before he died. He didn't say what happens to the stars if a person moves past the known world.

The girls in their twin beds, their breath soft, their bodies surrendered to sleep, are so perfect they break his heart. He tucks Lilly's bare leg back under the covers. He kisses Monica's forehead. He prays silently that they will be all right. Before closing the door behind him, he takes one last look at their dark eyelashes, their serious, stubborn faces.

For a while, he stands in the dark hallway, listening to Camila tell her mom about the meeting. Her voice strains against the seams of the house, filling the room with a shotgun of Spanish. He doesn't need to understand the words to know the real reason for her anger.

When the front door shuts behind his mother-in-law, he leaves the safety of the hall, pulled toward the light of the kitchen as if by draft. Pieces of Camila's hair fall into her eyes as she leans into the dishwasher. Her hair has been cut in the same style—bangs, shoulder-length—since she was fifteen. He focuses on this. He tries very hard to see her as stuck in the past, because someone stuck in the past is someone partly to blame for the future.

He picks up a plate. Camila snatches it from his hands. "Don't act like you want to help." She puts it away on the shelf.

"Mila."

She takes the broom from the corner and swipes at the floor. Her arm throttles the broom handle, her muscles defined against her skin.

"You've never once stood up for me like that, Ray." Camila runs the broom under the lip of the cupboards. "Not one time."

"You'd hate it if I got up like that while you were speaking. You don't like the way I do things."

The broom stops moving. Her stare is steady.

"Kimmy told me you left the bar with Susan the other night."

Ray sits down at the table. He takes a deep breath. "That's part of what we need to talk about."

Camila's eyes widen and her jaw drops. She leans against the broom handle. "You fucked her."

"No." Ray stares at his hands. Everything he once thought about the future shrinks to the size of a bullet. His voice is almost a whisper. "But I wanted to."

"You wanted to." She leans against the refrigerator and shuts her eyes.

Any hope Ray had held out that his wife might once look at him and really see something of his inner life, of the man he actually is instead of the man she has always wanted him to be, dies. Any hope that Camila will understand the seriousness of this moment and will find some inner compassion finally disappears. He moves quickly across the room until he is standing within inches of his wife. She still doesn't look at him. He leans over, his arm resting on the fridge; his face is level with hers, willing her to make eye contact.

"You act like I'm not a part of this family." Spit from his speech lands on Camila's cheek. "I did everything you wanted—became a deputy, bought this house in town, joined the guard—because you wanted to belong, to seem American. I've never known what that means."

"What were your great ideas, Ray? To be a rancher? To raise our kids without church? You like following my lead. It makes things easy for you."

"I'm not a piece of furniture, Mila. You can't just move me around when it suits you. Do you even love me?"

"You think sleeping with Susan Dunbar is going to help things between us? That's your plan to show me how invested you are?"

"I don't know what I want anymore."

"You never did. Don't pretend that life cheated you on some brilliant future with Susan because I got pregnant. You think this is what I wanted?"

"Do you love me? I need to know."

Camila throws a plate in the sink. It breaks in half.

Ray heads toward the door.

"Don't walk away from me." Camila's voice is quiet.

"I need some time, Mila. Give me a little time." He shuts the door carefully behind him.

35

HOME FROM THE MEETING, home like all the other sheep, Susan ignores the dark house, ignores Chicken whining inside the gate. She walks. Faster, faster, up the hill, over the ditch, and across the field until she is at the creek. The beavers should be working nonstop. The snow melts. It makes a flood. The beavers repair their dams. They should be out plugging post-flood holes. They should be damming up the ditch, making a headache.

But they aren't.

She paces back and forth above the creek. Fast enough, she can race her own thoughts. Fast enough, she can leave them behind.

Tick, tick, tick. Her dad's watch counts off the time she is wasting, has wasted, will waste. Sixty seconds on the minute. Sixty minutes on the hour. People are born with the same amount of luck. Susan must have used hers up to survive the accident that killed her mom.

Susan scoops some foamy sand from the bank and flings it at the beaver dam.

"Come out," she yells. "Let me see you."

Nothing happens. Tick. Tick.

The eagle isn't in the snag circling for fish, for her young. The scrub oak looks like it's been gassed at the roots. And the water bubbles.

The crumpled contract in her coat pocket doesn't make this right. This remains a mess of someone else's making, a mess that can't be fixed until it's understood.

Jackie doesn't know, and the people who might know don't live here anymore. They don't live anywhere. And Benny Fisk and Danny Jay might know, they probably know, but they won't say unless she makes them say.

What will you do, Susan?

Her dirty hand against her cheek doesn't help answer the question. She hits herself again. Harder. Again. It doesn't hurt near enough for someone who would steal someone else's husband; it doesn't feel like anything.

Ticktickticktick. Life doesn't change on its own. It stays this way. A tome of ticking. A tomb of ticking. There is no one on the bank, no one watching. She has checked. She should not be acting this way. She should not be acting. She should not be. Be aggressive, B-E aggressive. B-E-A-G-G-R-E-S-S-I-V-E aggressive.

The people in Canada were aggressive. The people in Canada defended their land. They knew exactly what to do.

This is not the journalist's way. The journalist's way is to stand on the sidelines, pencil in hand, detached, just the facts ma'am, but who is she kidding, she was never much of a journalist.

Her dead whisper to her through the trees: her parents, her unborn babies, her uncles and aunts and grandparents, all the old ones buried up top. She, Susan, is the only hope she has left.

The creek bubbles and pushes itself onward, through, around, making a mess of the beaver dam. She stares at it, thinking about what she will need. Anger moves through her, a force of its own making. She will need tools. And socks to cover her shoes, and that old Folgers can. And the Ruger. Drumbeats pulse inside her ribs as she runs to the shed.

36

JACKIE STEPS OUT OF the Skyline and night sears her lungs. Her hands shaking, her breath short, she tries to run, tries not to be slow, like something Tim would be, but her ribs ache and she finds after the end of a block that she has to stop. She walks in the empty street, past the hotel parking lot, over the bridge, muddy water flowing under her feet, bats hunting above. Soon she is out of town, onto the thin strip of dirt between Dry Hollow Road and an electric fence with fields on the other side. There is nothing and no one at her back.

A coyote howls someplace close and she is climbing the hill, past an old pump jack lifting its mechanical arm up and down, when the headlights of a car bounce past her. She jumps away from the road and trips. Her knees hit the thick weeds. Her elbow lands on a plastic bottle of motor oil. This is a good enough spot. She breathes the smell of dirt, her chest heaving.

For years, there had been a tube of purple lipstick, the exact color of Shorty's, on the top shelf of the bathroom cabinet. That was a specific Jackie had missed. Fay's lace cape was a specific she had missed. For too long she has focused on the bottom line, on the end game. Devoid of scientific scrutiny, she has missed the salient details. The specifics that expose the truth of things.

On the fridge is the timeline she made months ago: when to brand, when to bring in the bull, when to push the herd onto rangeland, when to hay. By the phone are the shear pins that need installing in the baler. There's a chunk of fence in the upper fields that's down. Two hundred and three cows have been pushed to a smaller piece of home; the turnout date is still weeks away. And the creek cuts across their land with god knows what running through it.

She considers the coffee she made that morning with tap water, the showers she's taken over the past seven weeks, the water irrigating the fields of grass, which her cows will eat. She feels sick. Jackie pictures Tim's smug face. Her own smug face. She lies there and tries to breathe, but it's as if another cow were trampling her. She rolls onto her back. The stars are cold and distant.

The same sky had been pale white one morning, all those years ago, when she woke not far from this spot, to the high-pitched call of Sandhill Cranes. Susie's warm body had been beside her, their sleeping bags zipped together. Nearby were Stark's pond and ash from the fire and some empty beer cans: their final campout. The next day she'd leave for college.

She'd roused Susan to see the birds before they flew into the white dawn.

"*What if school doesn't work out? What if I'm making a bad choice? I'll be so far away.*"

"*I can't see you making a mistake, Jackie. If you don't like what you're doing, you'll change it. You're entitled to a life of your own choosing.*"

Jackie listens very hard and she can hear those cranes. She can hear her sister, saying exactly what she needed to hear. Susan had been so confident then, already engaged to Kelly, already a star at the paper in Junction, fleet-footed and full of ambition. The pump jack in the nearby field thrums and bangs and whines in an incessant robotic pattern. The deer and elk that winter in this field are gone.

She once knew the names of every family who lived on this road but not anymore. Jackie shivers, cold. She doesn't matter to this place. This would've been obvious long ago, if she had been paying better attention.

Her dad would agree that being outside, that having a sense of place, is a salve for loneliness, but she sees now, hidden in all those Sunday phone calls from him, how the land was never enough. She had been a fool to consider it was, that it could be for her.

Carefully, gently, she remembers the camaraderie of the early morning meetings on the hospital ward, the chaos of the hallways when she'd carry a list of things to do in her pocket and another list in her head, the racket and stench of humanity.

There was the man with the handlebar mustache and the bad jokes, scheduled for an angiogram. She'd read his chart and, terrified, excited, wondered aloud to her attending whether he'd been misdiagnosed, whether he might not have a pulmonary embolism. And when they had run the CT scan, and when she had been correct, the patient had thrown his arms around her, as if she had saved his life.

Her longing is palpable, and it's not only from a deep love of science or wanting to do good in the world, but because it is simple. At medical school there are clear expectations. All she has to do is meet them. And if she fails, her failure is entirely her own.

She picks herself up and walks the hill. She takes it slow. She looks up at the stars and wonders about all the other constellations she has missed by staring too hard at the sun.

37

WITHOUT THINKING, HIS HEAD snapped shut, Ray coasts from his driveway, over the freeway, onto Dry Hollow Road. His hands shake. His knee bounces. He has been driving for ten minutes before he realizes where he's going.

At the turnoff to Amick's Quonset, halfway to the ranch, he pulls over onto the narrow shoulder. The derrick is gone. All that's left of the well that kicked all those weeks past, the well that started everything, is a silver pipe sticking out of the ground and the flags above the sump. If it weren't for the mess of his life, he could easily pretend that the fireballs had never existed.

The night settles in around him and all the unknowns about the future press against the window. The lights of town are far away. He longs for a drink. For anything but this darkness. He reaches under the seat, his hand groping the floor, hunting for a pint bottle or flask, forgotten somehow. He leans far forward, his face pressed to the wheel and he's ready to give up and head back to town, to the Skyline where he belongs, when a white shape passes outside the passenger window.

Jackie Dunbar is walking slow, glaring at him, her face muddy, bits of sage stuck to her hair. The usual pinch around her mouth is soft. Ray rolls down the window and leans out.

"You all right, Jackie?"

"I could ask you the same." Her eyes shine. "What are you doing up here?"

"I'm figuring that out."

"If you say so."

"You want a ride on home?"

She opens the door and slides in. For a while they drive in silence.

"Ray, I want to thank you. For what you did for Susie at the meeting."

"It wasn't much to do."

"No one else did anything. I sure didn't. I think it was a very big deal."

"Yeah, Camila thinks so too."

"I guess she would. That explain why you're driving around so late?"

"Something like that."

"Well don't expect Susie to lick your wounds."

"Jesus, Jackie."

"She's too forgiving."

"I'm not out to hurt your sister. You got to take my word on that."

Jackie nods and stares at him, water in her eyes. Ray has rarely seen her so soft, so slack in her movements. He isn't sure what to say.

"It's a pretty night," he says.

"I guess." She stares at the side of his face for an uncomfortable amount of time. He keeps his eyes on the road. "Hey, Ray?"

"Yeah."

"What do you think my dad would want me and Susan to do with the ranch?"

It's an easy question but Ray pauses, filled with renewed sadness. He can't help but think of his own dad, who he never talks to, who lives out east with a new wife and her grandkids to dote on. Ray had promised to never leave his daughters and what the hell is this drive up the road, away from them, if not this most basic pledge broken. He collapses against the seat.

"He'd want what's best for you girls. That's all he'd want."

It's true and it's not true. Ray tries and fails to imagine what his own dad might want for him, unclear since the man rarely visits or calls, a pattern made deep his whole life. And Ray knows what he wants for his own daughters is everything, the best of course, but what is the best? Is it best for him to stay at the house, a sliver of a man? It occurs to him that his own dad might once have felt this same confusion and the thought fills him with more heaviness.

"Hey, Ray?"

"Yeah?"

"I'm sorry for asking you to stop working for us. I didn't know what I was doing."

"I think you just wanted to protect your sister."

"I was wrong."

"You're just human, Jackie. We're all just making this up, best we know how."

He pats her knee and they both fall silent again for a minute while Ray pulls off Dry Hollow onto the ranch road where the concrete turns to gravel. The smell of dust and night fill the car; the cows are dark shadows in the lower fields.

Suddenly, the sound of gunshot slices through them.

"What was that?" Jackie sits up. "Stop the truck."

He rolls down the window, listening hard. "Sounds about thirty feet away to the northwest."

Again they hear the measured pop of a handgun. The sound sets his heart to flapping.

"Wait." Rays says, but Jackie is already out the door and heading up the field. Ray's muscles clench and his jaw tightens. He starts to breathe too fast and he needs to get up there, to chase Jackie across the field and sort what's happening but he can't get his arms and legs to move. He sits in the truck, stuck, the gunshots echoing in his head.

38

SUSAN SETS HER FEET apart and steadies her body, just like Dad taught. Scattered around her on the dirt pad are old rusty nails from the Folgers can in the shed. Two squat brown tanks, with signs warning about the chemicals, sit off to the side. The wind blows a sharp smell off the sump. Silver pipes with wheels attached to them stick out of the ground with all manner of arms, Christmas trees, Kelly used to call them. They wheeze and hiss.

You see something wrong, you do something about it. Dad said that.

She holds the gun in her right hand and balances the butt of the weapon on the palm of her left hand, and she puts her finger in the trigger. She doesn't lock her elbows. She finds her aim.

Johnson's house is hidden beyond the trees; the homes down below the mesa are far away. No one is watching. She fires. She aims. She fires. The gunshot in her ears is an anthem. She is a part of every sound, the hiss of the well, the highway traffic far below the mesa. She fires again.

Compared to writing or asking the right question or knowing how to be a wife, it's easy. Her body does the work for her. She is doing something. Maybe it was always true that she could do something.

A bullet ricochets off the wellhead and lands in the dirt, a few feet away from her sock-covered boots. It happens again, closer this time. Her younger self finds her, the one who was brave and strong and didn't care, who *wasn't attached*, in the words of a shrink she had once seen, to any potential outcome. That she has always been a lousy shot is not the point. One of these bullets is bound to make some kind of point. She squares her hips again. She squints and takes aim.

The sound of her own name startles her. She turns and sees her sister cutting a clean line from the gate that severs the Dunbar ranch from Johnson's, to the pad where she stands.

Susan turns her back and keeps shooting at the well.

"Dammit, Susie. Stop." Jackie's voice stumbles on itself. "People all over Dry Hollow Road can hear you."

"Since when do you care what other people think."

"Susie, please stop. I have to talk to you."

The Ruger is heavy but she lifts it up, aiming into the inky darkness, and shoots again at the well. The bullets spark and kick at the metal wellhead but nothing happens. Not enough. They bounce off and skitter across the pad. She is breathing heavy; the air from her body flies and circles.

Jackie grabs Susan's shooting arm. "You were right. Our water is contaminated."

Susan lowers the gun. "Say that again?"

"The state, the company, Tim, they hid data from us."

"What do you mean?" asks Susan, pulling her arm out of Jackie's grasp.

"There's crazy levels of benzene in the creek." She blinks too many times. She touches the sides of her eyes as if she were crying, which she never does in front of Susan.

Time slows down. One beat. Two beats. A drumbeat of minutes marching her way. Susan replaces the safety on the gun and shoves it into her coat pocket. "I was right. I wasn't crazy."

"Nope. Not at all."

"Holy shit. I was right." Her body goes slack.

"You're smiling a little." Jackie looks puzzled. "You're happy?"

"A little. I know that's strange. I mean it's awful news."

Jackie sighs. "I'm sorry I didn't listen to you. You were right."

"Say that again."

Jackie smiles through pursed lips. "You were right, OK?" Jackie takes a deep breath and stops smiling. "I'm going to stop fighting you on things. I can't take it. If you want to sell the ranch, I want us to talk about it some more. But I could be convinced."

Susan touches the gun in her pocket and takes pleasure in the unexpected shift in her own personal narrative. Life never makes any sense going through it. It's only by telling a story backward that it takes shape, meaning becomes clear from chaos.

Susan looks at the spent bullet shells, at the nails she's scattered around the well site. They are messengers. She'll leave them there.

"I'm not leaving. That's how they get away with it. It's just what they want."

"But Susie." Jackie looks apologetic. "I don't want to stay here. I don't want this to be my life."

She doesn't say, *you'd be alone*, but Susan hears it and waits to feel something awful. Instead she feels surprise. The question of how to run a ranch alone, how to make the land pay, is an easier question than why she should or what to do. *How* has never scared her. *How* requires only a good plan, only some doing. She pats her sister's arm. "I'll figure it out. There's so much to do."

They leave the well behind and head back down the hill toward Ray who is walking to meet them. He might have a list of reasons to be here and not one of them could have to do with her. Susan sets her mouth into a flat line. She has no questions for him.

"You both OK?" Ray lumbers toward them.

"Ask Annie Oakley over here." Jackie nods at Susan.

"What are you up to, girl?" Ray asks, looking at the old wool socks pulled over her boots. He sees the criminal intent; he should know enough not to ask.

"Go on home to your wife, Ray." She folds her arms across her chest. "We're fine."

"I hoped we might talk."

"There's nothing to say. I get it. Finally, I get it."

"Me and Camila are taking some space." There is no wind and no sound, and everything is still except for the wet of Ray's eyes in the dark.

Susan holds herself very straight. "Why would you do that." It isn't a question.

"A lot of reasons. But I'd be lying if I didn't say that you're part of it."

Susan tilts her head. She smiles a small smile.

"I'm such a mess though, Sue." Ray rubs his hand across his cheek. "Not sure I'm worth much to you right now."

She shrugs and glances at Jackie, something unspoken passes between them, before turning back to Ray. "Go ahead and camp out by the old pond if you like. Get yourself some time to get sorted."

His smile is a flash. "You're a rare find, Sue."

Jackie sighs. "Let's get out of here before someone finds us here having a tea party."

They load up into the truck, Susan beside Ray on the bench seat like she used to all those years ago. The cattle, round in a herd nearby, call to them as they pass, a low curious call. In the dark, the land is reduced to blurry shapes, the outline of things, but they find their way up to the house without trouble.

39

SUSAN AND RAY DRIVE the trailer over to Pete's to collect the first bull, a Danish Red with a semen test of 85 percent. He loads in easy; bulls are always optimistic about their futures. When they get to the upper field, which they've fenced off from the creek, and let him out the back, he runs over to the cows, and sniffs butts and bellows until he finds someone in heat and nails her. It takes all of three minutes.

"He'll do fine," says Ray.

"A real dreamboat."

The picnic lunch was his idea. Across the old cotton blanket, Susan spreads strawberries from down-valley, potato salad, apples, cheese, and white crackers. Ray pours lemonade from a thermos. They sit in the shade made by the trailer and watch the bull get it on. Susan studies the little hairs that cluster near Ray's ear. Serious questions, lots of them, flap their arms inside her belly, in need of answers she can't know.

For the past two days, Ray and she have worked together while Jackie works on her research proposal. Not once has he tried to kiss her. She has never felt more respected. She has no slim clue what's happening between them.

"Tell me a story, Sue." His long lashes kiss the skin of his lower eyelid.

"What sort of story?"

"Something that happened to you sometime." He smiles and settles in, making himself comfortable in the grass. "Just make sure it's got a good ending."

The sky is an endless pale blue and the light shines through the aspen leaves and the whole world is hers with this man lying beside her, wanting to listen to no one else. Her scalp buzzes.

She tells him about the time she went backpacking, the first spring she lived in Wyoming. They'd gotten a late start, and hadn't realized that the trailhead was on the opposite side of a creek swollen with snowmelt. They were young, sure that their love was protection against all threat, so they hadn't worried, just set off across. She doesn't mention Kelly's name as she describes following her friend into the cold water.

"It didn't look very wide from the shore, but as we were going across, suddenly water was up to my chest and if I kept going forward I knew it would keep getting deeper and all I could do to keep from getting pulled under was to lock my knees. I just kept telling myself that I was strong and that it would be OK."

Susan pauses. Ray has been to Iraq. His dad was an outfitter. "This is kind of a dumb story."

"No, I'm loving this. Keep going."

They had been lucky. A fisherman watching from the bank took off his pants and ran into the water, carrying a long stick with which to steady himself, which of course she should've known to use but had forgotten, it being spring and her being so out of practice, and he had ferried her to shore. It wasn't until several hours later, when they had hiked up and over the saddle, that they realized the tent poles must have come loose in the water. It was cold that night, and they squeezed themselves into one sleeping bag to stay warm. They had joked that it wasn't spooning but forking.

"I don't know why I told you that story."

"I like the idea of you in the river, keeping yourself together. I'll keep that with me."

Beyond the fence, far across the field, the bull is working another of the cows.

"You hear the one about the old bull and the young bull?" Ray says, snickering. He's sitting half up to rest his head on his hand like an underwear model, his muscled forearms flecked with scars.

"This is a joke?"

"Yes ma'am, a good one. They're up on a hill and they look down and see a bunch of cows. The young bull says, 'Let's run on down and screw a cow.' The old bull says, 'Let's walk on down and screw 'em all.'"

Camila would find the joke hilarious. She would laugh her Santa Claus laugh and then tell a dirtier joke.

Smile. Eat some potato salad and smile.

"What are we doing, Ray? What is this?"

"This is an afternoon without skeeters or black flies or rain." He puts a hat over his head and lays his hand on the top of her thigh. "I'd say we're enjoying ourselves. At last."

His hand is there, on her body, a real living thing, proof of something. She sits still for several minutes and watches the bull, which isn't afraid of anything. "Are you making a move on me, Ray?"

He throws off his hat and laughs. "I guess I'm out of practice at this." He sits up and kisses her lips, slowly. "You've always shone for me, Susan Dunbar." The air against her skin is neither cold nor hot but just an extension of her blood and bones and sinew. After a while, she climbs on top of him, her hips clicking, proof that she is out of practice, but he doesn't seem to notice or care. Afterward, they lie tangled together. Ray doesn't say: this isn't about loneliness, this isn't a rebound. But for once, Susan doesn't feel like asking questions. There's no wind, and sweat pools between her breasts, and she longs for water but it's not worth moving away for; there's no telling how long this will last. This could be the beginning of a story, or it might be the middle or even the end. In the future, whenever that is, this day and week might not even be a story worth retelling.

Ray snores beside her. Curled up against him, lying on the blanket that smells of dogs and dust and sex, she tries to sleep but can't. The deer Ray had freed from the fence that day, the one who had been hung on the wire—did it find its family? Did it drink benzene from the creek and die a horrible death? It occurs to her that possibly they set that animal loose for a worse fate.

The sound of an idling car rouses them from their rest. Susan stands up in time to see a patrol car making its way up the long gravel drive. "Ray. Look."

There were hidden cameras at the well site. Someone found her fingerprints on the nails. Jackie's shoe prints were found. Susan had wanted to send a message. She hadn't thought through the eventualities.

They throw on their clothes quickly and load up into the truck. Ray will resent her for this. He doesn't like to handle things. He wouldn't have to handle this for Camila. As he opens the door for her, the band on his ring finger glares in the sun.

"You think this is going to be bad." She tries to sound calm.

"We don't know anything yet."

She sees Ray watching her and has no idea what he's thinking. She feels sick. The air is too hot.

At the barn, they're met by the sheriff, idling in his car. Once sixty pounds lighter, with the kind of looks girls used to call pretty, he now has a puffy face fueled by cases of beer and french fries. Walnuts sit under his eyes. He rolls down his window a crack and raises two fingers, the nonchalant greeting given between men in rural areas.

"I heard you were up here, Ray." His nod is clipped, unsmiling. "Hello, Ms. Dunbar. This sun sure does plague the soul."

"What can we do you for, Sheriff?" Ray lets his arms hang loose at his sides, tilts his hat back off his brow. He's all smiles. He's not himself.

"Did you all hear anything coming from Johnson's the other night?"

"What happened?" Her voice is too high. Her body feels too big for her skin. Faking it and lying have never been the same thing. "Did anyone get hurt?"

"I heard you got some bad news about your creek. I heard those benzene levels were real high."

"Want me to poke around Johnson's for you?" Ray says, leaning into the car. "What are you looking for?"

The sheriff gives him a long look. He glances at Susan, at the inches between Susan and Ray. Before dinner the entire town will know that Ray is staying up here, that he is smiling too much and anyone can guess what that means.

"Come on by the office next week, son. We should talk."

Only when the patrol car has passed the lower field, when Chicken has quit barking, when she can't hear the engine, does she exhale, her hands trembling. "He knows."

"Hard to say, but I doubt it."

"Why does he want you to come by, then? Your probation isn't up for another month."

"Not sure. But it's not likely to have anything to do with this business."

"You don't know that. You don't know any more than I do, which isn't anything. I mean, what must Camila be thinking? Everyone knows you're living up here, and people are going to assume all sorts of things. And what about your kids, Ray? I just lost my dad, and now I'm going to be responsible for taking you away from your girls? How am I going to clean up the creek? What are we breathing from those flares?"

"You're freaking out?"

"I guess." She wraps her arms across her chest. He's going to take offense. He's going to make it about him and tell her how to be and it's going to be over. She has been through this before.

Ray picks up her hand and strokes her skin. "When I get nervous, I try to focus on the little things nearby, things I can see, like the notch in that tree or that rock over there by the lavender. And I try to breathe."

"That's it? That helps you?"

"Sometimes."

A sliver of moon rises against the pale sky. The poplars that Granny planted shake their green leaves in a frenzy of lust. Chicken lounges in the middle of the dirt road, his tail making clouds of dust. There's an aliveness on her skin, a wanting that is clear and sharp and a great relief. The irrigation spigots shoot water into cheerleader arms; they whisper *today*, *today*, *today*.

40

Ray pulls up in back of the department and parks beside four brand new Toyota Tacomas, black ones, the paint jobs shiny enough for him to catch his reflection. He's shaved and tried to get the dirt stains from his neck and hands. But his shirt is wrinkled, and he needs a haircut. Everything that doesn't matter at the ranch is important here. He licks his fingers and smoothes his hair.

"Stark, you're browner than the Mexicans pruning peaches over at my Pop's." Ty steps out of one of the trucks and comes over, his boots heavy against the concrete.

"Good to see you, man." Ray smiles and holds out his hand to his old friend. "Santa come early?" Ray nods at the new trucks.

"Something like that. Gas company made a big donation. These things are wicked. Even got Sirius radio in them."

They talk for a few minutes, catching up on each other's kids and the ball game, on the latest perps. Ty tells a long story about bringing in a guy who had a hundred pounds on him, who wasn't wearing any shoes, who was a biter.

Ray could stand here all afternoon. "I miss this."

"Good. We need you back here."

"Speaking of, I better get in to see the chief. Can you open the back door for me?"

"Shit, Stark. Can't do it. You know the rules. Probation gets public entry."

"Right." Ray steps backward and runs into one of the new trucks, its black hot on his elbow. "Cool. No big deal."

To enter in front, something he hasn't done in eight years, Ray cuts across the grass, getting hit across the chest by sprinklers. He keeps his head down. No one should see him like this. He buzzes for Judy to let him in and pretends to read the anti-meth posters plastered on the wall, the Plexiglas wall, bulletproof, meant to keep out the unwanted.

"Vacation looks good on you." Sheriff waves Ray into a seat on the other side of a big wood desk that's stacked with paperwork in leaning piles. "Coffee? Judy," he yells out the door, "get our man some coffee." His secretary hustles in with a Styrofoam cup and two cream, one sugar, just the way Ray likes it.

"Thanks for this." Ray nods at Judy. "It's good to be back."

The sheriff shifts his bulk in his wooden chair, a simply-made thing he insists on keeping to prove some point about discomfort and longevity. He watches Ray drink his coffee, as if to have a sip is not the correct thing to do. Sheriff has always been able to do this, to knock Ray slightly off balance.

"I hear those Dunbar girls aren't going to lease their mineral rights."

Ray shakes his head. "This town is amazing."

"What'll they do if they get force-pooled?"

"I can't say, sir. That's not my business."

"Stark, we're getting some pressure from the county commissioners, all three of them." Sheriff slowly unwraps a piece of gum, rolls it up, and starts chewing. It's an old trick. A mask of the unconcerned public servant. "No one appreciated your attitude at the meeting the other night."

Ray feels himself go cold, go quiet.

"It's our job to protect the citizenry." Ray is almost whispering. "I believe I was helping to do that."

"Just like you helped people that night at the derrick?" The sheriff moves three inches of paper from one pile to another. Sheriff squints when he's concealing something, and he's squinting at the stack until finally he looks up and meets Ray's eyes. Ray holds his gaze.

"What are you saying, Sheriff? Do you want me to quit?"

"Don't be an ass. Before you left for Iraq, you were one of our best. I think you still have it in you. We just need you to get in line."

"What's that mean? Get in line?"

"Oh you know. Go have lunch with the gas people and the commissioners. Tell them you appreciate our new fleet of trucks. That you intend to keep their wells and infrastructure safe in this county."

Ray's chest caves. All the lines he's stepped behind, kept behind, circled, for years, forever. It is another way to be stuck, to be scared, to not live a day for himself. He didn't move away from his sweet girls just to follow orders from someone else.

Life never just happened to his grandpa. The days never stacked up on his chest. He started out without more than a thin dime and tamed his land into a steady, rich parcel. He made something good.

Out the very small window cut from the old brick is the blue sky. A good day for haying. A good day for moving cows to the high country. He knocks twice with his knuckles against the desk.

"No thanks, sir."

The sheriff looks amused. He pops his gum. "What's that, Ray?"

"I'm done. I can't work for a political organization. I can't work here."

"That don't sound like you, Stark."

"No offense, sir, but I think it does."

He gets out of the building quick, unsighted. In the parking lot, he throws his cup of coffee at one of the new Tacomas. The coffee splatters across the windshield almost, but not quite, like blood.

That night, Ray and Susan lie naked in Susan's small bed, the lamplight shining on their heaving chests; he pulls back the sheet so he can better see her body. Unmarked by childbirth, her belly and breasts are firm. There is more strength in those skinny arms than he would've thought. That life can still be a surprise, that it can still make him happy, fills Ray with wonder.

"How you feeling now?" she asks, shyly.

"Better." He tucks a single strand of hair behind Susan's ear.

"You regret quitting?"

"Nah, not really. I'll figure something out."

"You will."

"What's happening with that article of yours?"

"I've been thinking about writing an editorial about what it's like to live surrounded by gas wells, sending it in to the *Post*. Seems more honest somehow than trying to report as if I don't care."

"I can see that."

Susan settles down under the covers and tangles her legs with his.

"Why don't you tell me a story this time?" She traces the lines next to his eyes and smiles at him, unafraid and curious. "You never talk about Iraq, about what it was like there."

"Lots of people go to war. I'm sure you've heard enough war stories."

"You aren't lots of people. What happened to you?"

"I don't have a good story about that place."

"We don't have to talk about it, but I'd like to be a friend to you. I'd like to listen if you'd let me. I think it helps to be heard."

Susan narrows her eyes at him. Her stare knows about loss, about defeat and hopelessness. And she kisses him hard, her mouth a life raft, and for the moment he dives into her and when they pull apart, he thinks, maybe she's right.

So he talks.

"It was September 7th and I was late for guard duty. I'd gotten dealt a month of night watch for telling my commanding officer what I thought about Iraq. He didn't care to know. But that night,

I'd stayed too long on Skype with Camila and the kids—Monica had this song she wanted to sing me, and then Lilly kept trying to kiss the screen—and I just didn't get out of there when I should've." He gulps at the air with loud effort. Susan touches his shoulder but he pulls back. "I fucked up. Because I was late, Marcus, my friend Marcus Wilson from Columbus, Ohio, he had to stay and so it was him, instead of me, like it should've been, who got hit. A bomb." Marcus had loved books about presidents and talking shit and basketball. His skin had been the color of rich soil. He wanted to be a teacher. He was a sweet kid. "There was nothing left of him but pieces of tissue on the wall."

He stares at the ceiling. His chest hurts and his eyes fill with water and everything blurs and he shouldn't cry, she doesn't deserve that, this is his burden to hold, so he holds his hands to his eye sockets, but it doesn't help.

"I killed my friend. I killed other people too, innocent civilians, people who did nothing wrong except be in the wrong place."

"It's what happens in war, Ray. You didn't make that bomb explode." Susan touches his face and the hair at his temples, over and over. "You didn't do anything wrong."

He shakes his head at the pillow but she turns his wet face toward her body and holds his head against her breasts, and she wraps her top leg over his back and after a while, his breathing steadies. A worn out, cleaned out feeling takes hold of him. Susan moves the talk to the ranch, asking him what it is he dreams of doing. And that is kind of her; it helps him. By the time Susan falls asleep, they've made a plan for moving cattle to range, for haying, for a new shed on the backside. Ray stares at the ceiling for a long time, wondering how it is he can feel better, grateful to Sue beside him, and how that feeling can make him also feel worse.

He can't remember the sound of Lilly's breathing. Monica will learn to roll her eyes at him. The loss of seeing them every day is like the loss of a limb. Memories of their laughter, the way they call Daddy across the house, the smell of their hair after a bath, follow him like phantom pains. He was never going to be the dad that wasn't around. He was never going to miss out on their lives.

He gets out of bed, throws on Susan's short pink robe, and walks to the kitchen to dial the number on the old rotary phone.

"What's wrong?" Camila's voice is breathy like it always is when she's half-awake. "Did something happen?"

"I just wanted to talk to you."

"What do you want, Ray?"

"How are the girls? Did Monica pass her science test?"

"Ray, I have to sleep. I have to wake up with the girls in the morning and get them off to school and then I have to go to work." She takes a sharp inhale and he can picture her sitting up in bed, her hair wild, her eyes flashing. "I don't have time for some bullshit father-of-the-year routine."

Ray shifts from one foot to the next in the dark kitchen. Again, he feels as if he and Camila were traveling the same road but in opposite directions. He wonders: if he is honest with her about everything, from this point on, if they can find some peace between them in this new place they're headed.

"I quit my job."

"I heard. Child support is not cheap, Ray."

"Could you please take the phone to the girls' room so I can listen to their breathing?"

"You miss them?"

"All the time."

He stares out the kitchen window at the moon, lost behind the poplars. He closes his eyes and listens to Camila breathing in his ear. He could identify the quiet rasp of air leaving her throat in a crowd.

When she speaks again, her voice is tired, worn out. "Our life wasn't perfect but it was good, good enough. Now it's wrecked."

"Mila. There's a lot of ways for life to look that can be OK. Even if we're not married."

"This isn't what I wanted."

He starts to say that he's sorry, but she hangs up on him. Outside, a coyote howls to his pack. Somewhere the elk are grazing together, bedding down in a clump. He holds the dead receiver in Bill Dunbar's kitchen. His feet are cold against the floor.

"Nice robe." Jackie stands in the doorway, her T-shirt and cotton shorts wrinkled with recent sleep, and stares at the sheer pink lace on the edge of Susan's robe. It just covers the hem of his boxers. "I thought you were sleeping in the tent."

Ray hangs up the phone awkwardly. They had not thought to tell Jackie that Ray would sleep inside that night. They had not considered her at all. He shifts uneasily.

"Sorry if I woke you." He puts the phone back in place and picks up a few dishes from the counter and moves them to the sink and wipes his hands on his boxers, trying to avoid looking at Jackie. "You want some tea or anything?"

"I wouldn't peg you a tea drinker, Ray."

"I'm not." What he leaves hanging there in the cool air is the fact that he has spent half a life making tea for his wife. "Go ahead and sit down. It'll help you sleep."

He fills the kettle with water and lights the stove and opens the cupboard to search for a tea bag, aware that Jackie is watching him, seeing right through his lacy robe, worrying about her sister.

"There's some in the very back. I think it's old."

"I don't plan to hurt her, Jackie." Ray looks into the dark, nearly empty cupboard.

"You said that before. I know that's not your intention."

The kettle hisses at him. He turns to see that there is a quiet searching in her stare. Jackie leans against the wall, running her fingernail under the faded cherry wallpaper, coaxing the paper back into place where it has started to peel. "And you're saying I can't control all the variables." He waits a while for her answer.

"You all right, Ray?" Jackie looks at the phone, at the mug he's pulled from the shelf.

"I look that bad?"

"I think the robe is a good look for you." She smiles and he laughs. Her kindness is a surprise. The water boils and he fills the mug with hot water and hands it to her.

"I don't know, Jackie. Could be worse." He thinks of Susan in the next room. Of Marcus Wilson's family. Of his mom dying in a place that smelled like piss and bleach.

"People always say that time helps with hard things, but that never helps me." She blows at the hot tea and takes a sip. "Why would you feel better to know that someday you won't care anymore about the things that you care about now? I'm sorry it's hard. That's all people should ever say."

"That's true. Thanks."

"Thanks for the tea." She nods and disappears into the hallway.

He stares out the kitchen window. He can picture the cows in the lower field. They'll be facing north, all piled together, their rear ends toward the wind.

At the crest of the hill, the land, growing out for hay, looks silvery. The afternoon rain that fell, and left just as quick as it started, has freshened the hay. The breeze makes it shimmy, like a woman dancing. The question Ray asks himself without thinking is, will it be enough. Will it give enough of itself to keep things going through winter. It's the training of his grandfather, to look at a field in pasture and think nine months away.

Out of sight, at the crest of the hill, high grass and clover become an aspen grove. He can picture where the pond smells of damp, the cool it gives the breeze, the fields that need extra irrigating in the summer. In the afternoons, light hits the creek and sparkles. *Betty's diamonds*. Ray pictures where the elk cross in December, where the coyotes den, where to sight barn owls. The pale green of spring, the brown of summer, the yellow of fall, and the white of winter. Every season offers its own kind of hardship and reward.

For a long time, he stands leaning against the counter, watching the stars through the window; the trees shift in the wind and he waits for the moon to slide into view.

41

JACKIE FIDGETS IN HER wrinkled blouse. It's seventy-eight degrees outside, but she's freezing. The air conditioning blasts from the vent without regard for cost. Across the wide mahogany desk, Larry Batjer, Esq., reads through the paperwork Susan has spent the past week assembling. His ruby pinky ring glints as he flips to another page. He hums. Something that sounds like "Uptown Girl" by Billy Joel. Wiry and small, his head shaved, Mr. Batjer doesn't look threatening enough to take on the oil and gas industry.

Beside her in overstuffed leather chairs are Ray, who only agreed to come after she and Susan had asked repeatedly, and Susan. Ray scowls at Mr. Batjer's yellow bow tie. Susan tucks her hands under her skirt. Jackie would bet money that her sister's fingers are crossed.

"You can see that the level of benzene in our creek is sixty times higher than the state's safe drinking water threshold." Jackie slides to the edge of her chair. It shouldn't take a professional this long.

Mr. Batjer nods his bald head slightly. "That level looks like an outlier. I'm sure they'd argue for retesting, but yes, I see it's interesting." Mr. Batjer talks with intensity, his accent almost

Midwestern, his words so full of air that they slow and stand still. He keeps humming.

Ray and Jackie exchange a long look. Susan had been sure that Mr. Batjer could help them. He had won several major cases on behalf of citizens against gas companies. He knows what he is doing. So she had said.

Jackie looks down at her polyester blouse with the peach blossom print, at her suede skirt and heels. Not one to usually pay attention to clothes, she dressed that morning with care, hoping for an outfit that would inspire this man to care about them, to take action where they could not.

The bull must be brought in soon; the cattle must be moved to range. The gate needs mending. Jackie has another thirty scientific articles about purkinje cells to review before she can complete her proposal. All three of them are too busy to sit around a stuffy office in Junction and listen to the humming of someone with the body of a pro ping-pong player.

"Just a few weeks before the creek started bubbling, our neighbor's well exploded. And there were several frack jobs conducted in the area within a mile of the creek. Did you see all that there?" Jackie asks. She taps her heel against the chair leg.

"Honey, give him a second." Susan pinches Jackie's leg.

Mr. Batjer clears his throat. "There's no doubt you've been robbed." He smiles for the first time, wrinkles making fists of his creased cheekbones. Jackie pays attention to that, to the sign that he is not a young man, that he has done this before. She leans forward as he goes on.

"Because you own your mineral rights, if a gas company, through any misconduct, enabled gas to escape to the surface without capture, that's a loss of revenue that the gas company owes you. We can try and do something about that."

"I don't think you understand, Mr. Batjer." Susan, unselfconsciously, clasps her hands together at her chest. Jackie would've expected her to use her reporter smile, the low voice that Susan uses when she wants someone's attention. But instead Susan is transparent, her eyes cavities of longing and fear. "We want our creek cleaned up. That's why we're here. We want them to fix what they've done."

"It's more than plausible that one of the new companies fracked a well nearby and that some of that chemical content didn't make it back up the well bore and ended up coming up through your creek. But proving causality, proving who is responsible, that's another matter."

He uses some legalese, his bow tie bouncing up and down, to explain the challenges of proving corporate poisoning of the environment. He points out that there are three different companies punching holes in the area, and many more now-defunct companies that once did business here. Any one of them could be culpable. Any one of them could blame the oil service company that fracked the wells.

Jackie has the feeling of falling. She grabs hold of the armrests and tries to sit up straight.

Money has a finite value, and it diminishes over time. No dollar amount can match the value of spring water or fresh hay or the cool of the riparian zone. The future prosperity of the land can't ever be distilled. Jackie stares out the slats in the blinds to the parking lot of the beige strip mall. There's a ripped awning on the sandwich shop across the way; there are weeds in the cracks of the cement. This place was once a sea of grasses as high as a horse's flank. There was nothing between the river and the mountains but open space. What an embarrassment to be human, to lead every time with hubris.

Mr. Batjer hasn't stopped talking. He smiles and nods his head up and down as if he were prodding them forward with his forehead. "We'd want to get all your neighbors who own their gas involved. It could be a huge class action, and if we won, you'd help people all over the country whose new neighbors are gas wells."

"Well now, that sounds all right." Ray looks at Susan, his face a question.

"It does, actually." Jackie feels her jaw relax. She smiles at Mr. Batjer and notices a picture on the bookshelf behind him of a younger him, his arms around two people who can only be his parents. The gray-haired man wears the same sort of wide-brimmed hat her dad liked. "It'd be nice to think we could make a difference."

Susan touches her hand and Jackie gives it a squeeze. They look at each other and smile.

"If it's a class action, we don't pay for that, right?" Susan asks.

"That's right. If we take on the case, and if we win, you won't pay a thing. You just need to put up the value of your land as collateral while we're in process."

"Wait. What?" Jackie's hands grasp the chair. "If we lose, you get our land?"

"It'd be to cover my expenses, but I won't take on the case unless I think we can win."

Jackie, Ray, and Susan all sit quietly, stunned.

"I'm on your side here, folks." Mr. Batjer's face darkens; he nods at their dismay. "It's the law that's not."

In the truck on the long drive home, past the new mall and the old mall, past the airport and the massage parlors, past the canyon carved by the Colorado, Ray sits between Susan and Jackie, passing out the BLTs he made in their kitchen that morning. They share a thermos of coffee. Jackie drives.

"I'm going to say it," Ray says with a mouth full of bacon. "It's stupid to risk losing your land in order to save it."

"I agree." Jackie eases off the gas. "It's a stay of execution at best. It saves nothing."

"So we do nothing?" Susan leans forward to look at them both, her forehead pinched in the middle. Her favorite blue dress with the butterflies now stained with mayo.

The weight of not knowing settles over the car. Jackie looks at her sister and at Ray and she can see the wrinkles that will come, that slump of their spines, how their bodies will betray them.

"Camila would know what to do," Susan says thoughtfully. She leans her forehead against the window.

"At least she'd have a very strong opinion," says Ray, and Jackie smiles, grateful to Ray for knowing what to say, glad to have him with them. It has been an unexpected pleasure to have him around for the past two weeks. He is always the first to the kitchen in the morning, making coffee, frying eggs. He has a way of taking care of them, like with the BLTs, without making a big deal about it.

They pass several mile markers before Ray breaks the silence. "You ladies are smart. You just need some time to think on it."

Jackie looks out the bug-streaked windshield and cringes. The brave thing is to ask the question that needs asking. She makes herself speak. "Do you think Dad would be disappointed? That I'm leaving?"

"It's normal that you want to finish medical school. It's good to know what you want." Susan shrugs as if to push off Jackie's guilt, which is nice, which only makes Jackie feel worse.

"Maybe we should let Batjer try. What do we have to lose?"

Ray coughs and looks at Susan, a question pulling his eyebrows toward his hat. She meets his gaze and looks quickly away.

"Speak your mind, Ray, please," says Jackie.

"I know it's not my decision to make of course, but I don't think you should rush on this. It's one thing to sell your land. It's another thing to lose it."

"I'm not planning to lose anything anymore. Not as far as I can help it." Susan in profile, her hair wild at the sides, looks just like their mom, the sort of person with agenda and sass.

It's quiet again for a while and when Jackie does speak, it's forced, too loud in the cramped cab.

"I'll come back in the fall to help with market. I won't be that far away."

"Sure. I know," says Susan, which isn't what Jackie needs to hear.

Ray coughs. "I've been meaning to ask you two a thing and I guess this might be a good time." He pauses again for what seems to Jackie around five minutes. "I was wondering if you might consider bringing me on as a partner in the ranch."

"What about the creek?" says Jackie. "The whole place could be worthless."

"Not to me. It's not ever gonna be nothing to me."

"No," says Susan, her eyes bright. "Me neither."

"I can get on with a place that's been through a hard time," says Ray.

The sisters look at each other and their smiles sink into their faces, the same smile. "What do you think, Susie?" Jackie keeps her eyes on the road. "It's your call."

"Let's give it a try."

The canyon wall outside looms over them, the sand-colored rocks perched high on the lip, threatening to slide. The clouds, bloated with moisture, are too high to do anything. The rain falls against the blue, dissipated before it ever has a chance to reach them here.

In mid-June, Jackie drives west on the highway; she is intentionally alone. At a one-lane ranch exit not far from Silt, she heads north, into the rolling flat lands of peach orchards and wide swaths of alfalfa, an area still free of gas development, until she comes to Clear Creek. From the back of the truck, she grabs the old fishing gear and wades back upstream. In the two months since she and Tim came here to fish, the promise of spring snowmelt has been replaced by the reality of a sullen summer day. The river is low and the wind is sluggish. It suits her mood.

Earlier that afternoon, she had emailed her research proposal to her attending. In another two weeks, she'll resume rotations at the hospital in Denver. If her proposal is good enough to impress her attending, if she gets the research rotation she wants, she can remain competitive for residency. Even if she doesn't, she'll finish. She'll have a place to go on from. To worry too much about possible failures is useless, but Jackie can't quite let it go. What will happen when she's gone, it badgers her.

She reels in. She casts. Her body orients itself to her raised arms with only a mild ache; her ribs are healed, spared, ready for the doing to come. Ten o'clock, two o'clock, her pole hits the empty sky.

She casts again and her line snags an overhanging branch and when she tugs, it holds taut. With the nail clippers hanging from the vest pocket, just where her dad had hung them, she clips the line, releases it to the trees. The plastic fly box falls from the lower front pocket and bounces open against a rock. She crouches into the water to pick it up.

The flies her dad made or bought are lined up in rows, hooked to Styrofoam. Their beaded heads catch the low light and glow. She unhooks the back of one with green thread and holds it in her palm. Her dad would've touched this. He would've known its name and its proper use. She holds it to her nose and smells. She throws it into the river, watches it leave her. This isn't something her dad would have ever done. This isn't something her dad would ever have understood. She throws another fly away.

When you're dead, you're dead. There are no angels. There is no grand order to the universe. This is what she's always thought. Today she wonders if she has been wrong. She feels him here with her, as if he were right beside her. In the snap of her line and the feel of the creek moving past her shins, in the smell of fresh pine and motor oil and sweat, in the cottonwoods and the piñon on the hills above, in hard work and quiet and sarcasm, in everything he ever taught her to love, she can sense his presence. She hopes that maybe, in this same way, he can feel her too.

"Giving the fish a break, Dunbar?" Tim's voice startles her. She slips into the stream, splashing. In his expensive waders, his rod in his hand, he stands on the bank smiling his landman smile.

She stands up, water dripping down her legs. The vest is too wide, but she wraps it close to her chest. "I didn't expect to see anyone here."

"I saw your rig at the turnout." He shrugs shyly. "I drive by here a lot. Hoping I might find you."

"You know where I live. You could always run into me up there."

"I figured you'd run me off." A flash of red colors his face to the roots of his hair. He looks small, uncertain, more like the teenager she once knew.

"I might've. Susan would've for sure."

He frowns and takes off his hat. He holds the wide brim in his hands and squints at it.

"I've thought about your creek. I was thinking you might try to ask for a settlement. The company gave some people in Wyoming six figures a few weeks ago. There was benzene in their creek too. They set it up where the company can't pull any gas as long as there's high levels in the creek. You might try. Could work."

"Thanks. I'm glad to know that. I'll have to talk it over with Susan and Ray."

"I've only ever wanted to help you."

Jackie considers this carefully. One of her dad's flies floats in a nearby eddy, stuck there, aswirl to itself. She puts her hand in her pocket around the plastic fly box. She watches Tim on the bank in the way she has come to watch the clouds and the fish that rise beyond her line. The edges of his clothing and his rod seem to flatten into the background, into the river and the trees. The sun slips behind the mountains and the wind brings the cool down from the high lakes. The low light catches beads of sweat on his forehead.

"It's all right, Tim. No one died. I'm OK. It seems like you are too."

"Well, that's true, isn't it?" Tim smiles, relieved. He walks slowly toward her place in the river. "I quit my job. I want you to know that."

"What will you do for work?"

"I've been talking to a mountain bike company about doing sales for them."

"Is that what you want?"

"As long as I can get outside most days, it'll be OK."

"I'm glad for you."

"I heard you're going back to school. The mountain bike company is headquartered in Denver. Could I look you up some time?"

"I don't know, Tim. I don't know how I feel about that." She shrugs. "We could fish a little bit if you want?"

"Sure. That sounds nice."

They fish in silence until the sunset bleeds into the cottonwoods, until the last rays of light slide across the valley and seep into the ground, turning the river silver. On the walk back to the turnout, Jackie carries two browns in her creel. The leaves make a canopy of blue shadow against the dirt path and she can taste the salt of her own sweat.

"You're a hell of a good fisherman," Tim says, glancing sideways.

The weight of the browns at her back is a kind of ballast.

"Thanks. My dad taught me."

42

They rise in the dark. The smoke in the air, from the forest fires down-valley, makes the moon a red claw, as if the devil had branded the sky. Ray makes breakfast while Jackie and Susan water and feed the cows for the last time of the season. After everyone has fed, Jackie loads the salt blocks into the back of the ATV. The cattle call softly to one another. They know what is coming.

Ray carries a rucksack from the house, filled with snacks and extra clothes and water for the long day ahead. Susan tacks up the horses they borrowed from Amick. Light eats away the shadow blanketing the forested mountainside. It's to those lush fields and dusky pine that they are going. The cattle will be safe there on the federal range, away from the creek and the gas wells. They will fatten. They will be one less thing that Jackie is leaving for Susan and Ray to handle. Jackie leans against the work corral, her arm resting against the middle rail, and feels the summer slide off her back.

Susan walks over and puts a foot on the bottom rail beside her sister. They watch the cows for a few minutes, listening to the sounds of their hooves against the dirt.

"I want you to have this." Susan takes off the watch from her wrist and hands it to Jackie.

"No way. I can't take that. Dad gave it to you."

"You know you want it."

"Of course."

"Then just shut up and take it already."

Jackie laughs and puts it on her left wrist. She holds it up to her ear; she studies the hands. "I'll take good care of it." She touches her sister's sleeve.

"I still miss him so much." Susan looks out toward the mountains. "I don't need a watch to remind me of that."

"I keep thinking of things I want to tell him before I remember that he's gone."

"I do that too. All the time." Susan looks at Jackie and smiles. "I'm going to miss you."

"You can always call me if you need anything." Jackie speaks quietly. "I'll come right away."

"I'll count on that." Susan takes off her ball cap and squints into the sun.

"I hope we don't have to sell," Jackie says.

"Yeah." Susan looks at Ray, riding over on the ATV. "Me too."

Ray shuts off the motor and sidles up beside them, leaning against the fence.

"All right." Ray grins. "You ladies about ready? I give us a few hours and we'll be up with the cool breeze."

"Just don't rush them," says Susan. "Remember it's best if they think it's their idea. We'll be there soon enough."

"All right, boss. You all about ready to think it's a good idea to get up on those horses?"

"You bet. Let's go."

Ray opens the gate, letting Blanca, the lead cow, head out on the well-worn trail to the south. Chicken takes a flank, Ray another on the ATV, and Susan and Jackie work a semicircle behind the herd. The sun settles on their backs and they move slowly into the hills, facing the long day ahead together.

Acknowledgments

THOUGH *KICKDOWN* IS A WORK OF fiction, many events that occur in the book are based on stories I heard while reporting on the rural West for various national magazines about natural gas development, among them *High Country News*, *Mother Jones*, *Salon.com*, *Orion*, and *Fortune*. Thank you to all the editors who sent me out into the field and thank you to all the good people who invited me into their homes, their patrol cars, their drill rigs, who let me walk fence line on their ranches and visit well sites and man camps. I am indebted to all of you who trusted me with your stories.

This book could not have been written without the support of Karen Fisher, Sterling Clarren, Sandy Clarren, Chris Dennis, Lee van der Voo, and Amy Rude. Thank you to my agent Lisa Bankoff for her tenacity and to Lilly Golden, my editor at Skyhorse, who truly has a golden pen. I also owe a great big thank you to Lance Astrella, Lisa Bracken, Jim and Sue at the Johnny Creek Ranch, Jon Clarren, Stevan Allred, Joanna Rose, all past members of the Eastside Literary Guild, Carter Sickels, Jason Maurer, Toby Van Fleet, Laura Veirs, Carolina Pfister, Alexa Weinstein, Shelby

Brakken, and Marc Cozza. To the many friends who patiently encouraged my efforts and answered all of my questions about everything from splenectomy to mountain biking, and to our babysitters, Emma Frantz, Meg Gibson, and Kristen Billous in particular, who made it possible for me to steal away and write. Thank you to the Alicia Patterson Foundation for the gift of enough money to spend a year researching the impacts of oil and gas development on rural places. Thanks to Craig Childs for the usage of his wonderful line on page 28 about the Colorado River.

A few of the excellent books I consulted in the course of writing *Kickdown* are *Exit Wounds* by Jim Lommasson, David Finkel's *The Good Soldiers*, and *Darkness Visible* by William Styron.

Finally, thank you to Jude and Lou, who have had to share their mom with this book from day one, and to my darling Greg, upon whom everything depends and thrives.

About the Author

AWARD-WINNING JOURNALIST REBECCA CLARREN has been writing about the rural West for twenty years. Her journalism, for which she has won the Hillman Prize and an Alicia Patterson Foundation Fellowship, has appeared in such magazines as *Mother Jones*, *High Country News*, *The Nation*, and *Salon.com*. *Kickdown*, her first novel, was shortlisted for the PEN/Bellwether Prize. She lives in Portland, Oregon, with her husband and two young sons.